ANGEL

Jon Grahame

MYRMIDON

Myrmidon
Rotterdam House
116 Quayside
Newcastle upon Tyne
NE1 3DY

www.myrmidonbooks.com

Published by Myrmidon 2014

A catalogue record for this book is available from the
British Library.

ISBN 978-1-905802-84-5

Set in 11.75/15.5 Sabon by Reality Premedia Services, Pvt. Ltd.

Printed and bound in the UK by
CPI Group (UK) Ltd, Croydon, CR0 4YY

1 3 5 7 9 10 8 6 4 2

This is for Antonietta Maria Colaluca.

Daily Telegraph, February 5, 2010

China's reckless use of antibiotics in the health system and agricultural production is unleashing an explosion of drug resistant superbugs that endanger global health, according to leading scientists.

Chinese doctors routinely hand out multiple doses of antibiotics for simple maladies, like sore throats, and the country's farmers' excessive dependence on the drugs has tainted the food chain.

Studies in China show a 'frightening' increase in antibiotic-resistant bacteria such as staphylococcus aureus bacteria, also know as MRSA. There are warnings that new strains of antibiotic-resistant bugs will spread quickly through international air travel and international food sourcing.

'We have a lot of data from Chinese hospitals and it shows a very frightening picture of high-level antibiotic resistance,' said Dr Andreas Heddini of the Swedish Institute for Infectious Disease Control. 'Doctors are daily finding there is nothing they can do; even third and fourth-line antibiotics are not working.

'There is a real risk that globally we will return to a pre-antibiotic era of medicine, where we face a situation where a number of medical treatment options would no longer be there. What happens in China matters for the rest of the world.'

Associated Press, February 10, 2013

An outbreak of SARS (Severe Acute Respiratory Syndrome) has been reported in Guangdong Province, China. It was discovered by Canada's Global Public Health Intelligence Network (GPHIN), an electronic warning system that monitors and analyses internet media traffic, and is part of the World Health Organisation's (WHO) Global Outbreak and Alert Response Network (GOARN). The disease comes on top of the problems caused by the violent earthquake that devastated the region two months ago. Members of worldwide aid agencies are still working in the area.

Guangdong Province previously suffered a SARS epidemic in 2002, although the Chinese Government did not inform WHO until four months later. It spread to 37 countries and there were 8,096 known infected cases and 774 fatalities. SARS is a viral disease that can initially be caught from palm civets, raccoon dogs, ferret badgers, domestic cats and bats. Initial symptoms are flu-like and may include lethargy, fever, coughs, sore throats and shortness of breath.

Les Knight, founder of the Voluntary Human Extinction Movement

(As quoted in *The World Without Us* by Alan Weisman, Virgin Books)

'No virus can ever get all six billion of us. A 99.99 per cent die-off would still leave 650,000 naturally immune survivors. Epidemics actually strengthen a species. In 50,000 years, we could easily be right back where we are now.'

The Rt Hon Geoffrey Smith, spokesperson for HM Government, UK

By now, you will all be aware of the terrible affects of the SARS pandemic. It is estimated that fifty percent of the population has already died of this dreadful virus and we fear that many more will succumb. Hospitals are full and medical staff have fallen victim at the same rate as the civilian population. All known medicines have failed to stop the devastating effects of what scientists have described as a virus aberration. No one could have foreseen this modern plague, and no one, it seems, can save us from it, not just here in Britain, but all around the world. We don't know when this pandemic will end. But we do know there are some who have a natural immunity. This small percentage is our only hope for the survival of the human race. All I can do is urge you all to make your peace with your god and remain in the safety of your homes as we truly face the apocalypse. God bless. And good luck.

Chapter 1

CLEETHORPES, ON THE EAST COAST, WAS FIRST
SETTLED by Danish Vikings in the eighth century. They
arrived with a reputation for violent conquest but they
stayed and made their homes. It was the latest occupiers
who were there simply for the rape and pillage.

Reaper and Sandra arrived in the early evening, travelling
through the Lincolnshire Wolds and heading towards the
town along a road that arrowed out of the countryside
towards the sea. They had seen no sign of life since Caistor,
once a small comfortable Georgian town a few miles back.
A door had closed silently in the market place as they
drove through. They had felt that their progress was being
watched and imagined the relief when they passed. Living
so close to the evil on the coast, survivors would be wary
of any intrusion into what life they held onto.

Reaper reversed the Astra into the drive of a semi-
detached house on the fringes of suburbia. The sun was low,
the sky blushing red. It promised good weather tomorrow.

5

He was in his middle forties, the girl still in her teens. They wore dark blue tee shirts, combat trousers and Doc Marten boots. Both wore Kevlar stab-and-bullet-proof vests. Reaper had two Glock handguns hanging from his belt, each in Viper drop-leg holsters strapped to his thighs. Sandra had only the one Glock in a similar holster on her right thigh. The guns held 17 rounds each. They both carried Heckler and Koch G36 carbines with twelve-inch barrels, fitted scopes and thirty-round curved magazines. More magazines were in the pockets of their police belts and vests. Both also had ten-inch Bowie knives in sheaths strapped to their lower right leg. Reaper also had three stainless steel throwing knives in a sheath on his left wrist. He had once asked himself how much armament he needed and had come to a swift conclusion: as much as he could bloody well carry.

They each put on a backpack, slung the carbines around their necks on straps and surveyed the empty road from the cover of a privet hedge. Nothing stirred. No cars, no people, no bicycles, no children playing in the late summer sun. Nothing had stirred down this road it seemed since the end of the world, five months before. Lawns and gardens were overgrown, and in the neat houses beyond the hedges would lie the occupants where the virus had taken them: in bed or sprawled on sofas to watch the news highlights of a dying world before they succumbed in their turn. Bodies that by now would be beyond putrefaction and breaking down slowly into bones and dust.

The two exchanged a glance and set off down the deserted road towards the centre of the seaside town, carbines held ready.

They kept to side streets and paused often to listen. At last they could see the flat line of the ocean between the houses, the reflection of the dying sun glittering upon its surface. Reaper had two locations fixed in his mind. He suspected the enemy occupied a prominent apartment block on the seafront to the south and, possibly, a nightclub or pub a mile or so to the north. That was where he had last encountered them. The sound of bottles clinking together made them freeze in the shadows of an alley. It had come from a small all-purpose store on the opposite corner of the road.

They exchanged hand signals. Sandra crouched and levelled the carbine at the store. Reaper crossed the street silently and paused, his back against the wall alongside the shop door, which he could see was not properly closed. Someone was moving around inside, trying to be quiet and failing. He risked a swift glance. One man. He was putting items into a cloth shopping bag. He risked a second glance but could see no one else. The man seemed unarmed.

Reaper looked back across the street and raised one finger and then held his palm out indicating that Sandra should stay in position. He slipped the strap of the carbine over his head and laid the weapon on the ground. As he rose back to a standing position, he took the Bowie knife from its sheath. The steel reflected the last rays of the dipping sun. A gun might cause someone to dive for cover. A long, wide blade was far more personal and terrifying and silent. They didn't want an alarm raised.

He moved into the shop quickly, the knife held forward at waist height. The man stopped, turned and his eyes widened in shock and horror. He dropped the cloth bag and the contents clanged on the floor. He raised his hands and said, 'I'm sorry. I'm sorry.'

This was no wolf. This was a sheep, doing the best he could to survive by grazing the remaining stock from out-of-the-way food stores.

Reaper put a finger to his lips to tell the man to be silent. He glanced around but there was nobody else. The store had a counter to the right and three cramped aisles. The section that had housed the booze was empty. Any frozen food still in the refrigerators would have been ruined since the electricity died, but there were still tins and packets on the shelves, and cans and bottles of soft drinks.

'I'm not going to hurt you,' Reaper said. 'I want information.'

The man was confused. He still expected to be hurt.

'What's your name?' Reaper said. *'Your name?'*

The man was perhaps forty, slim build, average height, average features. He wore jeans and trainers and a green tee shirt depicting the profile of a man with a Mohican hair cut and the words *Diesel: Home of the Brave*. The wearer wasn't very brave. He moistened his lips to lick away the fear and said, 'Bradley. Paul Bradley.'

'I'm Reaper.' The man was nervous but no danger. Reaper sheathed the knife. The man's eyes watched the blade disappear and he began to breath again but he was still nervous. 'Where do you live?'

'What?'

'Where do you *live*?'

'Erm. Nearby.'

'Do you live alone?'

'Er, no.'

'Who do you live with?'

'I look after someone.'

'Someone?'

'A girl. My daughter.'

'Just the two of you?'

'Yes.'

'Good.' He pointed to the bag on the floor. 'Get your stuff. Let's go.'

'Where?'

'Your place.'

'Erm …'

'Come on!'

The man picked up the bag hesitantly. It was obvious Paul Bradley didn't want to go with him but he didn't have a choice. Reaper and Sandra needed information and somewhere to stay for at least part of the night. Now they had found a possible informant, they couldn't let him out of their sight for fear someone else found him and learned of their presence. Near the entrance, Reaper noticed a rack of street maps of the town. He took one.

He opened the shop door, picked up the carbine and motioned for Bradley to come on out. The man did so, reluctance seeping out of every pore. Maybe he was so conditioned to the casual violence of the town that he still expected to become a kebab on Reaper's knife. His eyes widened again when he saw the diminutive figure of Sandra armed to the teeth.

'Which way?' Reaper said.

'Over there.'

Bradley pointed across the road to a row of red brick terraced houses. Further down the road, the houses became bigger and many had been converted into private hotels, but here they seemed to have been family homes. A curtain twitched upstairs in the house towards which they were heading.

The road was silent and deserted. They crossed quickly; there was no garden and the door faced onto the street. Bradley unlocked it with a shaking hand and Sandra pushed him unceremoniously to one side and went past him, carbine at the ready. Reaper closed the door and waited in the hall.

'Ground floor clear,' she said.

'We live upstairs,' the man said, his voice quavering.

'It's all right,' Reaper said. 'We're not going to hurt you. We're the good guys.' He gave Bradley a hard look to let him know that he could also get nasty and added, 'Are you sure there's only a girl up there?'

'Yes.'

'Is she armed?'

'Good God, no!'

'Call her. Tell her we're friends.'

Bradley looked at Sandra and back at Reaper. He licked his lips again and then looked up the stairwell.

'Meg? It's all right. They're friends. Meg?' Nobody answered. 'They're friends. You can come out. It's okay.'

Sandra edged past Reaper. He understood her logic. Seeing a girl might be reassuring. That is, if there was only a girl up there. He let her take the first two steps and then the girl appeared. She looked over the banister and took a half step back at the sight of their guns.

'It's all right, Meg. They're friends,' said Bradley, and she moved to the top of the stairs and Reaper saw that she was about fourteen. Bradley pushed past and went up to her, put his arms around her, whispered to her, calmed her. 'They're friends,' he said, in a louder voice, for their benefit.

Reaper and Sandra exchanged looks and followed.

Bradley and Meg lived in the back upstairs rooms of the house. The attic had also been converted into a third floor. Meg was slim and shy, dark hair, delicate features and about five feet tall. She wore a gingham dress, which probably made her look younger, ankle socks and trainers. She was nervous but seemed glad to have another girl to talk to. Reaper suspected she wasn't Bradley's daughter. If she was, they would be the first family survivors he had encountered. Maybe Bradley had made the claim for the sake of propriety. Maybe he was still worried by what people might think.

In the beginning, Reaper had told other survivors that they met that Sandra was his daughter – not because of what people might think, but because they both felt a bond and he thought that having a father might protect her from the attentions of a changed world. He suspected that this relationship was different.

Reaper took Bradley into the front bedroom for a private talk, but also to get him away from the girl. The man was reluctant to go but had no reason not to.

'Who runs the town?' Reaper asked.

'There were three gangs at the beginning. Now there's just one. There was a lot of shooting and screams at first. That's why we stay inside as much as possible. The gangs went looking for people. I think they went out of town, too – looking for people. Looking for women. The shooting died down until the other day. Then it all went off again but we kept our heads down.'

'Are there others like you? In hiding?'

Bradley nodded. 'I've seen people. When I've gone further than the corner shop for supplies. I've seen people who aren't with the gang.' He smiled sheepishly. 'They were as frightened as me.' He shrugged. 'I'm not good with violence. But I've done my best to look after Meg. To keep her safe.'

'Where did you meet her?'

'She …' Bradley stopped himself. 'She's my daughter. I said.'

'I don't believe you.' Bradley was too nervous, had too much to hide. Reaper said, 'Look. We come from a good place, it's called Haven. We've built a community there. All sorts of people. Working together. We've got other adults who found kids and looked after them. Now they're families, they have a chance again. You and Meg can come there with us when we leave. You can both have a life again.'

'She's …'

'Where did you find her?'

He sighed and said, 'I was a teacher. After it happened, I went to the school. So did Meg. She had nobody and things were starting to get wild. The gangs formed. I took her in and kept her safe.'

'You did the right thing. Don't worry. In these times, no one judges. Now, the gang … Tell me all you know about them. Where they live, where they drink. How many there are, what weapons they have. Can you do that?'

13

'Yes.' He was still hesitant, unsure. 'But why?'

'Because we're going to kill them.'

Bradley's look was one of disbelief but the longer he looked into Reaper's hard eyes, the more he realised that the intention was clear and unequivocal.

'There's too many,' he said.

'How many?'

'Maybe twenty.'

'That's not too many.'

'Maybe more. Then there are the hangers-on. The gofers.' He blinked and glanced away before looking back. 'And the girls. The women. When they get bored, they go looking for new ones. That's why we keep to ourselves, Meg and me. Nobody knows where we live. Nobody knows about Meg. They beat information out of people. If someone knew where we were, they would find and take Meg. That's why ...'

Reaper raised a finger. 'Is there a leader?'

'There's a biker, a sort of Hell's Angel. He's the leader.'

'What's his name?'

'Mad Dog. His real name is Bob Tyldesley.' He grinned nervously. 'I knew him before.' He meant before the virus. 'I taught him ten years ago. Nobody liked him. His nickname was Tilly. He was one of life's losers. Until now. Now he's in charge.' Bradley shook his head. 'He couldn't hold down a job before, didn't want to. Now he can do whatever he wants. And he does.'

'Where do they live?'

'They move from one hotel or pub to another. Drink them dry then move on. At the moment, Mad Dog and half a dozen of them are staying in a place called Bits and Pieces.' Reaper remembered the song by the Dave Clark Five from the early days of rock and roll. 'The pub was like a nostalgia thing. Swinging Sixties? It used to be the "in" place when things were normal. Bits was a young persons bar. It's attached to Pieces, which was a hotel with seven or eight bedrooms and a restaurant. It's the second time they've been there. He likes it because he used to be banned from it. They re-stocked it with booze and set up a generator. Sometimes, you would think everything was normal, you know, with the lights and the music. They don't do it every night. Only when they're in the mood.'

'Where do the rest stay?'

'Most of them sleep nearby. Wherever they like … guest houses, hotels. They have two other places. Sort of guard posts. One is a block of flats on the promenade near The Smugglers Inn. The other is a guesthouse on Isaac's Hill – the main road into town. It faces down the hill. There are always a couple of his gang in both places.'

Guard posts to the north and south guarding what? Anybody could enter the town along any of its other roads and avoid them, as Reaper and Sandra had done. Mad Dog – or Tilly, as Reaper preferred to think of him – didn't seem very bright.

'Has the gang killed anybody?'

Bradley laughed bitterly and said, 'Oh yes. Who's to stop them? They do what they like. They hang people from lampposts for fun. Have hunts. Let a bloke go, give him a start, and then shoot him down.'

'Why do they hang people?'

'Because they can.'

'Have any got away in the hunts?'

'No one has a chance. They let them go on the beach and take pot shots from the promenade. Have you seen the size of the beach? One bloke annoyed them, an old chap. He refused to run, just walked into the sea and drowned. Mad Dog was so angry, he pulled his body out of the water and shot him anyway, even though he was dead. I saw it happen. I was in a promenade hotel, looking for food.'

'And the women? Do they have a choice?'

Bradley shook his head. 'They do as they're told. They only keep the good-looking ones and a couple of older ones who can cook. And anyone is fair game if they catch you looking for food. Or even if they see you on the street. They just open up, like it's open season.' Bradley looked to be on the brink of tears.

'Why not move away?'

Bradley shook his head as if trying to shake his reasons together so they would make sense, even to himself. 'Some have. Some have been caught trying. It's more sport for them if they see you. They chase the cars and shoot them up.' He took a deep breath. 'I thought we could wait it out until it settled down, until … I don't know … something happened … like a diversion … and then perhaps we could sneak away. So far it hasn't happened.'

'It has now. Me and Sandra? We're the diversion.' He opened the town centre map on the bed. 'Now, show me where they are.'

Bradley marked the location of the flats on the promenade, the guesthouse on Isaac's Hill and the bar and hotel called Bits and Pieces. Reaper also had him draw a rough sketch of the floor plan of Bits and Pieces, so that he had an idea of the internal layout.

Bradley and Meg ate cold food from foraged cans. It was a diet they appeared to be used to. They had a camping stove but had run out of gas canisters. Reaper suspected it would be a major undertaking for Bradley to venture far enough to collect more, and that might never happen as the former teacher's nerves were on the verge of collapse. The house had fireplaces downstairs that could have been used for cooking, but the couple hadn't dared use them for fear the chimney smoke would give them away. Water still ran from the taps but, wisely they didn't drink it; purification systems had undoubtedly failed a long time ago. So they'd survived on lemonade.

Reaper and Sandra had flasks of coffee, bottled water and sandwiches. They shared their supplies and Bradley and Meg sipped the coffee as if it were nectar and ate the fresh bread with their eyes closed to savour what was, for them, a delicacy. Reaper and Sandra retired to the front bedroom to plan their moves; he sat in a chair and she sat cross-legged on the bed. Once behind the closed door, he looked at her quizzically.

'One bed,' she said. 'Meg hasn't said it, but they're sleeping together.'

'For comfort or sex?'

'Probably both.' She shrugged. 'Maybe it started as the first and became the second.'

Reaper stared at the floor. 'How old is she?'

'Thirteen and seven months.' He looked at her and Sandra added, 'The months are important. They take her closer to being an adult.'

'She's still a child.'

'She *was* a child. When it happened, people had to grow up quick. I was a child when you found me.'

Reaper looked at her. 'You were eighteen.'

'I still am. I'm also a widow and I feel I'm eighteen, going on death. How old do *you* feel Reaper? Like Methuselah? Forget the age of consent. This is the age of terror.'

He held her gaze. 'Before this happened Bradley would have been labelled, put on a register and sent to jail and we would all have said good riddance,' he said.

'That was then and this is now. Would it have been better if she had gone to the gangs?'

'It would have been better if he hadn't touched her.'

'But he did.' They continued looking into each other's eyes. 'Two lonely people.'

He began to snort his derision.

'Bradley's not strong,' Sandra said. 'He gave in to temptation. Maybe the girl needed the comfort? Maybe she instigated the comfort? Not everybody is like you, Reaper.'

'So he gets away with it? When this is done, we take them back to Haven as if it's all right? They set up home together? How does that fit in with our brave new world? What will the Reverend Nick say?'

'Nick won't be pleased. But these are new realities. The social order has shifted.'

'Morality hasn't. I can understand how it happened, but she is still a child and he shouldn't have crossed the line.'

'What are we going to do? Leave them behind? Take her and leave him? She's dependent on him, Reaper.'

'Stockholm Syndrome,' he said. 'Patty Hearst. She'll get over it.'

He could tell she didn't fully understand the references but she caught the drift.

'Girls who are nearly fourteen are not necessarily children,' she said. 'They weren't before it happened and they sure as hell are not now. Childhood is an endangered species, like polar bears used to be. In the wild, childhood doesn't exist, and this is the wild.'

He shrugged, uncomfortable with the situation and her words, and stared at the carpet again. Young people needed protection from older people until they could form their own opinions and thirteen – or fourteen – was no age for a girl to be seduced by a much older man. The knowledge of what had been going on between the teacher and the girl during their long days of isolation made his skin crawl. But was he being unreasonable, as Sandra suggested? Had times changed that much? What had happened had happened and the girl was, at least, physically safe and seemed content in Bradley's company.

If this had happened before the plague, the law would not have been understanding. And if Reaper had sensed the girl had been forced in any way into acquiescence, he would have had no compunction in taking Bradley downstairs and slitting his throat. But, of course, there were different types of persuasion and the girl had been in fear of her life ... Stockholm Syndrome ... Patty Hearst ... He might still slit Bradley's throat. It also left them with the problem of what to do with the couple when their mission was accomplished. How would they explain the arrangement to the ordered regime at Haven where childhood was still protected?

In the Middle Ages, marriages and liaisons with girls of thirteen had been considered normal. Sex was legal with girls that age until Victorian times. Jerry Lee Lewis married his thirteen-year-old cousin for chrissake, and still became a rock and roll legend. But that still didn't make it right. They hadn't slipped back to the middle ages yet, surely? And Victorian England had been a sexual cesspit. And this was not backwoods Louisiana.

'We'll have a problem when we've finished,' he said, and

looked up into her face again. He left the words hanging there for a moment: *when we've finished*. They both knew the challenge that faced them; they both knew one or the other of them might not make it to the finish. 'You sure?' He meant the mission.

'I'm sure.'

After devastation had swept the world, Reaper had been given a chance in a new life. A chance to make up for all the inadequacies he had displayed in the old. He had found and saved Sandra and taught her the skills of self-protection and she had become a warrior. They had gathered other shell-shocked survivors and led them to Haven, a former holiday village in a Yorkshire country estate between York and Scarborough that had offered them all a new beginning; the best chance for normality for two hundred souls in the cottages of the grounds and in the surrounding farms.

Once Haven had been established, he had allowed himself to fall in love again. This had been unexpected. He hadn't thought he deserved the right to fall in love. This wasn't part of the deal he had made for salvation with a god in whom he didn't believe. Kate had made the first move and he had finally accepted they really were in love. For a short time, he had found happiness again, even though it was tinged with guilt. He and Kate had planned to marry but, only three nights ago, she had been killed by marauders as wild and untamed as the gang led by Mad

Dog. The new despair had changed his outlook.

He no longer believed in salvation. He was now motivated by anger and revenge.

Sandra's joys had also been crushed in the same murderous incident, with the slaying of the husband she had married only weeks before. She, too, had taken refuge in the dark emotions that now ruled Reaper.

Maybe they were both suffering from survivor syndrome, the guilt of still living. For they had survived, not just the cataclysm that had changed the world, but the vacuous violence that had killed those with whom they had found love and hope for the future. Now, together, they were intent on removing violators wherever they found them, both to give the world a chance and because they wanted to wash their grief in blood. It was Mad Dog's misfortune that only a few days previously, Reaper had travelled through this town and discovered his regime.

Sandra looked at the map on the bed next to her.

'How are we going to do it?' she said.

Chapter 2

THEY DECIDED TO TAKE OUT THE GUARD POSTS FIRST and hope that any shots might be drowned by the noise of the disco in Bits and Pieces. Just their bad luck if Mad Dog decided to have a quiet night. Bradley was co-opted into their scheme, even though the teacher showed extreme reluctance. It was his bad luck that he'd admitted he had a car parked outside.

While Reaper and Sandra had been discussing their plans, Meg had changed into jeans and a tee shirt. The androgynous clothes made her look older and yet somehow less sexualised. The dress, Reaper realised, had been too similar to school uniform. Unsavoury suspicions lingered in his mind and he found it difficult to look at the girl without embarrassment. He sensed she felt the same, preferring to address any comments to Sandra rather than Reaper, and perhaps already distancing herself, ever so slightly, from Bradley.

They persuaded Bradley to help by giving him no

option, even when he cited Meg's safety as a reason why he should remain in the house to protect her. As protection, Reaper thought he would be as much use as an ashtray on a motorbike. The teacher surrendered the car keys and they bump-started his Ford Focus down the gentle slope of the road to avoid what might have been several noisy attempts to fire the ignition by key. It had been a warm summer. The car started sluggishly and with a groan, as if it resented the disturbance, but soon picked up to tick over quietly.

Sandra spent a few minutes with Meg alone before they left shortly before ten pm. The town was shrouded in dusk, the streets valleys of shadow. The lights from the generator-fed Bits and Pieces a glow above the roof tops to their left. Behind them, the front door to Bradley's house closed as Meg retreated to her sanctuary on the first floor. Bradley drove Reaper and Sandra towards the apartment block on the sea front. He parked two streets back and Reaper instructed him.

'You wait here. We will try and do this quietly but there may be gunshots. Whatever happens, you wait here. It's ten now. If we don't return, you can leave at eleven. Go back to Meg, look after her and try to leave town.' He held his arm in a strong grip that made the teacher wince. 'But we *will* be back. And you had better be here. Clear?'

'Clear,' he said, nodding his head.

Sandra and Reaper left the car and slid into the shadows, one covering while the other gained ground, then reversing the process so that they 'leap-frogged' each other silently towards the flat expanse of the sea, which sighed and gleamed in the soft moonlight. The previous occasion Reaper had been here, the doors to the apartment block had been open and unlocked. He wondered if they had improved their security. They had; the doors were locked.

The apartment block stood proudly overlooking the sea at a point where the main road kinked. It was a white-painted confection that, on first sight, had reminded Reaper of the sort of seaside accommodation where Hercule Poirot might have stayed in the 1920s or 30s. Tonight, he suspected it would not be occupied by anyone as cultured as the Belgian detective. The balconies at the front provided a clear view of any vehicles approaching from the south, while the corner windows of its upper floors had unrestricted views towards the town centre.

Light spilled from a flat on the second floor. Not electric light, but the dimmer cast of battery-operated camping lamps. They went round the front of the building and saw that the lighting extended to a French window and balcony. Reaper pointed and twirled his finger. 'Round the back,' he mouthed, and they retraced their steps past the locked entrance and shop windows, until they found a narrow alley, as dark as a cave. The service entrance was unlocked.

Reaper used the torch that hung on his belt to light their way along a corridor and through a door that led into the ground floor vestibule of the flats. There was a lift that was out of use without power and carpeted stairs. Dim light came in through the glass of the front doors and an even dimmer light could be seen from above. He switched off the torch and they went up quietly, carbines at the ready.

They had agreed what they would attempt but knew it might be difficult to achieve. No loud gunshots if at all possible. And, as they had no sound suppressors for their guns, that meant knives. Reaper felt his heart pounding as they climbed and wondered if steel was such a good idea. He had killed several times with the knife but Sandra? The eighteen-year-old had also wielded a blade with desperate efficiency when it had been essential, but in cold blood? He stopped himself glancing in her direction in case she thought he was questioning her commitment. That was never in doubt.

The light grew brighter as they climbed. The guards, it appeared, were afraid of the dark. They had left a camping light in the corridor on the second floor. From behind the closed doors, came the soundtrack of a film. Shots, tyres screaming. An action movie? Maybe a film; maybe a video game. Somebody in the room laughed. 'Look, look!' he yelled. Someone else shouted, 'Twat!' An item of furniture was kicked over.

A settee sat incongruously halfway along the corridor. Reaper put his carbine on the cushions; Sandra did the same. He removed the Glock handgun from the holster on his left hip and pulled back the slide to arm it. The safety was in the double action trigger. He depressed the trigger one click so the safety was off. Sandra did the same with her side arm and transferred it to her left hand. They took the Bowie knives from the ankle sheaths and held them in their right hands. No gunshots if possible but, once through the door, they would be relying on surprise and improvisation.

They exchanged a last look and Sandra nodded. Reaper kicked the door in with one well-placed boot at the level of the lock and led the way inside. Images came swiftly; actions were swifter.

Two men had been playing a video game on a laptop that sat on a coffee table. One was sitting on a sofa that faced it, controls still in his hand; the other was on his feet, a side table upended on the floor, where he had kicked it. Since the man on his feet was closer, Reaper stepped straight up to him and stuck the knife hard into his stomach, angling it upwards to dig beneath the rib cage and penetrate the heart. The man staggered backwards and crashed over the coffee table. The sound of the video game ended abruptly. Reaper followed the man to the floor, pushing hard. He realised that the man's breathing was heavy and that there was blood on his hand. He pulled the knife free and got to his feet. His victim hadn't made a sound.

Sandra reached her target before he could lift himself from the softness of the sofa's cushions. His arms were pressed at his sides for leverage as he attempted to rise, providing an unobstructed target for the deadly thrust of her blade: she pushed the knife deep into his throat, the serrated edge ripping both his vocal chords and carotid artery. The blood spouted; some of it onto Sandra, whose blonde hair was now partially crimson, her face a caricature of a 70s rock singer, only her face wasn't masked in paint. She pulled her knife free with a harsh grimace and, just for a second, Reaper wondered at what they were doing.

'What the …?'

A third man appeared in a doorway. He wore a tee shirt and nothing else and was rolling a cigarette.

'Don't move!' said Reaper, levelling the Glock.

The man dropped the makings of the cigarette and raised his hands. Sandra stepped past him and went into the second room with her own gun raised. Moments later, she returned, her gun holstered. The man in the tee shirt was taller than her by six inches. She kicked him behind the legs and he dropped to his knees. She grabbed his long hair in one hand and stuck the Bowie knife into his throat. Reaper sidestepped the arc of blood as she twisted the knife.

He wiped his own blade on the sofa and returned it to its sheath. He put the handgun in its holster. His mind was in turmoil. His own mission of revenge was one thing, but had it been necessary for him to transform Sandra into some kind of bestial killing machine? She pulled the knife free and kicked the still twitching corpse. Her breath was coming in short bursts as if she had run a marathon. She glanced at Reaper, her eyes without a semblance of normality – almost feral. Then she turned and went back into the other room.

The room where the slaughter had occurred was at the corner of the building and with the view towards the town centre. There was an open plan kitchen and dining area around the corner. He went the other way to follow Sandra into a bedroom that had open French windows and a balcony on which were placed a white metal table and two white chairs in art deco style. Very Hercule Poirot. The bed was large with a white metal frame. Upon it lay a girl who wore only a pair of black hold up stockings. Her small breasts looked as if someone had drawn around them with lipstick, until he realised that they were bite marks. A noose was around her neck and the end of the rope was tied to the top of the bed frame. Now he understood Sandra's second bout of violence.

He felt Sandra's eyes upon him. They had returned to normal but were filled with deep sadness and compassion. She had been there. She knew this girl's suffering. Reaper nodded to her and turned back into the other room. As he passed, he kicked the corpse of the third man.

Only now did detail expand the first impressions of entry. The man he had killed had been in his late twenties, unshaven, about six feet tall, no excess weight. He wore jeans and a sleeveless vest, presumably to accentuate his muscles, but which had done nothing for the body odour that had assailed Reaper's senses before the blood spilled. A reasonable specimen – for a bastard. The one who had had terminal trouble trying to rise from the sofa was shorter, but not by much, and fatter, which was probably why he had sunk back into the cushions as Sandra delivered the death blow. He had been early twenties, clean-shaven and in a fresh shirt. Even now, with the other odours taking over, he could smell the aftershave. What sort of twisted creature wore aftershave for a gang rape?

The third man was thin, weedy, and in his forties. Reaper remembered sunken eyes widening in horror in a skeletal face when he had walked out of the bedroom and seen them. The sort of downbeat piece of scum who would have found it difficult to get any half decent girl to look at him before the Happening. At times like this, Reaper hoped fervently that he was wrong about the afterlife. He might be an atheist but it would be good to think that these swine had gone straight to hell for an eternity of torment. He caught sight of himself in the mirror. He was blood splattered but not as drenched as Sandra. If anyone else walked through the door, she would scare them witless. He wondered how she was managing with the girl on the bed?

The girl was called Andrea. Sandra wrapped her in a pink raincoat that was too short and she wore flat black shoes. Reaper collected the men's weapons and put them in a small suitcase he found on top of the wardrobe. The apartments were plush and would have been expensive retirement homes before their owners died and the rooms were taken over by Mad Dog's animals.

Reaper led the way back, carrying the case in one hand, the carbine at the ready in the other; Sandra brought the girl, an arm around her in an attempt to diffuse her continued disorientation. The girl's face was blank as if desensitised by days, maybe weeks, of abuse.

The car was where they left it, which was a surprise. Reaper thought Bradley might have lost his nerve and deserted his post. He hadn't, but he almost did when he saw the state that Sandra was in. She looked like a survivor of a chainsaw massacre – or more appropriately, the perpetrator. He put the case in the boot and Sandra got in the back of the car with Andrea. Reaper got into the passenger seat.

Bradley kept glancing into the back and then at Reaper.

'Back to your place,' Reaper told him. 'That's Andrea. She's in shock.'

The teacher did as he was told. They drove to the house without incident and he parked in the silent street. They went inside and took Andrea upstairs. Sandra took her and Meg into the front bedroom and closed the door. They stayed together for long minutes. Reaper washed his hands; he wasn't bothered about his face or clothes. He counted any other stains as camouflage or deterrent. Sandra came out and nodded.

'They'll be okay. Meg is a resilient girl.'

'Time for Part Two,' said Reaper.

Bradley drove them to within two streets of Isaac's Hill, taking a detour to avoid going close to Bits and Pieces, which was now on their right. The night glowed with its lights. He was given similar instructions. Wait for an hour. If they hadn't returned by then or if he heard gunshots he should return to the house and wait. The man was becoming increasingly jittery. Much longer and he would be a liability. Much longer and he might break down and cry.

Reaper and Sandra approached the target carefully, taking their time. Shadows and silence. They glided through the streets. The flats were on a slight hill, facing any traffic approaching the town from the north. The entrance to the block was on a corner and to the rear. Lights showed from a first floor window. They crossed the road and inspected the entrance: a glass door that was locked. A dim light that glowed from somewhere above showed them a flight of stairs. Sandra faced outwards, at the ready; Reaper began to move into the darkness of a nearby alley, seeking another entry point, when she hissed to him. He turned and rejoined her and heard footsteps approaching. They both slipped back into the shadows.

Two people were crossing the road: a big man in front;

somebody slimmer behind and carrying a plastic shopping bag. Reaper placed his carbine on the ground and took out his knife. The back figure stumbled on the pavement in the dark and bottles clinked.

'Careful with those, bitch! Mossa needs his lube.'

'Mossa's a dirty sod,' a woman replied.

Another victim?

The man put a key in the lock of the door, both hands in sight. Reaper stepped from hiding, the man half turned, and Reaper put the knife in his stomach and pushed upwards.

'Jesus!' the man said, his voice turning to a whisper before the word was completed.

'It's okay,' Reaper said to the woman, over the man's shoulder. 'You're safe now.'

'Fuck,' she said and dropped the bag of bottles onto the pavement.

For a second, Reaper thought she was swinging her handbag into her arms and then saw that her handbag was an Uzi. He stared down the muzzle and she pulled the trigger. It clicked. The woman wore tight black leather trousers and a black leather vest. He could now see a tattoo on her arm that said *Evil Bitch* and here he was, still holding her boyfriend in an embrace of death on the blade of his knife.

'Shit!' she said, and Reaper knew she only had to move her thumb to find the safety.

Sandra shot her in the head with the carbine before she

could and the woman slid backwards with a neat hole in the front of her head and a larger one at the back.

Reaper pushed away the body he was still holding; the knife was still embedded. He pushed open the door and ran up the stair whilst pulling a Glock from his right hand holster. A door opened on the first floor and someone shouted, 'What's happening?'

'Mossa?' shouted Reaper, to gain a second of indecision.

He saw Mossa, silhouetted in a doorway. He was holding a handgun. Reaper shot him twice, chest and head, and kept on moving, stepped over his falling body and into the room, gun levelled. Sandra was a pace behind him. She slid into the room, her back to the wall, the carbine held in covering position. They were in the living room of a not particularly elegant holiday apartment. A fey young man sat on the sofa, his face a mask of terror. He was gulping for air and waving hands delicate enough for a Renaissance painting in front of his face.

'Who else is here?' demanded Reaper.

'No one. Just me.' He began to cry.

Sandra crossed the room to an open door, darkness on the other side. She kicked it all the way inwards.

'If there's someone in there, you're dead,' said Reaper to the young man.

'No one, no one,' tears on his cheeks, his whole body agitated. 'Just me. Just Mossa.'

Sandra went in low, kicked around, came out. He had

been telling the truth. Another door led into an empty bathroom.

'Who are you?' Reaper was becoming wary of assuming innocence, even from someone so camp.

'I'm Duncan.'

'What are you doing here?'

There were no other weapons in sight.

'I'm … I'm …' He cried again and then said with an effort, 'I'm Mossa's fuckpig.'

'What?'

'I'm his fuckpig. He fucks me.' The tears flowed. 'He fucking fucks me.'

For Reaper the tension went. He exchanged a look of sympathy with Sandra.

'No one will hurt you again, Duncan,' he said. 'Hide until this is all over. We're taking Mad Dog down.'

The man's tears and gulps paused at the enormity of what he had been told, as if it was beyond believable, and maybe it was. Reaper and Sandra left. They also left the handgun. Maybe Duncan would need it.

Downstairs, he retrieved his knife, wiped it quickly on the dead man's shirt and stuck it back in its sheath. He shouldered his carbine and took the Uzi. He pointed across the street and they took cover behind a parked car to wait and see if anyone came to investigate the shots. Two minutes later, they spotted three people dipping in and out of cover, coming from the direction of Bits and Pieces. One stayed on the far side of the road and the other two crossed cautiously. Reaper touched Sandra's shoulder and pointed to the man alone. She nodded and pointed the carbine, the red dot of the sight picking out the darker shade among the shadows.

'Your shot,' he whispered.

She took it, and the darker shade fell as Reaper stood up and blasted the other two with the Uzi in a four second burst that put them both down and twitching.

'Now let's go pubbing,' he said, sliding the empty Uzi beneath a car for safety.

Chapter 3

BITS AND PIECES WAS LIT UP LIKE A FAIRGROUND
RIDE. The pub had floor-to-ceiling glass windows that
could slide open in summer, so that the interior melded with
seating on the terrace. Tables and chairs spread all the way
to a chrome and glass bar that ran the length of the back
wall, lights shining and reflecting everywhere. A jukebox
played Presley singing *Love Me Tender*, the sound soft and
pensive. The door to the hotel was in the middle and to the
right was the dining room, where the lighting was dimmer
and more intimate. Next door was an alley and then what
had been an Indian restaurant.

They watched from across the road. Cars had been left
haphazardly, some double-parked. Men and some women
were in the bar. The men carried guns and all of them
looked agitated.

'Jesus!' Sandra said.

He looked at her and she nodded down the street. The
body of a woman hung from a rope attached to a lamppost.

It could have been mistaken for a bizarre Halloween street decoration except that it had once been a human being. From the clothes she wore, he would have guessed a middle-aged lady with a weight problem. Obviously not wanted by Mad Dog's gang and so used instead as entertainment. In the circumstances, the retribution he and Sandra were dispensing didn't seem so bad.

They exchanged another look, levelled the carbines, and started firing. Two males in the pub went down, sending furniture crashing, glass smashing, women screaming and everybody scrambling for cover. Shots were returned and they hunkered down behind engine blocks and wheels; the flimsiness of car bodies did not stop bullets.

The opposition was on both the ground and first floor and they fired indiscriminately but with enough frequency to make Reaper and Sandra keep their heads down. Some bullets came too close, sending showers of window glass over them.

'Shit,' said Sandra, as they crouched together.

'Okay?' Reaper said.

She nodded.

'Just take care.'

'You too.'

He placed his carbine in the gutter beneath a car, kissed two fingers and laid them on her blood-encrusted forehead. She gave him a tight smile and he was away, up the street, staying low, until the road curved and he could make a dash for the other side. From inside Bits and Pieces, the Righteous Brothers began singing *You've Lost That Loving Feeling.*

Sandra was alone. This was their plan. Reaper to go in and she to stay and provide a barrage of annoyance that would keep the enemy wondering who and how many they were fighting. She fired and moved, taking advantage of the double-parking that brought double protection, wary of the upstairs windows and the better elevation they afforded the defenders. She slid open the side door of a VW van that contained a mattress and ropes, shuddering to think what use it had seen, and fired through the driver's side window before retreating through the back door and taking another shot from the rear end of a double-parked Jag.

She noticed the preponderance of expensive cars that had been left haphazardly by gang members, rolled, and fired from behind the bonnet of a BMW. This was a crazy game she was playing and she didn't dwell too long on the possibility that it could get her killed. It shouldn't, she thought; she was a good shot, had trained hard and was focussed. The scum across the road had probably never been in a real fight and were showing a reluctance to show themselves for more than a snatched second whilst making their shots. *Go careful, Reaper,* she said in her head.

As Reaper crossed at the top of the street, he saw shadows flit across the bottom going in the opposite direction. A flanking movement. His heart sank.

'Incoming!' he yelled. 'Left!'

The odds facing Sandra were lengthening but there was nothing he could do other than continue with the course of action they had planned. Sandra was good. Probably better than anybody their enemy had ever faced. But still, the odds worried him.

He slid round the curry house and into the alley. After the bright lights out front it was like entering a cave. He closed his eyes for a few precious seconds to encourage night vision and then opened them again; he could now vaguely make out the sides of the alley. He went forward carefully and approached the yard at the back, a deeper expanse of space, a deeper darkness, so dark that he walked into a rubbish bin that was as high as his shoulder. The gunshots continued from the front, making his progress seem slower than it was, and then he stopped as a door opened from the back of the hotel restaurant. A dim light from inside illuminated a man coming out, a rifle in his hands. Reaper stepped behind the bin and took the Bowie knife from its sheath.

Even as he waited, the knife gripped at waist height, he reflected on how the changes wrought by the world had turned a normal civilian into a silent killer with a blade, who no longer minded the blood and the sharing of the last breaths of his victims.

As the man came around the bin, Reaper thrust the knife – in at the curve of the rib cage and upwards. His victim gave a yelp of surprise, dropped the rifle and, for a few moments, stood on tiptoes, his forehead resting on Reaper's shoulder. A shove to shift balance and the man slid off the blade and fell to the floor with no more noise than the slap of dead meat. Am I getting immune to death? Reaper thought. He hoped so, at least for the foreseeable future.

He went in the open door and closed it behind him. He was in a kitchen, two doors facing him: one into the hotel reception area, the other into the restaurant. Someone shouted from upstairs. 'Turn that fucking generator off!'

Someone else shouted, from downstairs. 'Baz! Turn the generator off.'

A voice from the hotel front door: 'I don't know how!'

'Shoot the fucking thing!'

Reaper stepped into the corridor and Baz, a small youth, ran straight onto his knife. He was going so fast that he took it out of his hand, spun around and fell face downwards onto it, driving it further into his body. Baz shuddered; a leg twitched. Reaper took out his handguns. He heard a noise in the restaurant. He went back into the kitchen and took the second door, the guns levelled, safeties off.

He was pointing them at a crowd of women and girls who were huddled in a corner.

'No. Please!' one shouted.

They held up their hands.

Victims.

'Stay here!' he said. 'No one will hurt you again. We're the good guys.'

He turned away and one of the girls screamed, alerting him to turn again, but too late. A man had been hiding in the middle of the crowd, crouched at the back. As he rose, the man fired a handgun. Reaper twitched his head as a bullet grazed his neck. Another hit him in the chest and he went down backwards, already sending a prayer of thanks to St Kevlar. The bullet hurt but didn't penetrate. The man must have thought he had killed him because he took three steps closer without administering the essential headshot. Reaper shot him in the right wrist, so that he dropped his gun, and again through the genitals with a bullet aimed up into his lower abdomen. A classic gut shot. See how he liked the pain.

The man fell to the ground as Reaper got to his feet and kicked away the handgun. The man crawled in a spiral, screaming and trying to hold himself with his left hand.

'Please, please,' he said.

Reaper looked at the crowd of fearful girls. 'Any more?'

'No more,' one said, and he could tell from her demeanour that it was true.

'Please, please,' the man whimpered.

Reaper leant over him and said, 'You should be pleading with God because She's the next person you're going to see. Just before She sends you to hell.'

He stepped back into the corridor and listened for the shots from across the road that meant that Sandra was still alive.

Sandra had heard his warning and had time to repress the momentary panic and work out what to do. Simple was best. Complex left too many things to go wrong. She fired across the street, rolled and took up another position. Fired again, grabbed an empty bottle from the gutter and went back into the VW van through the side door. She pulled back the mattress to reveal the metal base of the vehicle, tied a piece of thin rope around the bottle, which she balanced on the wheel arch, paid out the rope and hoped it would be long enough. She left the van by the open back door. Another shot over the double-parked Jag and she was back on the pavement.

Three shadows were moving closer, into and out of doorways and the cover of the vehicles. She laid the carbine on the ground and took out the Glock. Seventeen bullets, she told herself. She only needed three.

From one of the pockets in her vest, she took out a compact, opened it and held it low by the rear tyre of the van. She crouched silently and watched the men in the mirror. They were nervous: they moved slowly, staying foolishly together for the comfort of numbers. As they neared the front of the VW, she pulled the rope and the bottle fell, the noise echoing in the emptiness of the van's interior, and Sandra stepped sideways onto the pavement in a crouch.

The men had half turned at the noise, a half turn that gave her a second of advantage. She shot the nearest in the right arm and he went down; her second shot hit a small

43

man at the rear who carried a sub-machinegun. He had begun to face forward again and the impact tightened his trigger finger and from close range he blasted a third man, fat and middle aged who was carrying a sawn-off, sending him banging along the side of the van.

Sandra let out the breath she didn't know she had been holding and straightened up – and the first man she had put down fired a single shot with his left hand that hit her squarely in the chest and knocked her to the ground. She rolled, pointed and fired again. This time a head shot. Chest and head. The man no longer moved. She sat up, flexed her shoulders and wondered how Reaper was doing.

Reaper took a glance from the hotel reception into the well-lit pub. Two men: one over to the right by the jukebox that was now playing Pat Boone singing *Love Letters In The Sand*; another to the left. Everyone else had to be upstairs.

He stepped through the doorway, both guns raised. He didn't have a clear shot to the right but opened up with both guns, smashing mirrors, tables, glass panes, until a bullet caught the man in the corner and lifted him upright so that he could provide the coup de grace of chest and head. He bounced sideways into the jukebox. The jukebox hiccuped. Pat Boone was cut off short and Jerry Lee Lewis burst in abruptly and loudly with *Great Balls Of Fire*.

The bullets he had fired to the left had kept the other occupant of the room behind cover. Reaper fired twice more and a table spun sideways revealing his enemy.

The man squealed – he actually *squealed*, dropped his weapon and raised his hands. Reaper shot him twice, same formula. What would he do with prisoners? What remained of society could do nothing with murderers and rapists except execute them. They could not put them in jail, punish or rehabilitate them and they could not allow them to go elsewhere and pollute another part of what was left of the world. Death was the only clear answer.

A glance behind the bar, to make sure no one was hiding there, and he went up the stairs.

As he neared the top, he heard footsteps running, and when he gained the right hand corridor, saw someone disappearing through a window at the end. He ran past three open doorways without pausing to check if anyone was inside. He leaned out of the window and shot the escapee in the top of the head as he negotiated a metal fire escape. More shots to make sure as the body tumbled. The upper glass in the window shattered and he turned to face a man who had come out of the far bedroom holding a handgun. A burn on his left thigh and another thump in the Kevlar vest. Reaper staggered but kept his footing and fired both guns – never mind chest and head; his adversary was too close for niceties. Reaper sent him tumbling down the stairs.

Four steps to the first open doorway. Inside a man crouched, his back to the wall by the window, his knees drawn up, a gun on the floor by his feet, his hands in the air waving like white flags. Four shots to penetrate the knees and arms to ensure the kill. Two more for good measure to stop him twitching.

Reaper was breathing heavily. His senses were heightened although he was deaf from all the gunfire. Through the vibration of the wall, he had the impression that a scuffle was taking place next door. As he turned, someone took a shot at him through the open doorway, missed and started running. Three steps to the doorway and his attacker paused at the top of the stairs: an ordinary-looking bloke in jeans and a sweatshirt that said *New York*; copious sweat on his face as if he'd been in a shower; mouth open; breathing laboured; fear in eyes that darted everywhere, still hoping for freedom. Almost as an after-thought, he raised the handgun he carried and pointed it. Reaper already had both Glocks levelled. Two shots from each threw the man backwards into the wall and then he fell down the stairs, free at last.

'Where are you Tilly?' he roared, even though the words sounded as if they were coming through soggy cardboard.

From the room next door, the one the last shooter had left, came a reply. 'Bastard. Who are you?'

'I'm the Reaper, Tilly. And I've come for you.'

The door of the room was partially closed and bullets from a sub-machinegun smashed into it, smacking into the frame, and turning the panels into matchsticks. Reaper waited until the burst had ended, kicked in what remained of the door and stepped forward with both Glocks levelled. Mad Dog Tyldesley was at the other side of the room, changing the magazine of an Uzi.

'Say hello to the devil,' Reaper said, and pulled the triggers of both guns. Both clicked on empty.

Fuck. How had he used 34 bullets? Thoughts filled his mind fleetingly. He hoped Sandra was okay, that she would get away, maybe even finish the job. At least he'd done his best. If there was a God and She was in a good mood, he might be reunited with Kate.

Tyldesley smiled and displayed a gap where his two upper front teeth should have been. He was maybe thirty, a sloppy six feet in height with a shaved head, his body already going to seed. His arms were flabby in a black vest. He raised the Uzi, and fell flat on his face in front of Reaper, who heard the sound of the carbine a fraction after the bullet had hit the so-called Mad Dog in the back.

His brain took a second to return to live mode. Tyldesley was still breathing. Sandra had shot him through the window. Reaper kicked away the Uzi and slowly and with deliberation reloaded both Glocks with new magazines. Tyldesley was twitching and breathed heavily at his feet. Both hands were stretched in front of him; on the knuckles of one was spelled the word LUVE, on the other HATE. Even the tattooing had been DIY and poorly done. It seemed to sum up his life. Reaper pointed one of the guns at his head and ended it.

He went to the window but stayed out of the line of fire.

He shouted, 'Good shooting, Sandra. You got Mad Dog!'

'You okay Reaper?' He could barely make out her voice.

'I'm fine. You?'

'I'm good.'

'Stay put. I may flush some out of hiding!'

Downstairs, the jukebox had become silent.

He tried the other bedrooms. The front ones were empty. In one of the rear bedrooms, he found a girl sitting in bed, hysterical and holding the duvet as if it were a steel sheet to divert bullets.

'Are you alone?' he said.

'Yes,' she whispered. 'Don't hurt me.'

He lip-read the words and, when she pointed with a shaking finger to a wardrobe, he fired six shots into it and a man fell out. He put a final bullet in his head.

'The other girls are downstairs,' he said, scarcely able to hear his own voice. 'You're safe now.'

He walked through the gun smoke and silence of the stairs, stepping over bodies as he reached them, feet crunching on glass and expended shells. The girls were still in the restaurant. Their numbers seemed to have grown. The man he had shot in the gut was dead; a kitchen knife had been stuck in his throat. His memory prompted, he went to the body of the small youth, rolled it over, and retrieved his knife.

He stood in the doorway of the restaurant and one of the girls said, 'Is it over?'

Again, he had to read her lips.

'It's over,' he said. His voice distant even inside his own head, and yet even now he was working out percentages. 'I need to know how many of them there were. We visited the flats first. Work out how many there were and we'll see if the body count matches. If there are any left, we'll hunt them in the morning.'

The girl was the same one who had spoken to him earlier. She looked to be in her twenties but the room was in shadow.

'We also need to collect all the guns. The weapons.' He wondered why he was drifting into details that none of them needed. He waved his right hand in a dismissive gesture to discount the last instruction and realised it still held a Glock. Instead, he shook his head and said, 'It's over. You're safe.'

'You're wounded,' the girl said.

'I'll live.'

He walked into the bright lights of the pub.

'Sandra,' he shouted. 'I'm coming out. Cover me.'

He crossed the road in lights still ready for a premier but no one shot him.

Sandra stood up from behind the car where she had been waiting and he finally holstered the guns.

'You okay?' he said softly.

'I got hit in the tits again,' she said.

He pulled her to him and they embraced and she began to cry.

'I don't know if we can do this again,' he said.

'Only if we have to.'

'I love you,' he said.

'Mutual, Reaper.'

They broke apart and he walked back into the street.

'If any of Mad Dog's people have survived, this is their time to leave!' he shouted. 'You have thirty minutes amnesty! After that, you're dead! Thirty minutes to leave! This town is back in the hands of its citizens! The gangs are finished! Twenty-nine minutes to leave. Your amnesty is running down!'

Still no one shot him.

Chapter 4

REAPER TOOK COLD BOTTLES OF PERRIER FROM THE generator-operated fridges in the pub and then he and Sandra left the women in charge and walked to Bradley's house. The wound in his thigh was raw; the one on his neck annoying and his ribs ached.

The teacher had packed the car with belongings and was trying to persuade Meg to get in. Andrea, the girl they had rescued from the sea-front apartments, was standing wide-eyed and fearful on the doorstep. At least she was better dressed, wearing a tracksuit provided by Meg.

Bradley's nerves had not improved when they walked out of the night.

'I heard the shooting,' he explained. 'Lots of shooting. I thought it best to leave while we could. You said ...' Meg pulled free from his grip.'I wanted to get her somewhere safe.'

'We can't leave Andrea,' Meg said, stepping back to the doorway where the two girls embraced.

Bradley stared down the street past Reaper and Sandra, as if expecting pursuit.

'There's no need to leave,' Reaper said. 'We killed them.'

There were stares of disbelief.

'Killed them?' Bradley said.

'All the bogeymen have gone,' Reaper said. 'Tomorrow is a fresh start. But we're tired.'

'We need to sleep,' said Sandra.

She walked into the house and the two girls followed. Reaper trailed behind, leaving Bradley on the pavement with his half-packed car. He could go where the hell he liked. The girls needed to be able to believe that what Reaper had said was true. Sandra reassured them. Reaper splashed water in his face and handed the girls two spare bottles of still-cold Perrier. He was not at all upset that he didn't have one left for Bradley, who had followed them reluctantly upstairs.

Sandra said, 'Do you have a first aid kit?'

Reaper was not surprised when Bradley said he did. It was an item, he said, that he had acquired early in what he described as the 'interregnum', the period that had started after the mutant virus had swept the world. Perhaps he thought Reaper was the new Prime Minister who would impose a fresh democracy with the power of the Glock automatic.

'I'll need you first thing,' Reaper told Bradley.

'What … Why? You said it was over.'

'It is. I'll need you to take me to our car. I'm buggered if I'm walking.'

The two girls went up to the attic room, leaving Bradley to go into the back bedroom.

Sandra took Reaper into the bathroom to tend his wounds. The graze in the neck she anointed with some kind of unction. The thigh wound was more severe and might have chipped the bone. As it was, it had removed a chunk of flesh.

'Trousers,' she said.

He removed the Kevlar vest and his weapons and dropped the trousers. He winced when she probed the rawness and she said, 'I thought you were a tough guy?' After a moment or two, she said, 'This probably needs stitching or a flesh transplant. I'll bandage it for now.' She applied more unction, gauze, bandage and tape. 'You'll have to see Greta when we get back.' Greta Malone was their doctor: as far as they knew, the only doctor in Yorkshire.

Reaper pulled up his pants, picked up his kit and followed Sandra into the front bedroom. She took off the Kevlar vest and the gun belt but nothing else and lay on the far side of the bed, facing the window. Reaper stacked his weapons and the vest and climbed alongside her.

'Hold me, Reaper,' she said.

He rolled on his side and he held her as he looked at the night sky through the window over her shoulder.

'That first night,' she said, 'you held me like this. Remember?'

'I remember.'

She cuddled into him and her breathing eased; tension began to seep away.

'I miss him, Reaper.'

'I know. I miss him, too. And Kate.'

Jamie and Kate had both been killed a few days before. Without being over-dramatic, they had laid down their lives to protect the Haven they had been building together.

He could hear her crying softly. After a while, after the tears had stopped, when he'd thought she was asleep, she said, 'What we did tonight. It was crazy.'

'Yes it was.'

'Were we crazy?'

'Probably, we were very crazy.'

'But did we do right?'

'We killed some bad people. We freed some innocent people who now have the chance to be good.'

'But that's not why we did it, is it? We did it for revenge.'

'Yes, we did it for revenge.'

'After Jamie, I didn't want to live, except for revenge.'

'And now we've had it, love. We've had more than enough.'

She lay silently in his arms for a while and then said, 'Will we do it again?'

He kissed the back of her head and said, 'Only if we have to.'

'I love you, Reaper. I'm glad I'm your daughter.'

'Mutual,' he said. 'I love you, too. Now, get some sleep, daughter.'

Sandra was still sleeping when Reaper slipped out of the bedroom at six. He kitted up on the landing and tapped on the door of Bradley's room. While he waited, he drank from a bottle of water. The teacher had also slept fully dressed, if he had slept at all. His hair was tousled, which made him look younger. But still not young enough.

Bradley drove Reaper through empty sunlit streets without speaking. He dropped him by the Astra on the outskirts of the town and drove immediately away. Reaper felt liberated to be in his own car, away from the presence of their reluctant host. He sat for a moment and reflected that he and Sandra had attempted the impossible because of their need for righteous revenge and had, against all odds, succeeded. He didn't know whether to feel relief that they had survived yet again or dismay at the depth of malevolence they had displayed. Maybe a mixture of both. But it had been cathartic for them and a necessity for the people they had liberated.

By the time he got back to the house, Sandra was kitted up and the two girls were dressed and ready for what the new day might bring.

'We'll go back to the pub and see the girls,' Reaper said. 'The whole town will have heard the shooting and know something major happened last night. Maybe we can entice some of them out.'

'We'll follow you,' said Bradley. 'After we've finished packing the car.' He shrugged. 'No point staying here, now.'

Reaper wasn't sure of his motives and Meg seemed more eager to visit the scene of the previous night's mayhem, but she agreed with his suggestion. Andrea came with them in the Astra.

'Don't be long,' Reaper warned.

Reaper drove the short distance to the pub and hotel and the bits and pieces that remained of Bits and Pieces. He stopped the car in the middle of the road and, for a moment, they didn't get out. The generator was still on and the girls and women had cleared some of the debris and were eating breakfast on tables in the sunshine. The body of the middle-aged woman that had been hanging from the lamppost had been removed, but three more women had been hanged from other lampposts in her place. The people on the terrace, a few men among them, stopped eating. Some got to their feet and nervously held guns.

They got out of the car slowly. Three women came from the pub and called to Andrea and she ran into their arms. Someone shouted, 'They're back,' and someone on the terrace began clapping and this built up into a general round of applause. Reaper had experienced bizarre moments since the end of the world but this had to be among the weirdest. He and Sandra self-consciously acknowledged the rather restrained acclamation. Two of the women led Andrea away and the third approached them. She was the spokeswoman from the night before. She offered her hand.

'I'm Tanya Metcalfe. We met last night.'

Reaper shook her hand. 'Reaper,' he said. 'This is Sandra.'

The two girls shook hands and Tanya said to Sandra, 'You were brilliant.' She glanced back at Reaper. 'You both were.'

The women probably needed a heroine more than a hero. Reaper could understand that. He glanced at the bodies that swayed in a gentle breeze.

'What happened?'

Tanya's eyes slid away for a moment. She didn't want to look at the bodies.

'Not all the women here were reluctant. Most suffered and some were coerced. Some took to the life with enthusiasm. They embraced it. They were part of it.' She shrugged. 'Retribution got out of hand. Maybe someone should have tried to stop it.' She meant she should have tried. 'This morning, I think everyone is sorry it happened.'

Reaper could hardly complain if the survivors had instigated their own justice in the euphoria and probably hysteria of deliverance from a living hell. His own justice had been dispensed with righteous finality the night before. What was done was done. Time to move on. He raised his nose at the smell of cooking. The men and women at the tables had resumed eating.

'Who are the men?' said Sandra.

'They were captives. Used to do work the gang didn't want to do or couldn't do. One's a motor mechanic, another an engineer. We've got a dentist, too. And a baker. There are nine of them. The others were used as labourers.'

'How many women?' Sandra asked.

'Twenty-two. Three are in their forties. They were used for washing, mending. Domestic duties. Useful stuff. The rest of us are aged from thirteen to twenty-eight.' She looked at Reaper defiantly. 'We were used for entertainment.'

'Not any more,' he said, his nose still twitching.

'Hungry?' asked Tanya.

'Very,' he said.

She led them across the terrace to a table inside the pub.

'Omelette okay?' she said.

'Sounds good,' said Sandra.

The young woman left them to go to the kitchens as they took their seats. When she returned, she joined them.

'We collected the guns, like you suggested. They're in the dining room. We moved the bodies from down here. They're in the yard at the back. We did a count. There were twenty-six in the gang, including Tyldesley.'

He was pleased she hadn't referred to him as Mad Dog.

'We did a body count, too,' Reaper said. 'We got twenty-five. So we're one short. All things considered, that's not bad. If the one we missed has any sense, he'll be hiding or running. Either way, I can't see him being a threat.'

A man in his forties came from the kitchen. He carried a tray on which were cups, knives and forks, butter, condiments, a pot of coffee and a loaf of bread that was still warm. He unloaded it onto their table and shook their hands.

'Malcolm,' he said, in introduction. 'Thank you. Thank you. I don't know how you did it but what you did was a wonderful thing. I'll bring the omelettes.'

Sandra and Reaper exchanged a bemused look. Then the food came and they ate.

Once the edge had been taken from his appetite, he said to Tanya, 'It might be useful touring the town and letting people know the old regime is dead. Some kind of loudspeaker would be good. Get them to come out of their hiding places. You'll have to get together to start organising.'

Tanya said, 'What about you? Where will you go? Where did you come from?'

Sandra said, 'We're from a community near Scarborough. We've gone back to the land. People from all over, different occupations, lifestyles. We're farming, starting schools, finding energy sources.' She laughed. 'We've got a mad scientist who wants us to use wind power and solar energy.'

'That sounds incredible. How many of you are there?'

'Two hundred?' Sandra glanced at Reaper. 'Three hundred?'

Reaper said, 'We're based at what used to be a holiday village on a country estate. The place is called Haven. We've expanded into the farms and villages nearby.' He took another mouthful and interpreted Tanya's look. 'If you want, you can join us. You all can. There's strength in numbers.'

Tanya nodded. As well as liberation they were being offered a new home that had already been established.

'But first, you should get local citizens to come out of hiding. Tell them Tyldesley is gone. That they have to decide what they want to do.'

'There's a loud hailer Tyldesley used. When they had sport on the beach.'

'We heard about that,' Sandra said.

'If you'll excuse me, I'll get someone to start touring the streets and telling people the news.'

She left and they continued eating and drinking excellent coffee.

'Do you think they'll come with us?' said Sandra.

'I think it's their best option. We've already got a toe-hold; they'd be starting from scratch.'

They finished the food and strolled out into the sunshine. A man and a woman were standing across the street, watching what was happening at the pub with fascination. Two women and a child were further up the street, approaching slowly and warily, as if ready to run if the vibes suddenly changed.

'They're coming out already,' said Reaper.

'Do you think we might scare them away?' Sandra said, and he had to admit that, kitted up and draped with guns and knives, they were probably an intimidating sight.

They returned to the terrace where they could watch what was happening unobtrusively. Others had finished eating and were rummaging through the upstairs rooms of the hotel and in the nearby guesthouses where Reaper supposed some of them had been living.

'I'll go and get some more coffee,' he told Sandra, and found Malcolm in the kitchen. He noticed Tanya was in the dining room, holding what looked like a meeting. When he returned with a tray Sandra said, 'Two cars have gone out to spread the news. I suppose now, we wait.'

'Seems like a good idea.'

They sat and drank coffee and watched the world organise itself. After a while, Reaper said, 'Where's Bradley and Meg?'

'They'll be here. He daren't not be here.'

As if the words were an invocation, the Ford Focus turned into the street and stopped. Meg jumped out and began walking quickly towards them. Sandra raised an arm in greeting. Bradley got out of the driver's side but, before he could catch her up, the girl was grabbed by somebody who leapt from between two parked vehicles.

'Who the hell …' said Reaper.

The man held Meg from behind with one arm around her shoulders. In the other hand he held a gun that was pointed at her head.

'Christ,' said Sandra. 'Is that …'

'Duncan,' said Reaper.

'Come on out, you bastard! You know who I want!' shouted Duncan towards the pub. His voice was close to hysteria. The hand holding the gun shook. Although Reaper had thought him fay, he was tall, and his grip around Meg's shoulders seemed firm.

Behind them, Tanya said, 'Oh God. It's Duncan. He's the one that got away.'

Not a victim, then.

Sandra slipped away to one side, Tanya the other. Reaper, now alone, got to his feet and walked to the edge of the terrace.

'It's me you want,' he said. 'Let the girl go.'

'I'll let her go when I'm ready!' Duncan screamed. 'When I'm ready. You are a bastard. You have ruined my life! And now I'm going to ruin yours. Get down here! Now!'

Reaper stepped down from the terrace, leaving his carbine behind. He took two paces and stopped.

'You bastard!' hissed Duncan, his mood switching from high hysterics to pure viciousness. 'Who asked you to come here? Who sent you a fucking invitation to the feast, eh? You were not wanted, not needed.' Spittle came from his mouth and suddenly his mood switched again and he was crying. 'You killed him. Shot him. You shot Mossa! My Mossa.'

'Let the girl go,' said Reaper. 'You can have me. Just let her go.'

'I will,' he shouted, almost back in control of himself.

'Well, I might. It depends how I feel.' He snarled the words. 'But first you have to do what I say. Simon says. We're going to play the game. You know it? And Simon says drop that gun belt.' Reaper hesitated and Duncan screamed, 'I said drop it!'

Reaper took his time unfastening the belt. Then he held it in one hand while he unclipped the straps that held the holsters to his thighs. Slowly, he held out the belt with the holstered guns in front of him to gain Duncan's attention, crouched low, despite the pain from his thigh, and laid it on the ground. The longer this pantomime lasted, the better chance Sandra would have of getting a shot at this madman.

He stood up and held his arms away from his side. If Meg gave him half a chance, he might be able to take him with a throwing knife. He had practised the move often enough: grasp one of the knives ensconced on his left wrist in the fingertips of his right hand and one backward flip with accuracy and strength, and he could make him a new windpipe. He had done it before. But not with an innocent in such close proximity.

'Now take off that vest!' Duncan said, a shade calmer and less strident now that the handguns had been relinquished. He began to laugh. 'I'm going to strip you, you bastard. And then I'm going to shoot your dick off.'

Reaper pulled apart the Velcro fastenings on the Kevlar vest, held it out in front of him, and dropped it on the ground. Meg struggled and Duncan pulled her more viciously and ground the barrel of the gun into the side of her head. The girl screamed in pain and fear and Bradley stepped forward.

'No,' the teacher shouted. 'She's done nothing. Let her go.'

In the periphery of his vision, Reaper saw Sandra behind a vehicle, the carbine at her shoulder, waiting for a clear shot.

'Fuck off!' Duncan shouted at the teacher, momentarily diverted, but Bradley stepped forward, arms outstretched towards the girl. Duncan moved his gun hand, pointed the weapon at this new threat – and shot him. Bradley was flung backwards. Duncan looked surprised at what he had done as Meg wriggled from beneath his arm and flung herself sideways, causing him more consternation and confusion.

Now, Sandra! Reaper urged silently, but he saw that Tanya had stepped forward and was blocking Sandra's line of fire. He plucked a throwing knife between his fingertips but, before he could launch it, Tanya was blasting Duncan from close range with a revolver. It looked like a .38 snub-nosed Smith and Wesson, notorious for its inaccuracy but which, from three feet, was totally deadly.

Tanya kept firing until all six chambers were empty, each bullet dancing Duncan on his tiptoes with a look of confusion frozen on his face. After the final shot, he fell backwards and was still, his blood pooling around him.

Reaper returned the knife to its sheath on his left wrist, picked up his belt and put it back where it belonged around his waist. He picked up the vest and carried it in one hand as he walked towards the tableau before him. Sandra had joined Tanya and put an arm around her shoulders. Tanya was crying silently, tears flowing down her cheeks as they both stared at the body of the man she had killed. Meg was crouching near Bradley who lay on his back, blood bubbling from his chest. He reached out a hand but the girl didn't take it.

'I'm sorry,' he said, and his fading gaze found Reaper. 'I'm sorry,' he said again, and died.

Andrea came from the crowd and took Meg by the shoulders and led her away. The girl was dry-eyed and composed.

Reaper looked down at Bradley without emotion. At least it was one problem solved.

Chapter 5

THEY HAD A CONVOY WHEN THEY LEFT. Forty of the town's hidden citizens abandoned the shadows in which they had lived and gathered outside Bits and Pieces. They came singly, in couples and small groups. Others, they said, still preferred to stay safe and anonymous until they were convinced that Mad Dog's gang had really gone. The former captives kept to themselves. The divisions were already apparent. Did the abused feel shame at what they had suffered or anger that those in hiding had escaped? Did the newcomers feel superiority, guilt or gratitude at not being victims? Reaper knew the complex emotions that could follow the end of a tyranny. It needed time before a normality of sorts could prevail.

He told them about Haven. He said anyone who wished could return there with him and Sandra. Or they could stay in the town and create their own community or go travelling, as others had done, in a search for their own peace of mind. There was a lot of empty countryside out there, he told them, and the future lay on the land. He warned them that towns and cities would not be totally empty; that there would be survivors like themselves who might be possessive over warehouses and stores. Whatever their wish, the choice was theirs.

Of those who had remained hidden for the duration of Mad Dog's reign, only two men opted to come to Haven. The rest decided to stay and build their own lives. Seven of the captive men also chose to stay, along with the three women in their forties who had been used by the gang for domestic duties. They had no sexual history to complicate their rehabilitation. One of the men and two of the women opted for the open road, perhaps to seek a place where no one knew their past. Seventeen of the women, plus Meg, wanted to go to Haven. They were taking home twenty-one new souls.

The next morning, that number was reduced to twenty when they found the body of one of the women who had made a different choice. Unable to face a future after her horrific recent past, she had taken an overdose of pills on her first night of freedom.

They formed their convoy of vehicles and took only bottled water and food for the journey north, as well as the armaments and ammunition. Sandra took the lead vehicle and Reaper the rear, so that they would lose no one on the way. But when they reached the bridge across the Humber, a car containing three women pulled over.

He stopped alongside, lowered his window and looked at them questioningly. The driver shook her head.

'We've changed our mind,' she said. 'We're going south.'

He nodded and did not attempt to dissuade them.

'Don't forget where we are,' he said. 'You'll always be welcome.'

She nodded her thanks.

'Good luck,' he said. He thought they would need it.

'You, too.'

He drove on and didn't look back.

They reached Haven and he followed the last car through the entrance in the high stone wall. James Marshall, the fourteen-year-old they had found in a public school near Scarborough, closed the gates behind them and wrapped the chain around the metal to make it look as they were locked and the place abandoned. James was young but he was a deadly shot. He had trained at his school as a military cadet.

On the hill in the lee of a copse of trees, was the camper van in which Reaper and Sandra had left their own inland city behind and headed here, picking up survivors along the way. The van was now used as a guard post. Standing outside it was Jenny, the blonde schoolteacher, delicate as an English rose, still only in her twenties.

Both she and James wore the same blue combat trousers, tee shirts and Kevlar vests as Reaper and Sandra.

They carried sidearms and carbines. *Special Forces*. Sandra had given them the name when it had all started and that was how they were known: Special Forces. Arif, the young Asian with attitude and a sense of life, had been one of them. That life had ended on the grass outside the van, the first victim of a night assault by superior forces. Reaper had found his body. In the same action, when they had fought back, Jenny and James had stood side-by-side, exchanging fire with the enemy. In the same action, Sandra had lost Jamie and he had lost Kate. Had it only happened a few short days ago?

He hadn't thought returning would be this hard. He drove to the top of the hill along the narrow road and stopped. The original manor house was in the bottom of the valley with farm buildings and stables spreading from its rear. A purpose built village of twenty holiday cottages had been created on the near slope. The road ran between them and ended in a village square and crossroads that was marked with a six-foot stone cross on a plinth. The last building at the bottom of the hill was The Farmer's Boy. That was where Kate had lived.

All was activity outside the manor house as the new arrivals disembarked. In the fields beyond, people worked. In the cemetery they had created on the other side of the barn, lay Kate and Jamie. They had been laid to rest in a communal grave along with Milo, garrulous, warm-hearted Jean Megson, Arif and the rest. His eyes misted but he had to control his emotions. He saw Sandra down below looking up the hill towards him. She, too, would be suffering at her own loss. He drove down the hill and joined her.

The new arrivals were welcomed and briefed by a reception team that included the Rev Nick Waite, in charge of spiritual guidance, Pete Mack, in charge of acquisitions, Judith, in charge of home comforts, and Ashley, the former Para who was in charge of Haven's defences. Together, they had achieved so much in such a short time, but at a great cost.

England might be under-populated, Reaper reflected, but those who had survived the virus included rogues and killers as well as the innocent. It was inevitable that for every two or three communities like Haven, you would get a robber baron with ambitions of empire or a Mad Dog Tyldesley.

Everyone at Haven had survived not just the end of the world, the virus, the plague, the Happening or whatever anyone chose to call it; they had survived the personal loss of partners, children, parents, friends. Reaper and Sandra did not consider themselves special when it came to the scales of suffering, although Reaper had been a victim even before everything had changed.

Back when life was normal and people paid taxes and grumbled about work and the price of a pint, his daughter had been the victim of a rape. Even though her attacker had gone to prison, she had been unable to live with the shame. Perhaps it was the derisory jail sentence that seemed to suggest that she had in some way invited the attack, or the way it had been reported in the Press, or the knowing looks of neighbours. Perhaps it had been the memory of what had happened, or a combination of them all, but she had taken her own young life.

When her rapist was freed from prison, Reaper had killed him. If he had waited a couple of weeks, the pandemic would have done the job for him, but he did not regret his action. It had been righteous and the bastard had died in pain. Reaper had been in a police cell waiting to be sent for trial when the virus took its final grip and the world died.

Sandra had lost her mother early in the pandemic as the disease started to wreak havoc. Afterwards, she had been a rape victim herself, the plaything of a gang of three. Reaper had killed them, too. This is why they were bonded as closely as father and daughter.

They had undertaken the recent trip with total disregard for their own lives. Maybe that was why it had been successful. The pair of them had trained hard in the last few months, faced and overcome dangers, and had become extremely proficient and deadly. To all intents and purposes, they *were* Special Forces. They were far superior to any enemy they had faced thus far.

Their small commando group could undertake dangerous tasks, escort duties, explorations and special operations, and were always under arms. They had been a team of six: Reaper, Sandra, Arif, Kate, Jenny and James Marshall. Now they were four.

Reaper and Sandra did not have to look far for new recruits in the following weeks. Tanya, the girl who had put six bullets into the grief-stricken Duncan, volunteered, along with three other women and two men. Reaper and Sandra put them all through basic training. Not all were suited to the role, but those not selected accepted the decision without rancour.

Tanya was twenty-eight, an IT designer in her previous life, who had lived in Leeds. She had been looking after her parents in a village in the Wolds when the epidemic began to rage. Both died. She stayed, but was captured by the Mad Dog gang during one of their 'fresh meat' tours. 'That's what they called it,' she said, with an edge to her voice that could cut steel. 'I was fresh meat.' She was dark haired and vividly attractive and Reaper sensed she nursed a deep well of anger. If it could be channelled in the right direction, she would be an undoubted asset.

Also accepted was Anna, a thirty-four-year-old American. She arrived at Haven alone on a motorbike, with a shotgun strapped to her back and a knife in her belt. Dark brown hair was cut close to her scalp so that small tufts stuck up in an irregular pattern. Reaper couldn't tell whether it had been professionally coiffured or if she had done it herself.

'I was a personal trainer at a fitness centre in Manchester,' she said.

'What were you doing in Manchester?'

'I married the guy who owned the gym. We met in Oregon. He was touring up the coast from LA. I was touring down the coast from Seattle. We met in a small place called Cannon Beach. It's pretty. Six months later, we went back and got married there and I came to Manchester.'

'A bit of a culture shock?' Reaper said.

'Not really. We get rain in Seattle, too.'

'When was this?' said Sandra.

'A year ago.' She pursed her lips. 'It wasn't working out. I was going back to California. But then the shit hit the fan.'

'What was it like in Manchester? When it happened?'

'We had an apartment in the middle of town. Opposite the Printworks?'

They shook their heads. They didn't know it.

'Great place. Bars, movie theatre, restaurants, clubs. One of those conversions you Brits do well, you know? Old building, new life. Brian – my husband – he got sick in London on a business trip. He never came back. I stocked up with food and stayed put in the apartment. I could see through the windows that it was pretty wild out there at first. Later, I went out. Found a few normal people, a few who seemed to have gone crazy in the head. Bad guys were still about, but I avoided them, mostly.' She smiled to herself.

Sandra said, 'Mostly?'

73

'Just the one time. It was my own fault. I went in a bar for a drink. Sitting there on a high stool, sipping warm vodka. These two guys came in. Thought I was easy. I did three years in the military, one tour in Afghanistan. I also learned taekwondo. I took the shotgun from them. That's the only trouble I had, although I saw what the bad guys could do.'

'Did you kill the two men?' Reaper asked.

'No.'

'We kill them,' said Sandra. 'So they can't hurt anybody else.'

'Could you do that?' Reaper said.

'I could do that.'

She returned his stare with an even gaze. He believed she could.

Both Anna and Tanya were motivated, had the emotional strength that was essential, and a true sense of reality. They knew this was not a time in history for self doubt or philosophical debate about the right to life and the right to kill. They had to accept justifiable homicide to keep themselves and their fellow citizens safe.

Both Sandra and Jenny had been rape victims; that knowledge and shared experience helped Tanya's assimilation into the group. Anna was a natural. During her military service, she had served as a medic in a combat unit, carried a gun and been involved in firefights. She had learned to survive in a man's world, ignore discrimination and bigotry, and fend off unwanted sexual advances. That was one reason she had learned taekwondo. It was inevitable that she became known affectionately as Yank.

Reaper had never had any qualms about accepting women into a front line role. They had proved on many occasions already to be deadlier than the male. They might not be as physically strong but they were quick, mentally adept and could be utterly ruthless.

One man also made the cut. Kev Andrews was fifty, a former electrician, who, like everybody else, had seen his fair share of horror. He had lost his wife and daughter to the virus and had lived alone and on his wits before reaching Haven. He was muscular, six foot tall, had a strong face and a head of tight blond curls that were going grey. He had been in the Royal Navy for twenty-two years, having enlisted as an eighteen-year-old, and his face looked as if it had been lived in by several generations of carousing matelots. 'All this natural beauty didn't just happen,' he said, pointing to his worn features. 'It was carefully nurtured in some of the worst bars in the worst ports in all the world.' Kev had a dangerous calmness, a way of using jackspeak – navy slang – and a sense of humour that appealed to Reaper. He had developed the quaint habit of addressing people as 'me hearty', as if trying to capture the lost camaraderie of the Navy.

Tanya, Yank and Kev all donned the distinctive blues and became Special Forces. As well as duties, all undertook daily training that included physical exercise, arms drills and the use of longbow and crossbow, both weapons they had been stockpiling for the day when the bullets ran out.

After all the action came peace. Sandra stayed in the apartment in the manor house that she had shared, so briefly, with Jamie. Reaper returned to the camper-van-come-guard-post on the far side of the hill.

Old Bob, the elderly farmer, became estate manager, aided by Cassandra Cairncross, the widow of a Squadron Leader, who they had found at an abandoned RAF station to the north. Cassandra was a refined lady in her forties, a twin-set-and-pearl type from Sussex about whom you made assumptions at your peril. She was used to organising and giving orders, in a quiet, understated manner that brooked no argument. People did what she told them, even though she told them in the nicest possible way. Her father had been a gentleman farmer and she had grown up helping him run the business.

The roles taken by Bob and Cassandra soon evolved to the satisfaction of both. Cassandra, in effect, ran the place with Bob's advice, while he gave hands-on practical training in husbandry of the land and animals to Haven's newcomers. They instructed that as many animals and livestock as possible should be rounded up and saved, and Pete Mack was told to find enough agricultural feed to augment what they had, to see them through the winter.

Rev Nick kept schedules and inventories, managed the calendar and maintained paperwork that helped organise the widespread activities of the community, aided by Judith, a handsome woman of sixty, who had been a retired vet. Now she was out of retirement and, as well as working with animals, she used her formidable organisational skills to arrange meetings and committees and develop the forward planning that was needed for all aspects of life: school; library; refuse; stocks; health. She arranged for the largely cosmetic fireplaces in the holiday cottages to be converted to burn fuel during the winter to come.

Pete Mack with his shaved head, big and tough enough to look stocky even though he was five ten and with the tattoo of a bulldog on his forearm, was their quartermaster. He organised the wagons that went out to warehouses and stores to salvage petrol, diesel, tinned food and anything that could be useful. They had commandeered a complex of industrial units in a nearby village close to the A64 for storage and easy access.

Ashley had virtually saved Haven single handed when he had wielded an M60 machinegun to suppress the attack in which Kate had died, fighting alongside him. He was an Afro-Caribbean former sergeant in the Paras who had served in Iraq and Afghanistan, an experience that had left him disillusioned with wars fought for no reason other than politics, but he had realised that the new reality demanded self defence. He had instituted and ran training sessions for part of the population that would form a militia in times of danger.

Haven would eventually have to hold elections but, at the moment, everyone seemed happy to let the ad hoc committee in charge continue running things. They had professionals, trades people, housewives, students, shop assistants, academics, market gardeners, construction workers and Ronnie Ronaldo from Castleford, a self-confessed reprobate who hadn't worked in fifteen years, who had become their prime scavenger. They all worked together for a common purpose, cultivating land, caring for sheep, cattle, horses, pigs and hens, and preparing with some trepidation for the winter ahead.

Cassandra suggested they instigate apprenticeships. Judith helped organise it and, at first, it was done on a voluntary basis, with former townies choosing which new trade or profession they would prefer to follow. The system would later become more complex, and abilities and aptitude had to be taken into account when finding candidates to learn the rudiments of medicine, dentistry, plumbing or bricklaying.

Haven had become a collective name for the estate and its surrounding villages and was now home for 249 men, women and children. It was part of a wider network of colonies that existed at Scarborough, Filey and Bridlington along the East Coast of Yorkshire and with whom Haven had close ties and agreements covering mutual aid and commerce. They also maintained good relations as far as Driffield in the South, Pickering and Malton in the West and Whitby in the North. Reaper and Sandra had travelled further afield to make more tenuous contacts, but had left the inland area towards York as a natural barrier between them and the major conurbations of Leeds, Bradford and the industrial heartland that nestled on both sides of the Pennine range.

They tried walkie-talkies for communication but found them unreliable and expensive to maintain; batteries were in short supply and maximum range was from two miles to as little as a quarter of a mile if buildings or hills were in the way. It didn't help that they had no radio ham or expert among their ranks. The permanent guard at the gate of Haven was equipped with a handheld transceiver – which is what Ashley insisted was the correct terminology – so he could be in communication with the manor house and the Special Forces' vehicles carried them, but they were not relied upon and were rarely needed in a world where urgency no longer seemed essential.

Travel was easy because cars were available and petrol was still plentiful, but acquiring it could also be dangerous. No one knew what regimes ruled inland in the major urban centres and they preferred not to advertise their own existence for as along as possible.

York was a city they avoided. The ancient county capital had attained a disquieting reputation that had been passed on by travellers who had visited and hurried on. The Minster had become the centre of a religious colony led by a cleric named Brother Abraham who proclaimed that the plague had been God's punishment for allowing Sodom and Gomorrah to flourish across the world. They guarded the city walls to keep out intruders and the rumours included accounts of self-flagellation. Abraham, it seemed, had gone back to basics and had gathered around him a steadily increasing flock of tortured souls.

Twas ever thus, thought Reaper, who was a born-again atheist. He was happy to blame science and mankind for what had happened, and leave God out of it. Haven tried sending envoys but they were rebuffed. Brother Abraham and his followers wanted to be left alone.

Reaper was also concerned about what might be happening in the South of England. He and Sandra had visited army and RAF camps looking for survivors, and had heard stories of morse code messages being received by units, asking for service personnel to proceed to Windsor. They had been instructed to take all armaments and ammunition with them. A national government was being formed at Windsor under the aegis of Prince Harry.

If this was correct, it could be good news, but there were doubts about the veracity of the message. Cassandra and a handful of others had remained behind at RAF Lemington to look after two sick children. Most of the camp survivors had gone south in response to the call and they had intended following later. They had kept a radio watch and had received a brief message from Flight Sergeant Harry Babbington, who had led the convoy south. The message had said: *Returning. Stay where you are. Imperative. Stay where you are.*

They had heard nothing more.

This had led Reaper and the committee to speculate on what exactly waited at Windsor and whether Prince Harry had actually survived. Perhaps someone was simply exploiting his name to attract men and armaments? Perhaps this was being done with the best of intentions: to bring trained men and women together and to give a new embryonic nation the best chance. But if it was a deception, it could be used for baser motives: by someone who wanted to raise an army and seize power in the fragmented country that was left.

The problem of Windsor would not disappear of its own accord but neither was it pressing. Reaper believed that, even if worse case scenario was correct, those behind what was happening would wish to first establish themselves in the south. Conquest of the rest of the country would come later. Still, it was a doubt that needed resolving, and Reaper knew that, before too long, he and other members of his team would have to drive south and investigate.

Time passed, and travellers tired of an itinerant life that could be all too dangerous joined Haven. Some came looking for somewhere to spend the winter. Their ranks swelled to 480, relationships were formed, new families were created. Children usually stayed with the adults who had found them in the after-days, that bond of attachment often being as strong as the familial one had been before. Two more villages were cleared of bodies; the cottages fumigated and occupied; cats and dogs always part of the new occupancy, to combat rodents. The few academics they had, became a scientific team to help them plan for the future. They became known as the 'Brains Trust'.

Dr Greta Malone, who had worked at Scarborough General Hospital, joined them at Haven. She had originally been with a small group based at Scarborough Castle under the leadership of Richard Ferguson, a physicist with plans of regeneration through renewable energy. When the oil supply ran out, we would need, he claimed, solar and wind power. Reaper did not disagree. Greta was black and, as the only doctor Reaper had met during all his travels, she was also gold. She realised her own value and had decided to base herself at the biggest centre of new development, whilst making herself available to all the other communities as a general practitioner.

Ferguson accepted the logic. Reaper suspected Ferguson also realised that the Scarborough Castle base was unlikely to be productive and that it wouldn't be long before he moved inland or to one of the fishing-based centres.

Greta had warned that the future would be bleak from a medical point of view. The cushion of the National

Health Service had gone. In future, people would die from illnesses or injuries that, before the pandemic, would have been treatable. Surgical procedures that had been taken for granted, were no longer available. She was not a surgeon, although she would be willing to undertake simple operations and attempt more complicated ones in cases of last resort. At the moment, she had a good stock of drugs and antibiotics but they would eventually pass their lifespan and no more would be available.

The Rev Nick held non-denominational services on Sundays. He had started by using the dining hall in the manor house but, as the population increased, he moved to the parish church of St Oswald's in the nearby village of Westfield. Many attended, including a Sikh, two Muslims and three Jews among their multitude of occasional Christians and non-believers. He also officiated at weddings as relationships were gradually formalised.

As the summer wore on, they reinstated Saturday night socials at the pub to which all were invited. Alcohol was served in moderation and a live group formed around Shaggy, a talented middle-aged singer, guitarist and keyboard player. Reaper had first met the long-haired rock musician in Scarborough, where Shaggy had been working his way through the town's alcohol and drugs supply. He had also been quietly looking after a quartet of emotionally damaged survivors. Eventually, Shaggy had agreed to move inland.

'Might as well, man. I've smoked all the weed.'

Among the newcomers were a variety of musicians. Two guitarists – one classical, one rock – a trombone player from Black Dykes Brass Band, and a percussionist. They coalesced around Shaggy.

Autumn came with no vicious surprises and a gentle dip in the temperature and another relationship formed among the Special Forces themselves. English rose Jenny, the former teacher from St Hilda's Public School, moved in with Tanya. They did not ask the Rev Nick for a service to sanctify their union but he gave them a blessing anyway, one Sunday morning in October, before a packed congregation that gave them a round of applause.

Tanya told Reaper, 'Me and Jenny … it's not because of what happened. It didn't put me off men. Truth is, I never was attracted to them to start with. This is just natural selection.'

'And you've made a great selection,' Reaper told her.

Anna teamed up once or twice for patrols with Reaper and she made her interest in him plain.

'It's not good to be alone, Reaper,' she said.

'I'm not.'

'I don't mean being close to your daughter. Let me, in my North American way, be more explicit. Everybody needs sex.'

She was so direct that Reaper didn't see her as a threat to Kate's memory or his celibacy. He grinned at her.

'Even you, Yank?'

'Particularly me. I'm a West Coast girl. Land of liberation. Shit, I had to buy a bra to burn one.'

'That was before your time.'

'You get my drift. We invented free love.'

'I thought that was the Swedes?'

'No, they invented the duvet.'

'Are you propositioning me?'

'Damn right, I am.'

'I'm very flattered, Anna. But no thank you.'

'To turn me down, you get personal? Before I'm Yank and now I'm Anna? You Brits are so polite.'

'You're a beautiful young woman, Yank. But let's keep this professional.'

'Okey doke, Reaper. But you can't blame a girl for trying.'

Chapter 6

HAVEN HAD A WHITE CHRISTMAS. WINTER CAME, snow fell and closed the roads, and they survived. The Rev Nick held services in St Oswald's church. They ran a generator in the manor house for two days and the community got together for a low-key celebration of survival; with food and drink being supplied from buffets in the dining room of the manor house and at the pub. They played board games. Monopoly was popular because it was played with real money: £20 and £50 notes were stacked for casual use, having been liberated from a bank by Ronnie Ronaldo simply for the fun of it.

Ronnie was wiry, no taller than five six and had an unhealthy pallor. His hair was thin and slicked straight back and he smoked, constantly – roll-up cigarettes for preference. Even when he was in conversation, his eyes never stayed still, as if checking the background or his peripheral vision for enemies, of which he had had a few in his past life: rent collectors, tally men, police, an ex-wife.

He was forty-three but had an ageless quality, as if he had been born old and would stay that way until he died.

'I had a job when I got married,' he once confessed, as if it was not a fact of which he was particularly proud. 'But my money went nowhere. It had its hat and coat on as soon as I got paid. I was better off on benefits, the black, the blag, the fiddle and the five-finger discount. I was better off without the wife.'

He had adapted better than most to the new challenges of a new life, probably because his previous one had been so dysfunctional.

As well as cash, Ronnie had collected a sizeable hoard of diamond rings, necklaces, jewellery, precious stones, gold and silver, and Kruger Rand. He had handed them over sheepishly to Judith.

'I don't know why I took them,' he explained, a little abashed that she might think he had been stealing. 'I mean, I wasn't on the rob. But you would, wouldn't you? Take them? It's not that they're worth anything right now, but they might be, in the future, when things get normal. Well, they'll get a bit more normal, won't they? Stands to reason. I mean, I thought we could put them away and save them and, maybe sometime in the future, start a bank.'

Judith had smiled to ease his embarrassment and said, 'I think that's a brilliant idea. We'll call it the Bank of Ron.'

'By heck,' he said. 'That sounds grand. Like Rockefeller, you mean? The Bank of Ron.'

He was delighted and, thereafter, he would frequently return from scouting or scavenging trips with a suitcase or bag filled with jewellery, gold and silver. Judith never asked where it came from and stored it away in the cellar of the manor house for the future.

For the children, at this festive time, there were showings of *How The Grinch Stole Christmas* and the animated films *The Snowman* and *Arthur Christmas*. For the grown-ups, the old Hollywood classic *White Christmas* proved a surprise hit, with its Irving Berlin music and nostalgia and the evocative title song. It was shown five times.

Reaper hadn't meant to watch it but had stepped into the back of the hall as it started. He stayed to the finish. As he left, Greta Malone joined him. They stopped on the steps of the manor house and watched a fresh fall of snow cover the slush and footprints and restore the beauty of the winter. The pub across the square and the nearby cottages were full. It was open house to mark a tradition as well as a Christian celebration. Greta pulled the collar of her parka up to her ears.

'Cold?' he said.

'Yes, but it's worth it, isn't it? For a while you can let the silence settle and forget.'

'I suppose so.' He knew he didn't sound convinced.

'Where's Sandra?' she said.

'She's looking after the kids. There's another showing of *The Snowman* in the library.'

Greta smiled at him and said, 'How about buying me a drink?'

Reaper returned the smile at the notion. No one bought drinks anymore. That time might come again but, at the moment, they were a collective; tins and bottles of beer, wine and spirits were still readily available for free, and few abused the system.

'Why not?' he said, but she put a hand on his arm to hold him back, as he was about to walk down the steps.

'Before you do, can I have a word?'

Reaper stopped. For a rare two hours, he had lost himself in the movie, hoping that the on-screen misunderstandings would be cleared up in time for a happy ending between Bing Crosby and Rosemary Clooney. Hollywood schtick but it worked. Now he could tell that Greta wanted a serious word, possibly on a personal level, that might in all probability ruin his mood.

'Go on.'

She sensed his antipathy and smiled to ease his fears. She hooked her arm through his.

'Don't worry. It's nothing terrible. It's about Sandra.'

'Sandra?'

'You two are very close, even for father and daughter, which I know you are not.' Being a doctor, Reaper accepted that Greta would have worked out how unlikely it was that their relationship was not as they wished people to believe. 'And don't worry, I haven't told anybody. Although

I suspect one or two have guessed.'

'So?' For a moment, he had the terrible thought that people might believe he was having an intimate relationship with Sandra. 'People don't think …?'

Greta read the panic in his voice. 'People think you are two good people. They think you have strong feelings for each other, genuine father-daughter feelings. My point is, that you can be too close. And I don't for one second mean in a sexual way. The relationship you two have excludes anyone else. That, in the long run, could be unhealthy. You need to give her space to breath, Reaper. Maybe the space to meet someone new, at some time, somewhere, in the future. That's all I wanted to say. I hope I haven't offended you. You are two special people. Believe it or not, you have a lot of friends, a lot of admirers. What you and Sandra have is very special, but maybe, just maybe there will come a time, when you should ease away from each other.'

She squeezed his arm and smiled.

'I don't think I've put this very well, at all. I know you are both still grieving. You will always grieve. The pain may get less over time but you will always grieve. But the two of you together compounds the grief, amplifies it. It makes you strong. After it happened, that grief sent you into dangerous situations, places where you maybe shouldn't have gone. Risks you shouldn't have taken. It'll still happen because you feed off each other's grief. Do you see what I'm trying to say in my very clumsy way?'

He actually did, although he didn't want to acknowledge the fact. They did feed from each other's grief. Maybe they wallowed in collective suffering. He nodded. 'I think I do,' he said.

'I thought maybe you were too close to see, so me and my big mouth took the chance of giving you an outside perspective.'

'A diagnosis.'

'Hardly. But a different viewpoint.' She leaned forward, so that her head was against his. 'No one will take the place of Kate. No one will take the place of Jamie for Sandra. But she's young and she deserves the chance to maybe find somebody else.' They exchanged a look and he held her gaze. 'Now,' she said. 'How about that drink?'

He would have preferred to have walked away alone, go over the hill to the guard post, spend an hour contemplating past mistakes, losses and present complications in that wonderful gentle silence brought by snow, but he didn't. He liked Greta, admired her. If he left abruptly and walked back over the hill, she would be upset at upsetting him. He didn't want that. It was Christmas, after all. So they went to the Farmer's Boy for a drink and he saved his contemplation for later.

The winter was short, spring seemed to start in late February and Haven emerged from its semi-hibernation. A party crossed the Humber again. Sandra and Kev

Andrews provided protection for Pete Mack and Ronnie Ronaldo, who made contact with a group ensconced in an oil refinery at Immingham. The people were defensive but open to parley. They had been attacked by others, envious of the fuel they were holding.

Pete Mack explained that, while the reserve they were protecting might well be worth a great deal eventually, there was little demand at the moment when it was easier to syphon petrol and diesel from garages.

'They were suspicious,' he reported. 'But we did a deal as a basis for the future.'

The group had been living mainly on food salvaged from supermarkets and the sight of the fresh meat and home-grown produce that Pete had taken, as a taster of what they had to offer, proved decisive. They exchanged a van-load of beef, pork and lamb for a tanker containing 34,000 litres of petrol.

'They have a row of trucks in there and tanks containing God know's how much,' Pete said. 'They thought it was a good deal.'

While still plentiful, fuel was becoming a tricky subject. Each community was eager to preserve the integrity of the garages and fuel stations within their sphere of influence, although these boundaries were never precise. This could, the Haven hierarchy realised, eventually lead to fuel wars. The previous summer, Pete Mack had acquired two 1,000 litre petrol bowsers with electric pumps which they used to drain the tanks of other petrol stations and top up the two garages within their boundaries, in the villages of Westfield and Twin Acres, as well as the diesel tanks at Haven community farms.

Every official vehicle from Haven had a rotary pump in the boot so that fuel could be obtained direct from a garage forecourt, as well as a length of plastic tubing to syphon it from any abandoned car. They had time yet, but the time was getting less.

Richard Ferguson, their tame boffin, worked out simple figures. The Special Forces now drove Range Rovers with 3.6 litre diesel engines; all were the same model to make them interchangeable. They were excellent off-road vehicles that did 0-60 in under nine seconds and an average of 25 miles to the gallon and the tank was big enough to take them 580 miles without refueling.

Those four vehicles, driving an average of 400 miles a week each, would use 3,328 gallons of fuel a year between them. Which meant that a tanker of 34,000 litres – or 7,500 gallons – would last just over two years. Add the scavenger trucks, the farm vehicles and tractors, and the other vehicles the community used, and they could begin to understand that, eventually, it would run out. The timeline was finite.

The committee took the warning seriously and the fuel held within the community became rationed. It was only available for agricultural purposes, official vehicles and Special Forces. People began to get used to using horse transport and bicycles. They could, of course, continue to use cars, as long as they refilled their tanks by syphoning from abandoned vehicles when they were out.

A month later, Pete and Ronnie went back and made another trade, this time for a similar amount of diesel. They parked the trucks near their industrial compound of supplies.

Ferguson wanted to start fitting solar panels. Ronnie Ronaldo located stockpiles of them at Scarborough and Selby, and Ferguson, who soon acquired the nickname of 'Prof', organised a team and began to fit them on the manor house. Eventually, he wanted to equip all the cottages and houses in the community with them.

Reaper tried to lighten his relationship with Sandra. They no longer teamed up every time they went out. She had seen action; some of the others had not. So it made sense for them to partner with the newcomers. It came as a shock when he discovered she had become nineteen on 28th March. She told him on the morning of her birthday in her apartment in the manor house.

'I thought you ought to know,' she said, 'seeing as you're my father,' and he held her.

And they both cried.

The tears came unexpectedly. They came and didn't stop, as if they had been waiting since Jamie and Kate had been killed, maybe even before then: maybe since the death of his other daughter, Emily.

They allowed composure to return in its own time and

sat together and held hands. They didn't need words to explain the grief and regrets or the words to explain the anguish they both felt because no one knew her birthday. No one had needed to know her birthday or had taken the trouble to discover it. At that moment, Reaper saw the world afresh and wondered why they bothered.

'One thing I want for my birthday,' she said.

'Anything.'

'Don't push me away.'

'I haven't …' He saw her face. 'Was it so obvious?'

'Why?'

'We were too close.'

'We can never be too close.'

'Claustrophobic. I thought I might be smothering you. You're a teenager, for chrissake.'

Sandra started laughing and, like the tears, couldn't stop.

'What's wrong?' he said.

Eventually, she said, 'Teenager?' She was still laughing although not as severely. 'Nightclubs, high heels and a dropped shot in a Crabbie's Ginger Beer? I'll get my party frock out and see which band's on tour. Maybe it will be Madness. Madness would be good.' The laughter stopped. 'Madness would be totally appropriate.'

They sat and stared at each other, the tears drying on their cheeks. She reached out and brushed away the stain on his face.

'We'll always have each other,' she said. 'And bollocks to claustrophobic.'

'I was worried.'

'Don't be. I loved Jamie, I miss him, but I know I might meet someone else. In the meantime, I've got you. Now and forever, whether you like it or not. Dad.'

Now he laughed, too, and they held each other again and he revised his earlier opinion of the world. It was not such a bad place after all.

They got another recruit to Special Forces on April 1st. Keira O'Dowd was thirty-two and had arrived with three others a month before. She had a mass of unruly auburn hair, startling blue eyes and a soft Irish accent.

'I hope this isn't a mistake,' she said.

'What? Applying to join?' Reaper said.

'On April Fool's Day?'

'You don't look like a fool.'

'I'm not.'

'What did you do? Before?'

'I was in PR in Dublin. Married and moved to Manchester. Still in PR. Different city, same game. Became a widow, hustled, survived and ended up here.'

'No problems on the way?'

'Several. But as I said, I survived.'

His look invited further explanation but she didn't provide any. 'And you ended up here.'

'Luck of the Irish.'

'Then we'll give you a go.'

'Happy days,' she said.

Keira O'Dowd proved to be an extremely able recruit and the force formed itself into regular teams, that matched an experienced member with a newcomer. Jenny was naturally with Tanya, and fifteen-year-old James was teamed with Kev. Reaper and Sandra took turns at partnering Anna the Yank and Keira.

They were all proficient, they had suffered past experiences that had left them tougher than before, and they were committed to each other and the community. Of course, four of them still had to face a bullet in anger, but Reaper thought they would cope admirably.

Chapter 7

ANNA AND KEIRA EVENTUALLY TEAMED UP. They were similar ages and shared the same sense of humour. While Anna was blatant about looking for male companionship – and not necessarily of a lasting nature, Keira was prepared to wait until the right man came along.

'And what if Sir Galahad doesn't show up?' Yank asked.

'There are alternatives about which a good Catholic girl does not speak.'

'You've got a Rampant Rabbit?'

'Shut up, Yank! Your libido is dragging on the floor.'

'The Rabbit bit doesn't bother me. The Catholic bit does. Are you still religious?'

'Only when I'm on my own in the dark. Anyway, I have insurance. I did the first Fridays.'

'The what?'

'You go to mass on the first Friday for nine months. It guarantees you get a chance to repent before you rattle off the mortal coil. It's like a VIP pass into Heaven.'

'You went to mass on the first Friday of every month for nine months? What were you? A Nun?'

'I was nine. I hadn't discovered sin or a Rampant Rabbit. Still, it got me noticed in the right quarters. Me and God?' She intertwined two fingers. 'We're like that.'

'I don't believe in religion,' Yank said. 'But if I'm wrong and you're right, put a good word in for me when Peter blows his horn.'

'There you go, talking dirty again. Anyway, it's Gabriel, not Peter. But don't worry, I'll leave the stage door on the latch for you.'

'This guy Gabriel? Is he a good looking dude?'

'Hair like a surfer. Looks like an angel.'

'Sounds cool.'

'Of course, he has to be at least 2,000 years old.'

'I don't mind older men. Experience counts.'

'You tried it with Reaper?'

'I got knocked back.'

'Are you surprised?'

'Nope. But I had to try.'

They travelled down the coast from Bridlington, visiting those in villages within Haven's sphere of interest and with whom it traded and to whom it offered protection. It was a trip one of the teams made once a week. Some of the hamlets only had three or four people, determined to go it alone. Skipsea had a larger group, farming the rich lands to the north of the picturesque village. A couple of weeks before, they had been augmented by two men and three women who had arrived from the south. It had boosted the population to thirty-five.

'Tell me,' Keira said. 'Do we time our visit for Auntie Dora's baking day, or does she time her baking for us?'

'Who cares? She makes great scones.'

They stopped at Butternab Farm on the edge of the village, placing their carbines in the boot and locking the vehicle. People had been working in the fields they passed but something was not quite right. Normality seemed to have been nudged out of place.

'Michael?' Yank called, as they walked across the farmyard to the back door. 'Dora?'

There was no smell of baking as they reached the open door.

Yank put her head inside and stepped back as the large shape of a man emerged from the shadows. He stood in the doorway, a big man but overweight, in moleskin trousers, check shirt that was open at the neck, and a yellow waistcoat. He carried a double-barrelled shotgun, broken open for safety, in the crook of his arm.

'Good morning, ladies,' he said. 'Nice of you to call. Pity everybody's out working.'

Yank recognised him as the leader of the newcomers.

'Boris, isn't it?'

'Boris Walker.'

He was well spoken; a public school accent that she

didn't think was assumed. His fellow travellers had looked to him for instructions.

'Where's Michael?'

'Out. He'll be sorry to have missed you. Do you have time for a cup of tea?' He leaned back inside to shout. 'Dora? Tea for the two ladies.'

Keira said, 'I'll go help,' and tried to pass Walker, but he didn't move.

'I'm sure she doesn't need help. Probably resent it. You know how old folk can be so sensitive. Sit down.' He indicated the garden table and bench in the yard. 'Enjoy the sunshine.'

'I'll take a walk,' said Keira, not wanting to exacerbate a situation that might only be in her imagination, although her glance at Anna told her that Yank's instincts were similar.

Keira went round to the front of the house. In the fields on the other side of the road, she saw two figures. She waved and one of the men acknowledged her but then turned away. She was hot in the Kevlar vest and rubbed the back of her neck, feeling the sweat there. Never mind tea, a cold drink was what she wanted. But where was Michael? She turned abruptly and saw someone who had been watching her duck back behind a bedroom curtain.

As she walked back towards the farm, she took the Glock from its holster and worked the slide to put a bullet in the chamber. She depressed the trigger one click to remove the safety and replaced it in the holster.

Yank had not accepted the invitation to sit in the sun and was standing with legs slightly apart, hands on the buckle of her belt, like a gunslinger waiting to be called out. Boris Walker was talking.

'So it need not concern you in the slightest,' he said.

'What shouldn't concern us?' Keira said.

Yank said, 'Mr Walker was explaining that now he is farm manager everything will operate so much more smoothly.'

'It operated fine before,' said Keira.

'Efficiency, time and motion,' said Walker, as if about to embark on a lecture.

'Time and motion that doesn't apply to you?' she said. 'Where's Michael?'

Walker stepped into the yard to allow Dora, a small lady in her late sixties, to move past him carrying a tray on which were tea pot and cups but no scones. She put it on the table in the yard without looking up and began to head back for the kitchen.

'Dora?' said Anna, but the old lady kept walking.

Keira stepped in her way, causing her to stop.

'Is everything all right, Dora?'

Dora looked up, fear obvious in her eyes, and a bruise on the side of her face.

'Yes,' she said. 'Everything's fine.'

Yank took a pace forward, her hand moving to the butt

of her gun, and Walker sensed the meeting was not going to plan. He snapped the shotgun closed, but before he could level it Keira took her Glock from its holster in one swift movement and pointed it at his head.

'Put the shotgun on the floor, Mr Walker,' she said.

He snorted in disbelief that she might actually pull the trigger.

'Now don't be an idjit, Mr Walker,' she said, in a quiet voice. 'Put the gun down.'

When he still hesitated, she raised the barrel an inch over his head, and fired. The blast seared his ear and she lowered the gun to point at his head again

'Jesus Christ,' he said, crouched and laid the shotgun on the floor.

Yank picked it up and put it on the table.

'That should bring them running from the fields,' she said.

Walker blustered.' What right have you got coming here and throwing your weight around?'

'You know, that's exactly what I was going to ask you,' said Yank.

Without taking her eyes off Walker, Keira said, 'Dora, where's Michael?'

'He's inside. They have him inside.'

'They?' said Anna.

'Mr Walker's foreman.'

Yank said, 'Does he have a gun?'

'Yes. He has a gun.'

'Too right, I have a gun.'

The voice came from behind Keira. It was edgy with tension. This was the man who had probably been watching her from the bedroom window. Yank was staring past her, at him, but had made no move to draw her weapon.

'He's got an Uzi,' said Yank, in a voice that was a lot calmer than Keira felt.

Walker grinned and made as if to walk into the yard.

'Stay!' said Keira, as if ordering a dog.

'Your position is hopeless, woman. He has a gun pointing at your back.'

'I'm Irish. I'm used to hopeless. The thing is, if he pulls the trigger, it won't just be me he kills, it will be you, as well.'

'You said this was going to be easy,' said the man, his voice now whining as well as edgy.

'It would have been if they hadn't been so bloody nosey,' said Walker. And he snarled at Keira, 'Why can't you leave people alone? We weren't doing you any harm?'

'You hurt Dora,' Keira said. 'I like Dora. I like Dora's scones. It upsets me when I don't get my scone.'

She was talking partly from bravado and partly to provide a distraction so that Yank might try something.

Yank said, 'Why don't we all sit down and talk about it? We've got the tea, we've got the sunshine …'

'Why don't we put the show on right here,' said Keira,

lapsing into Judy Garland nonsense, but Yank laughed and Keira chuckled and, as if the humour made it all right, she stepped around the front of Walker, pushing Dora with her, until she was on his other side. Now she was holding the Glock in two hands and he was between her and a thin young man with an Uzi, whom she vaguely remembered from two weeks before.

'Dora, where are the three women who came with Mr Walker?'

'They're working. They're all right. They were being bullied, and probably worse, before they got here.'

'I hate bullies,' said Yank. She turned, ignoring the Uzi, and walked to the other side of the yard and looked over the wall. 'You were right. That shot has got them running.' She turned to the thin man. 'What's your name, by the way? I'm Yank.'

'Redford.'

'Not Robert?' she said, and put her head on one side to take a better look. 'Nah. You're too tall and too thin. I'll call you Slim.'

'This is getting us nowhere,' said Walker. 'You're right. We should sit down and talk it over.'

Without warning, he walked to the garden table. Keira let him go, her gun now pointing at the man with the Uzi. She felt this was leading to an inevitable conclusion and somewhere in the back of her mind was glad that she had completed the first Fridays.

'Yank?' she said.

As Walker reached for the shotgun on the table, she heard Yank slide the chamber of her Glock and the first click that removed the safety.

'Dora,' Keira said, in a soft voice. 'Go and keep the others away while we talk.'

The elderly lady left the yard and she heard her shouting, 'Stop, stop!' Walker was now cradling the shotgun. In her periphery vision, she could see his finger was on the trigger although the gun was not pointing at anyone.

'This is all very silly,' said Yank.

'All I wanted was a scone,' said Keira. And then, in a harder voice, 'Put the fucking gun down, Slim. My arm is getting tired.'

Walker's arm twitched as he began to move the shotgun, which might have meant nothing. It might have meant his arm was tired, too, and he was moving the weapon into a more comfortable position. But at the same moment, came a very clear memory of the basic training instructions drilled into her by Reaper and Sandra. Don't hesitate. She didn't, and neither did Yank. Both girls fired almost simultaneously.

The thin man with the Uzi screamed as he went backwards, the gun shaking in his dying grip and throwing a burst of 9mm bullets up the side of the farmhouse, bringing brick chippings down in a shower.

Keira still pointed the Glock even though her target

was on his back, arms wide, the gun still in his grip but its magazine now empty. She didn't know how many times she had fired and her ears were ringing. She was aware that Walker had moved backwards, then sideways across the yard, as if concentrating on the steps of a dance no one else could hear, before collapsing in a heap. Before he had started his solitary gavotte, he had discharged both barrels of the shotgun. Anna?

'Yank?' she shouted, turning.

Yank was standing across the yard, the Glock still gripped in both hands, still pointing across the table at Boris Walker.

Keira's cry broke the trance and the two girls stared at each other.

'Okay?' said Yank.

'Okay,' confirmed Keira.

Yank let out a huge breath, as if she had been holding it in for an hour, and put the Glock in its holster.

'Shootout at Butternab Farm,' she said. 'Not at all like the movies.'

She turned away, leant against the farmyard wall and was sick on the cobbles.

Keira kept her gun at the ready and checked the bodies. Another instruction from training: *make sure*. The thin man, Redford, had three bullets in his body and one in his head. Had she fired more? She wouldn't know until she checked the magazine. Still on her guard, she moved on to Walker, the bully who thought he had found himself a comfortable roost to rule. Another four hits. She didn't look too closely at the headshot. Now she put the Glock away and crossed the yard to Anna, who had recovered enough to stare over the wall.

Ten or twelve farm workers had stopped in their tracks at Dora's shouts. They stared towards the farm, consternation etched in their faces.

'It's all over!' shouted Keira.

The people began to smile and move again, towards the farmhouse.

'Happy days,' said Keira.

They had tea – but no scones. Michael, the middle-aged farmer the others all looked to with affection and for leadership, had been beaten, threatened and locked in a bedroom in the farmhouse. He would soon recover, he said. The rest of the small community showed their gratitude. The three women, who had arrived with Walker and Redford two weeks before, were even more relieved. No one mourned the passing of the two men.

Eventually, the two girls took their leave and drove on towards Hornsea, which was the furthest south they would travel, but Keira stopped the car after two miles. She got out, put both hands on the side of the vehicle and took several deep breaths. Yank joined her at the side of the empty road.

'I thought you were the cool one?' she said.

'I'm good at impressions.' Another deep breath before

she stood upright. 'Shit,' she said.

They looked at each other, laughed and went into each other's arms and held each other tight. Friends, comrades, survivors and glad to be alive.

The committee met to decide an anniversary date. The Rev Nick invited Reaper and Sandra to attend. The anniversary they wanted to fix was the date when the SARS virus reached that critical point the previous year from whence the world was doomed. There were several opinions as to which date might be appropriate.

First reports of the outbreak of the virus in China had come in February. The final official broadcast by a surviving member of Her Majesty's Government had been in the middle of May. Reaper remembered it well. He had watched it on a TV in the deserted bar of a hotel. He had heard the voice and thought it was another human being, then found the TV and realised the broadcast was being repeated on a loop. The official was a minor politician he had only vaguely heard of; apparently the only one left, or the only one with the bottle to face a camera and tell the nation that the virulent form of SARS that was sweeping the world was a virus aberration, a modern plague, to which only a small percentage had a natural immunity.

'Make your peace with your god and remain in the safety of your homes as we truly face the apocalypse,' he had said. 'God bless. And good luck.'

Good luck? Reaper had made his own luck. And he didn't understand the need to commemorate the disaster, like Christmas, every year. The discussion was desultory; others sensed his apathy to the proposal. Pete Mack said, 'Wouldn't it be better to celebrate the new beginning?'

'What do you mean?' said Nick.

'The date we came here. The date we founded Haven.'

'Of course,' said Judith. 'Far more appropriate.'

'When was it?' said Reaper.

Nick looked at a diary and said, '20th May.'

'Haven Day,' said Sandra.

At first, no one noticed when Ronnie Ronaldo went missing. Their chief scavenger had a habit of making solo runs on his Yamaha off-road motorcycle that might keep him away for up to two days. He never went armed and would quietly discover new sources of goods and equipment, then return to take Pete Mack back with the proper transport. Pete reported his concerns to Reaper on the fourth day.

'He has a low profile habit,' said Pete. 'He's stayed below radar all his life so this may be nothing more than him taking an extra couple of days off. Lying low, because he can. It's in his personality.'

Reaper knew what he meant. Going AWOL for a time could be Ronnie's idea of confirming his own individuality. The world might have ended but Ronnie Ronaldo was unchanged. He would continue ducking and diving, as if evading a police warrant, whenever he felt like it.

'The thing is,' added Pete. 'He wasn't going far. This wasn't a scouting trip, as such. He'd heard of a factory on the outskirts of York that had solar panels. That's where he was going. But York's an hour up the road, not three days away.'

'You think he went into the city?' said Reaper.

'He's a curious sod. If somebody wanted to keep him out, he'd want to go in through sheer bloody mindedness. He could be a prisoner of the mad mullah.'

'Brother Abraham.'

'Same difference.'

'Then we'd better have a look.'

Chapter 8

THE ROMANS HAD ESTABLISHED YORK AT THE JUNCTION of the Rivers Foss and Ouse. Later it was occupied by the Vikings and then fortified by William the Conqueror. Its castle walls were the most complete of any city in England. Reaper read about it in a guidebook in the manor house library. The walls did not completely encircle the city and, in ancient times, the rivers and marshland had been added protection. There were four main entrances in the fortifications: Walmgate Bar; Monk Bar; Bootham Bar; and Micklegate Bar, as well as at least four other main access roads into York.

Reaper led two teams. He partnered Sandra, and Jenny went with Tanya. They approached the city from the northeast along Malton Road, past the Holiday Inn and numerous hotels, pubs and guest houses. York had been one of the foremost tourist cities in Britain. As they came closer to the walls, the road became Monkgate and led to Monk Bar, one of the medieval gateways into the city. The central white stone tower had four storeys, arrow slits and an arched entryway beneath. Two other archways were beneath short stretches of castle wall on either side. The walls then disappeared behind more modern buildings that had been built on the short approach road.

Signs indicated that the main archway beneath the tower was a cycle lane. The small arch on the right gave access for pedestrians. The wider arch beneath the wall on the left, had been for vehicles.

They drove around the city: one team going south, the other north, without attempting entry. The limestone walls were still handsome after hundreds of years protecting a centre that was the cradle of two thousand years of history. The Minster towered above them in the northern quarter and Clifford's Tower was imposing at the southeastern, overlooking the River Ouse.

The teams passed each other and continued their circumnavigation until they met back on Monkgate. They parked the Range Rovers a hundred yards up the road, opposite the Tap and Spile public house. The road began to curve here and they were almost out of sight of the gatehouse. They could see the dead traffic lights at the junction where Monkgate met the road that paralleled the city walls. Further along on their left was the Viceroy of India restaurant.

Both teams confirmed that all gates, bridges and roads into the city were blocked with cars and lorries. Driving in was not possible. Neither, of course, was driving out if anyone needed to make a swift escape. They had a tourist street map of the city but no idea where Ronnie might be held, if he had, indeed been captured, or how many followers Brother Abraham had. Reports suggested any number from thirty to three hundred.

They walked across the road and Reaper studied the entrance through binoculars. People stared back at him from the crenellated castle walls.

'They're carrying crossbows,' he said, in amazement. He refocused. 'And pikes.'

'We could go in at night,' said Tanya. 'There are plenty of places. They don't have enough people.'

'But we don't know the city and we wouldn't know where to look for Ronnie,' said Sandra.

'The only sensible thing is to go and ask,' said Reaper. 'I'm inclined to try diplomacy before anything else.'

'Who's going to ask?' Sandra said.

'I will. I'll ask Brother Abraham.'

'What if he's as mad as people say?'

'I'll humour him.'

'And if that doesn't work?'

'If I don't come back, you're in charge.'

'If you don't come back, I'm coming in. And I won't be asking permission.'

Reaper put his carbine in the back of the car and shared a look with his three companions.

'It's two o'clock. If I'm not back by six, treat them as hostile. I should imagine Brother Abraham will be in the Minster. Be careful. They might send out a raiding party.'

He removed the belt that held his handguns and put them in the back of the car, too.

'Take care, Reaper,' Sandra said.

He walked down the middle of the road with his arms wide in the universal gesture that said he was unarmed and wished to parley. When he reached the traffic lights, maybe twenty yards from the barricaded entrance, he stopped and shouted.

'My name is Reaper! I'm from a settlement near the coast! I'm looking for one of our community, a man called Ronnie Ronaldo! Have you seen him?'

He kept watching the walls. A large woman holding a pike stared back at him from the wall to the left. A figure was sitting behind a low crenellation holding a crossbow that was pointing at him. The bolt was released and he had no time to jump for safety. He had fired a crossbow himself in training and knew the power of the weapon and the damage that could be caused by a steel tipped bolt fired with 150 lbs draw weight travelling at a speed of more than two hundred feet per second. The thought rooted him to the spot in momentary fear and resignation. The bolt hit the road surface by his feet and skipped away and he breathed again.

A voice shouted angrily from the tower, perhaps in

reprimand, perhaps at wasting a bolt. Behind him, he heard the click of carbines being readied.

Reaper didn't move. He didn't retreat and he didn't make any gestures that might be construed as provocative. He realised that the day suddenly seemed more crystalline, the air that he breathed seemed sweeter. Being so close to death certainly cleared the head.

'Is this the way you normally treat guests?' he shouted.

'You're not a guest!' a voice said. 'You're contamination!'

He had been called many things, but contamination was a new description.

'Can I see Brother Abraham?'

'Go to the pavement entrance!'

Reaper did as he was told.

Vans blocked both the other entrances beneath the wall. Not singly, but in an untidy clump with no apparent order or reason except to make them impassible to other vehicles. The pedestrian entrance was protected by a chicane of stacked steel beer barrels that looked solid until he reached it and saw he could slip in sideways. A sign on the wall pointed the way to the Richard III museum in the tower.

On the other side, he was confronted by a big man in a monk's black habit who had a lot of hair and body odour that would incapacitate at twenty paces. Reaper braced himself and tried to breath shallowly through his mouth. The man's beard was full and unkempt, his hair thick and wild as if he had been struck by lightning.

'I'm Brother Mark,' he said.

He wore a wooden cross on a cord around his neck. He was about thirty years of age and bristled with physical strength and an inner belief.

'I'm Reaper.'

They took each other's measure for a moment. Brother Mark did not look impressed. Reaper did not offer to shake hands. For one thing, he didn't think the monk would take it and, for another, he didn't want to catch anything. If he was contamination, this bloke was probably contagious.

'This way,' Brother Mark said, and strode off down the street, legs bare beneath the habit, black Nike training shoes on his feet.

Reaper had half expected them to take his knives from him but they either hadn't noticed or thought they were of acceptable vintage, seeing as they sported pikes and crossbows. He followed, taking a look up at the wall as he went. The walkway had originally been open but now had a metal railing, erected to stop tourists falling off. The woman who was holding the pike stared at him. She wore a tracksuit and was of uncertain age. A small man in a black sweater and black trousers sat with his back to the wall nursing a crossbow that he had reloaded. He also had a beard and his hair was long but the most striking thing about him was his smile: it was pure evil. Perhaps he had escaped from the Richard III museum.

With their attitude, Reaper couldn't see tourists returning any time soon.

Brother Mark strode out with long steps and Reaper had to speed up to catch him as they walked along Goodramgate. Coming towards them was a group of four men on bicycles. They wore tracksuits, beards and long hair and carried either longbows or crossbows on their back. Reinforcements, heading to Monk Bar. They passed without looking in his direction. Maybe they were frightened he'd contaminate them.

The street was a mixture of ancient and modern and seemed to get older the further they went. The Minster was to the right but Brother Mark stayed on Goodramgate, which turned to the left: old pubs, betting shops, restaurants, black and white timbered medieval buildings.

A man on horseback rode towards them. He was middle-aged and wore long boots, black velvet trousers and a cloak over a black shirt and a clerical collar. He had a gold cross on a chain around his neck. Brother Mark raised his hand sideways and indicated that Reaper should stay back, out of earshot.

The monk walked to the rider and they conversed for several minutes. Neither seemed happy with the way the discussion went. The man on horseback had a paunch that his posture in the saddle only served to emphasise. He was clean-shaven but had a wart on his chin and a veined nose that indicated a fondness for strong alcohol. Reaper thought this was what Oliver Cromwell might have looked like.

The horseman eventually turned his mount with an

angry gesture and rode away, the hooves echoing in the street. They continued walking until Brother Mark turned abruptly right through an arch in a high stone wall and led Reaper into a small enclosed churchyard. A stone path led between patches of long grass and, to the right, a few ancient gravestones leaned with the weight of time. Ahead was a grey church with a red tile roof and a short tower. A sign said this was the Church of the Holy Trinity.

The city they had walked through had been almost empty, but Reaper could imagine that, in the years before the virus, when its narrow streets had bustled with tourists and shoppers, this hidden garden churchyard must have been a haven. Sunshine slanted off the ancient stone of the church and graves. Beyond this small and beautiful place of worship, over the roofs of intervening buildings, could be seen the towers of its grand neighbour, York Minster.

Two men sat on a bench outside the church. They wore tracksuits, like almost everyone else, and had beards and long hair. Incongruously, they carried cricket bats. No ball was in evidence.

'Wait here,' said Brother Mark, and left Reaper outside.

Reaper felt as if he had stepped back in time. The men were wearing biblical length hair and the monk had the hygiene of an era before soap. They clearly did not use motor cars nor carry guns, but a crossbow was an effective weapon. As was a cricket bat. He suspected Brother Abraham might not have a total grasp on reality. Mark returned.

'Brother Abraham will see you,' he said, and led the way inside.

Whilst walking outdoors, Reaper had managed to stay upwind of the monk's body odour, but entering the small building together, it was once more overpowering. For a moment, he held his breath but the interior of the church was so beautiful he let it out again. Sunlight burst through stained glass windows to spill warm colours over the untidy confusion of irregular box pews.

They were at the back of a church whose roof was supported by octagonal stone pillars. They were standing at the start of an aisle that led down to a side altar or chapel. A central nave led to the main altar and there was a third aisle on the far side, and yet the whole place was not much bigger than a front room; an Alice in Wonderland church where he wouldn't have been surprised to meet a white rabbit and a mad March hare. Instead, he met Brother Abraham.

'Welcome to the city of Godliness,' he said. He glanced at Reaper's guide and said, 'You can wait outside, Brother.'

Mark left the church and closed the door behind him and the air began to clear.

Abraham waved his hand in front of his face to dissipate the smell.

'He does take it to extremes,' he said. 'But he has a good heart. Please, would you come this way?'

He led Reaper down the nearest aisle of uneven stone flags, past the higgledy piggledy pews, down wooden steps and into a small sunken area in the southeast corner of the church. The altar was a few feet away, up more steps, to the left, but here, in this depressed corner of the church, carpets covered the stone floor and cushions of many colours were scattered around a low table. The aroma was of incense and candle wax. The monk indicated Reaper should sit and they chose cushions facing each other.

'Now, how can I help you, Brother Reaper?'

Abraham was as tall as the departed Brother Mark, but aesthetically better proportioned. He was in his mid-thirties and wore a white woollen habit with a hood that hung down his back. His feet were bare. His brown hair was clean and well looked after, parted in the middle and hung to his shoulders. His beard, whilst full, was trimmed and well cared for. His face was well defined: high cheek bones; aquiline nose; blue eyes; a mouth that was both strong and sensual and was now smiling at Reaper as if to say, well, what do you think?

Reaper thought Abraham looked like a Renaissance Christ. Brother Mark had glowed with an inner fanaticism, but Abraham glowed with an inner charisma. It was easy to see why he had followers.

'I come from a community called Haven towards the coast,' he said.

'I've heard of it.'

'One of our people has gone missing. Ronnie Ronaldo.' Reaper shrugged at the name and Abraham smiled. 'We believe he came here some days ago and we haven't heard from him since.'

'Brother Ronald is, indeed, with us,' said Abraham. 'He is our guest – although, I have to admit, a reluctant one. He intruded into our domain without permission and resisted apprehension.'

'Resisted?'

'Oh, nothing too serious. He pushed one of our fellows off the castle wall whilst trying to escape.'

'Was the man hurt?'

Reaper had visions of a long drop onto concrete.

'It was upon a stretch with soft turf below and a gentle slope into a stream. Our brother survived with a sprained wrist and dampened enthusiasm. Others were nearby and subdued Brother Ronald, although, from what I was told, he accepted his containment readily enough. The good Lord tells us to turn the other cheek but, sadly, not all my followers are as assiduous in following the teachings of the Lord as they should be. I regret Brother Ronald received a few kicks and cuffs whilst being restrained.'

'Is he hurt?'

'Merely bruised.'

Reaper really had walked through a time warp. He felt he was in a different past, an alternative reality. Abraham was using language that was not quite archaic but not of the real world, either.

'If your man is hurt, we have a doctor,' he offered.

'Do not be concerned. The injury was nothing serious. Pride was hurt more than anything else. He has been tended by our own apothecary.'

Apothecary? 'Where is Ronnie?'

'He is in jail. The castle cells, you know, once housed Richard Turpin before his execution.'

Reaper said, 'You're not going to execute him?'

'Not on this occasion. It is my hope that Brother Ronald might appreciate the gravity of his situation because of the historical context of his confinement. We have told him he occupies the same prison cell once occupied by the highwayman so that he can contemplate Dick Turpin, his own transgressions and the possibility of the long drop. He also receives daily visits from a cleric who instructs him in appropriate passages from the Bible. I hope that he now understands that he committed grievous trespass and, once released, will not do so again.'

'So he is not actually in Turpin's cell?'

'He is in a storeroom of the Castle Museum. Bare stone walls, a barred window and a solid door, so the subterfuge is believable. Turpin's cell still exists but has no door. It was removed to make access easier for tourists.'

The hint of a smile permanently lingered around Abraham's mouth as if he was mocking both Reaper and his own position. But he had to be taken seriously. At this precise moment, Abraham held the power of life and death over both Ronnie and Reaper.

'So you will release him?'

'Of course.'

'When?'

'I will release him into your custody on the condition that no one from your community invades our society in the future. Not just here in the city, but amongst our brethren who work the land along the river to the northwest. All we desire is to be left in peace to commune with God; to make amends for the sins of the world and sow the seeds of a more humble future.' For the first time, the smile had gone. These sentiments, Abraham believed in.

Reaper looked around. 'I thought the Minster would be a more suitable place for your devotions.'

'Oh it is. We have services there twice a day and thrice on Sunday. This modest but holy dwelling is where I live. This is the Church of the Holy Trinity. God has been worshipped here since the 12th century and this church has existed since the 15th. These walls have heard a lot of prayers. At night, I hear them still, reverberating from the stones and in my dreams. They give me comfort and certitude in my belief in God's mysterious ways.'

'Mysterious ways?' Reaper said.

'The plague.'

'Forgive me,' he said. 'I don't believe in God.'

'What do you believe in, Brother Reaper?'

'Survival? The human spirit?'

'Don't you think God resides in the human spirit? In that part of a man or woman that we call the soul? That part that makes him different from the animals and wild beasts?'

'I've met quite a few wild beasts in the last twelve months who claimed to be human. I killed them. Was I killing God?'

'You were killing the devil.'

'I don't believe in the devil, either. I believe that a man can be a right bastard without any help from anyone or any god.'

'Satan was once part of God's holy horde, His holy alliance, until he and a third of all the angels rebelled against God's word. Ever since then, they have lured man from the path of righteousness through temptation. They have driven men, through greed, ambition and lusts, to wage wars, to commit genocide, to hate.' He smiled. 'This is the simplified version. It can be taken as an allegory of the human spirit. Good and evil are intertwined within us in perpetual conflict. Small inner battles that govern small personal decisions, in trying to lead the best life we can without harm to our fellow man. But it is still good and evil. God and the devil … good and evil. See how closely the words are. God is in the spirit of man, Brother Reaper. And the devil is the unholy aspect of this alliance.'

Reaper did not respond. He suspected getting involved in a philosophical discussion about good, evil, and God might be unrewarding.

Abraham smiled. 'Let's have lunch. Rebecca?' he called.

After a moment's hesitation the door to the vestry on the other side of the church opened and a young woman entered, bare feet slapping on the stones. She wore a full-length dress of white cotton and, from the way it moved against her body, very little else. Her hair was tied behind her head and she wore no make up. She looked fresh and lovely. She carried a tray upon which were two glasses and a bottle of wine that had already been opened.

Rebecca knelt on a cushion, placed the tray on the floor and transferred the glasses to the table. She poured wine into both, stood the bottle on the floor, and went to kneel beside Abraham.

Another, similarly dressed, young woman also emerged from the side room. She carried a bigger tray loaded with food. She was a plainer girl, although pleasant to look at and the drape of the dress showed her shape to be attractive. After placing the tray on the table, she knelt on the other side of Abraham.

He put an arm around each and, with a smile, said, 'Mary and Rebecca. My Trinity is complete.'

The men ate and the girls watched. Fresh bread, cheese and slices of ham. The wine was a Burgundy and extremely palatable, even to Reaper, who knew nothing about wines. The meal – and the wine – invited conversation and Reaper explained how and why he had travelled to Haven and how the community had formed. He described the attack it had survived.

'You fought?' Abraham asked.

'We fought.'

'And you vanquished your foes?'

'We vanquished them.'

'Permanently?'

'It's the only way. Turn the other cheek and they'll come back and kill you.'

'I'm afraid what you say is true.' Abraham was reflective. 'I had hoped it would be different, that the world would learn. But it hasn't.'

'It's getting better. The good guys are winning and settlements are growing.'

Abraham nodded and said, 'But there are still dangers. Envy and greed still stalk the land. Rapists and murderers still look for victims.'

'True. That's why all the settlements near us help each other. There is strength in numbers, in federation, in a common spirit.'

'That may be so. But we, in this blessed city of York, have put our trust in the Lord and in the past.'

'You mean, no motor cars, no petrol, no guns?'

'I mean we have put our trust in an age before greed and jealousy were lauded. Before people had a 42 inch effigy to Mammon in their front room, spewing out enticements to buy more, acquire more and forsake true Godliness in the pursuit of a perceived happiness that only came from possessions.'

He sipped wine.

'Humanity lost its way. The populace was confounded and confused. Religion became bigger car, bigger house, bigger breasts, bigger debt, bigger sins. Sin became the norm,' he said, in a quiet voice. 'Godlessness was rife. The commandments were shattered. God's vengeance was a plague.'

Reaper said, 'And so you arm yourselves with bows and arrows and Brother Mark doesn't wash?'

'That is only the surface manifestation of a deeper belief.'

'The plague happened,' Reaper said. 'Whether the virus was man's mistake or God's vengeance, it happened. But those who are left have to plan for the future with whatever they have available. Surely that includes cars, petrol, tractors. Even guns for protection. Bows and arrows will not protect you from an Uzi sub-machinegun.'

'Then we will die. In the meantime, we will pray to God and try to cleanse our souls of past misdeeds and misconceptions. And if we don't die, we shall thrive because we started our new lives in the simpler times of the past, without cars but with horse power, without guns but with arrows for hunting. How will Haven cope when the petrol runs out, when there are no more bullets?'

Reaper picked up the wine bottle and held it so the label could be read.

'But you make exceptions?' he said

Abraham smiled.

'It would be sinful not to,' he said. 'God would not wish us to waste a good bottle of Burgundy, nor indeed any tinned food that may still be edible. Brother Mark, however, is a purist. He refuses the wine in preference of our own brewed beer which, to be honest, is less than palatable. He has embraced the past so completely that he has forsaken washing and personal hygiene, as you have noticed. His only concession is the shoes he wears. Mark has bad feet and needs the comfort of his blessed trainers. Yet even there, he assuages his conscience by choosing Nike, named after Ancient Greece's Winged Goddess of Victory.' Abraham smiled anew. 'Nike, you might say, is protecting his soles.'

Reaper grinned in response.

'It seems that in your new religion, you can pick and choose.'

His gaze went from Rebecca to Mary.

Abraham laughed.

'There is personal choice. There has to be. We are a community of contradictions. All I do is preach and pray. I try to set an example and hope that others may follow. That's all I ever did, and the people came.' He put his arms around the two girls and gave their shoulders a squeeze. 'Mary and Rebecca came and I chose them to make my Trinity because my choice was not to cast out beauty but to revere it.' He kissed each on the head in turn. 'I revere them but I do not sully them. I am celibate, Brother Reaper, in the face of this daily temptation.'

'Why?'

He shrugged.

'Because I have free choice. Because I have the strength to be celibate. Because by being celibate, I prove my fidelity to God, to a higher commitment. So that I can eliminate lust and practice love.'

'Gandhi slept with naked disciples to test his celibacy,' Reaper said.

'Brachmacharya,' agreed Abraham. 'The philosophy of spiritual and practical purity. But I'm not Gandhi. We don't sleep naked together. You can take temptation too far. And I do not impose celibacy upon those who follow me.'

'Will you always be celibate?'

Abraham raised one eyebrow and the smile returned.

'Who knows what God plans.'

'His mysterious ways?' said Reaper.

'Exactly. Perhaps he will speak to me among the prayers I hear within these walls every night and give me new directions.'

Reaper chuckled.

'I founded this community by accident, Brother Reaper. You founded yours by design. Perhaps God spared you to help others. Perhaps we are more alike than you would like to think?'

'Why are you so certain you know God's will?'

'Because I am following God's orders. He told me to pray and to preach. Others interpreted what I said in their own ways and, before I knew it, I had a following. The way we live has evolved through trial and error. I started with an Amish ideal. You know of them?'

'I've heard of them.'

The Amish are ... were? ... a Christian religious sect in America that believed in simple living without modern conveniences. They often banned such devices as motor vehicles, radios or electricity. They practised humility and submission to the will of God. They kept their contacts with the outside world to the minimum, so as to avoid temptation and contamination. The Amish ideals are still here, in York, but have been adapted. Our personal beliefs within these city walls may take many different forms, but our lifestyle comes from consensus and tolerance. There are 182 men, women and children living here, and they have all chosen to live this way. But with discretionary contradictions.'

He nodded to himself and gazed into his wine glass for a moment as if considering his words.

'I pray, others organise, and a sort of order out of chaos was founded around me.' He shrugged. 'If I wanted to change it, I doubt I could any more. I am a victim of my own success.'

He grinned, almost sheepishly, and Reaper couldn't help but like him.

Abraham indicated the dishes and the two women rose, cleared the trays and returned to the vestry, closing the door behind them. They left the bottle of wine and the glasses and the two men alone.

Reaper said, 'Who organises the city? The defences, food, day-to-day life? Obviously, you look after the spiritual well-being, but who looks after the rest?'

'We have the Council of York,' he said. 'It makes most decisions. As I said, they are usually based on consensus. Brother Barry is a more practical person than I. He leads the Council.'

'Wears a cloak and a dog collar and rides a horse?'

'You've met him?' Abraham seemed concerned.

'I saw him in the street. He spoke to Brother Mark.'

'He will have been piqued that you did not ask for him.'

'Barry doesn't sound a very religious name?'

'Barry Foster. He used to be a theatrical medium. He's been talking to the dead for years.' Abraham smiled mischievously.

Reaper said, 'Then he had plenty to talk to after the virus finished.'

'He now prefers preaching his message to the living.'

'Where's he from?'

'He lived in Boston Spa. Lost his wife in the plague. They didn't have children. He came here because he had a booking at the Theatre Royal. Would you believe it? The world had ended and he turned up because the date was in his diary. *An Evening With Psychic Medium Barry Foster*. I think, like many, he was living in shock immediately afterwards. I'd been preaching, and holding non-denominational services in the Minster for about a week, when I noticed him because of the cross he wore around his neck. It was a plain wooden one, then. Now he wears a gold cross he found in the Minster. As I said, he is more practical than I am. He began organising and started holding services of his own, sort of ... *ancillary* to mine. For some reason, he made me the figurehead.'

'Because you look like a prophet?' Reaper said.

Abraham laughed. 'I suppose you have a point.'

'What about Brother Mark?'

'Brother Mark would have joined the Crusades if he had been born at the time – and what did they ever do but consolidate an enmity between Muslim and Christian that lasted a thousand years. Thank goodness there are no crusades left. But he does have a great belief in good and evil.' He smiled. 'He was a second year student of theology at the university. A mature student. His application to become an ordinant in the Anglican Church had been unsuccessful and he hoped this would prove to the bishop that he was serious in his desire to join the priesthood. I suspect he fights his demons every day and every night. This place is right for him. He would be lost anywhere else.

'Everyone here, I suppose, is damaged in one way or another, as are people everywhere. But through work and routine and prayer, they are learning to live again in simplicity. They have inhabited the older parts of the city for this very reason. We keep animals, grow vegetables, make cheese, brew ale, make candles. We have a blacksmith and farrier and a fully working forge. You should have a blacksmith, Brother Reaper. Plan for the future.'

'Do you weave?' said Reaper.

'We have ambitions in that direction.'

'We have sheep. We could trade you wool, if you didn't consider trade a contamination.'

Abraham smiled.

'We have principles but there is no point cutting off the nose to spite the face. Trade could be acceptable. What would you want in return?'

'How about allowing one of our people to work with your blacksmith? To become his apprentice and learn his trade?'

Abraham nodded.

'That seems a reasonable request. I shall put it to the Council.'

'As well as wool, we could offer fresh produce.'

'That, too, would be welcome.' He smiled. 'I feel we have come to an understanding, Brother Reaper. An exchange of ideas is always welcome. I have tried not to preach, but to explain. Besides, I rather think preaching would fall on stony ground, as far as you are concerned. So I shall pray for you, instead.' He got to his feet. 'Now, your companions outside the gates will be worrying about you. Perhaps it is time to reunite you with Brother Ronald so that you can go home.'

He led the way to the door and, in the porch, he slipped his feet into a pair of open toed sandals.

'Dr Scholl may not be a god like Nike but he made damn fine sandals,' he said. 'I may raise him to the sainthood.'

Brother Mark waited outside, along with the two guards. Two horses were tethered to the porch. Abraham handed the reins of one to Reaper.

'Do you ride?' he said.

'Not very well, but I can manage.'

'You should learn.' Abraham smiled. 'It's the future.'

They led the horses into Goodramgate and mounted, Abraham with ease, despite the habit. Reaper more carefully. He had had only a couple of lessons back at Haven. He knew horsepower would be the future eventually. Maybe he should take more lessons. They rode at a gentle pace. Brother Mark followed behind on foot; the two guards remained behind. Reaper wondered whether they had been there for his benefit, or to restrict Brother Abraham?

Abraham set a gentle pace to a pleasant square, with trees and a flagged centre. The monk reined in and pointed down an impossibly narrow lane, where the upper stories of old timber-framed houses butted out and overhung the cobbles, almost meeting to keep out the sunshine.

'The Shambles,' he explained. 'Before the plague, most

of the houses were cafes or gift shops. Now people use them once more as modest dwellings.'

Reaper checked the upstairs windows in case someone might decide to empty a chamber pot, but the monk led them a different way, through an open area with empty market stalls, into a wide thoroughfare called Parliament Street, with trees and a central paved area. The city felt empty, despite Abraham's followers, but it still looked good after a year of stagnation. But then, what was one more year on top of all the history that it carried in its stones?

At the end of Parliament Street, they turned right past another church and then left, down Coppergate, a narrow pedestrian way of modern red brick that opened into a wide and attractive piazza with a Starbucks on the left and the entrance to the Jorvik Viking museum on the right. Overgrown shrubs were in the centre, crowding round a solitary tree in a planted area that was surrounded by seating. On the right was another ancient church of white stone. The remnants of a burnt-out fast food kiosk, was in front of a Boots store, a Marks and Spencers and Topshop, its windows still filled with last year's teenage fashions.

Brother Abraham led the way up a sloping exit lane between the church and an art shop, turned left, and they emerged in front of a large car park and an open space that was dominated by a thirty foot high, turfed mound upon which stood a white stone fortification.

'Clifford's Tower,' Abraham said.

The imposing edifice was hundreds of years old and looked battered, as if by siege. It was defiant and impressive. The mound that raised it high had been built on an elevated position that looked down a slope to a main road and the river beyond.

They crossed the car park that in normal times, would have been packed with the vehicles of tourists and shoppers but was now only a quarter full. As they approached the front of the tower, Reaper saw that a flight of narrow stone steps led up the grass embankment to its entrance. A woman was partway up the steps. She wore a tracksuit, like most of the others he had seen in the city, and was climbing the steps on her knees, pausing on each one to dip her head in prayer.

Reaper looked at Abraham for an explanation.

'Brother Barry,' he said. 'The woman is Sister Alice. Barry regressed her. He's also a hypnotist. Do you know the history of the Tower?'

'No.'

'The Jews of York died there," the monk said. "In the 12th century, the Tower was made of wood. The Jews took refuge there when the town's citizens attacked them.'

'Why did they attack them?' said Reaper.

'Religious fervour – King Richard was raising a crusade. Plus religious bigotry, of course, and to rid themselves of debts. The Jews had loaned silver to everybody from the

King and his barons to the tradesmen of the city. The hatred was whipped up by a mad priest and they laid siege to the tower.'

'What happened?'

'The Jews fought, despite the odds, but the situation became hopeless and the wooden tower was set alight. Many of the Jews killed their wives and children and then themselves. Mass suicide. Like those in Masada, in Judaea, when faced by the Romans. Those who were left, either died in the flames or were massacred by the honest citizens of York.' He nodded towards the woman on the steps. 'Brother Barry says that in a previous life, Sister Alice was one of the perpetrators of the genocide. To make amends, Barry told her to climb the fifty-five steps every day on her knees.'

'Religion has a lot to answer for,' Reaper said. 'So does Brother Barry.'

'It does indeed,' said Abraham, ignoring the comment about the medium. 'Religious madness has been around for centuries. I hold a service here once a week in remembrance of prejudice and the Jews. And for the glory of the one God. York is the perfect city for recovery. It's full of history, monuments, churches, reminders. Signposts for the soul.'

Reaper had no answer to that. At least, none of which Abraham would have approved.

They passed the Tower and rode towards a three-sided square of imposing buildings. The central area was a circle that was overgrown with grass that rose thigh high, a single tree at its centre. Ahead of them was the Castle Museum: an older structure with a modern glass fronted addition to serve as the entrance.

The monk pointed and said, 'These used to be prison buildings. Built in the 18th century on the site of the castle. The Crown Court is to your right. There used to be geese here. Sadly, they were eaten.'

Below the Crown Court was Tower Street, a main road that provided another entrance to the city. Vehicles blocked all lanes. Here, there was no formidable castle wall or gateway. Here, you could drive over a grass border or make your way along the river embankment to enter the city. Here, more than anywhere else, Reaper thought, the security of the city was shown to be an illusion.

But then, as Tanya had pointed out, the city was vulnerable at many places. The blockages and occasional guards were meant as a psychological deterrent rather than a barrier. Perhaps to stop people leaving, as much as to make new arrivals think twice about their motives for entering.

They rode along the road to the left, towards the museum entrance. On a raised area was an artillery field gun that was obviously long out of use and part of the museum display. They stopped at the entrance, dismounted and a young man came from inside to take charge of the horses.

'Brother Mark,' Abraham said to their companion, who had walked at a discreet distance behind them. 'Perhaps you would be good enough to prepare Brother Ronald for his deliverance?'

'Straight away, Brother.'

Mark disappeared inside. Abraham indicated with a hand that they should follow. They entered a foyer in which there was a pay desk, a cafeteria and a gift shop.

'I like it here,' said Abraham. 'I often take a walk through time. When it actually was a museum, all the rooms inside were blacked out. We've removed much of the interior cladding, reclaimed the windows and the natural light. Of course, there are parts where you still need a lamp, but it remains an interesting experience. Although I wouldn't say it is inspirational, it reflects the history of a very turbulent city through centuries that have often been violent. Times when life has invariably been unfair and death arbitrary. If nothing else, it provides an incentive to try harder next time. This time. To try to build a society that is fair and godly.'

Reaper wandered into the gift shop. Abraham followed and picked a selection of guidebooks and tourist maps.

'Please,' he said, handing them to him as a gift. 'No charge.'

He smiled and Reaper, glancing at the dead tills and the empty shelves of the cafe, smiled back.

Abraham led him through a staff door, along a gloomy

ground floor corridor, and down a short flight of stairs. A door that led outside into a yard was open, letting in daylight. Brother Mark waited there. A man in a cassock, who held a book and cross in clasped hands, was standing by another open door that Reaper presumed, was Ronnie's cell.

'Is all well, Father?' said Abraham.

'I would have liked more time with him, Brother, but I think this experience may have done some good.'

Reaper and Abraham looked inside. Ronnie Ronaldo was sitting on a stool. His narrow face was full of contrition and had bruising around the left eye. Dim light filtered through a barred window. A palliasse and blanket were on the stone floor and a bucket covered by a piece of wood was in the corner. The wood cover was unable to contain the odours that leaked into the confined space.

'Boss?' Ronnie said, with surprise.

'How are you, Ronnie? How have they been treating you?'

'They've treated me fine, boss. Why are you here?'

'To take you home. We've missed you.'

Ronnie suppressed a smile. 'Are we going now?' he said. 'I'm taking Bible classes, like, and Father Michael says I need a few more.'

'We'll get the Reverend Nick to carry on the good work back at Haven, if you like.'

'Nick?' The voice of the priest queried the possibility. 'I

pray this is not a euphemism for Old Nick? You hear such stories from beyond the walls.'

'Certainly not, Father,' said Reaper. 'The Reverend Nick is a God-fearing man like yourself, properly ordained and well versed in the word of the Lord.' Just for a moment, he wondered whether Nick actually was ordained. After all, anybody could pretend to be anything and no one would be any the wiser. Like Abraham. Like Brother Barry. Maybe like Father Michael. 'He'll be happy to see to Ronnie's welfare.'

Abraham said, 'Shall we go, brothers? The staleness of the air is getting a little oppressive.'

A combination of Brother Mark and the bucket was making breathing strained, even with the open door. But, if it came to a choice, Reaper would have picked the bucket.

Brother Abraham left Reaper at the Castle Museum to ride back to Holy Trinity alone and prepare for the six o'clock service in the Minster. Reaper declined his invitation to attend. Abraham again said he would put to the Council the possibility of trading, which might be undertaken on neutral ground outside the city walls.

Brother Mark led the way back and they retraced their steps down Goodramgate. As they approached Monk Bar, Reaper saw that the small man in black with the crossbow was still in place.

'Who's the little chap in black?' he asked. 'The one who tried to skewer me?'

Mark looked up at the walkway on the wall and said, 'That's Brother Cedric. If he had tried to skewer you, you would have been skewered.'

Cedric was watching Reaper again, the malice apparent in his eyes.

'Happy little soul, isn't he?' Reaper said.

Reaper and Ronnie slipped between the barrels and walked along the middle of the road towards the two parked cars.

As they increased the distance, Ronnie said softly, 'You're right about that Cedric. He's an evil little bastard.'

'You know him?'

'I met him. Him and a mate came to the cell and gave me a kicking.'

'Why?'

'Light entertainment?' Ronnie said.

Reaper glanced sideways at the skinny man, to confirm what he meant. He didn't look back. He knew the crossbow would be pointed at him. Neither did they increase their pace. And Brother Abraham thought he led such a wholesome little community.

Then they were beyond accurate crossbow range and met the three girls, who embraced an embarrassed but happy Ronnie. While Tanya and Jenny questioned him about his experiences, Sandra stayed with Reaper as he once more fastened on his weapons and caressed the carbine. He hadn't realised how much they had become a part of him and that without them he didn't feel complete. Did that make him sad or safe?

He took a deep breath and blew it out.

'Difficult?' Sandra said.

'It's just nice to breathe clean air again.' He looked back from where they had come. He had seen no signs of self-flagellation but he had sensed something else. 'Something behind those walls has a bad smell about it.'

And it wasn't just body odour.

Chapter 9

REAPER WOULD HAVE BEEN HAPPY TO LEAVE BROTHER ABRAHAM and his strange followers alone but others at Haven were intrigued by the practices of a group of what had presumably once been rational people.

'Mind you, who's rational now?' commented Doctor Greta Malone.

'There have always been cults,' said the Rev Nick. 'Particularly in modern times, when people were looking for alternative beliefs.'

'You mean New Age religions?' said Cassandra. 'Stonehenge, Glastonbury Tor? Gazing into crystals?'

'I mean much more sinister ones. Better organised ones. In the 1960s, the Process Church of the Final Judgement worshipped both Christ and Satan and attracted mainly middle class followers. They had a Christ-like leader, whose name escapes me now, but he fitted the Western image of Jesus.'

'The Western image of Jesus has always confused me,'

said Judith. 'He's a six foot tall white man with perfect features, often with blond hair, when the actual Jesus was a Middle Eastern Jew who was probably about five foot one.'

'That doesn't mean he wasn't a nice person,' said Pete Mack.

'Children,' said Nick, in a tone that suggested mockery was not appropriate, and continued. 'The Process Church was said to have influenced the Manson Family. You remember them? The Sharon Tate murders? Manson preached a doomsday religion.

'Then there was Scientology, invented by a writer of science fiction, and derided as totally crackpot, but it still became powerful and had famous followers. The preacher Jim Jones? He took nine hundred people to Guyana and got them to commit mass suicide. Waco, Texas? Those people were not alone. Others committed suicide – Heaven's Gate, the Order of the Solar Temple. These are just in the West. There were many others in Russia, Eastern Europe, South America, Africa. Satanic cults, vampire cults. Fringe religions you wouldn't believe. So why do we find it difficult to believe that, after an apocalypse, people would follow Brother Abraham's message of love and cooperation?'

'Abraham talks about love and cooperation,' said Reaper, 'but it didn't feel like such a happy place.'

And Ronnie shed a different light on life behind the walls. The priest who had attended to him had been charitable enough, but he hadn't experienced much godliness from others he had encountered. Two jailers had visited him briefly, twice a day, to deliver food and escort him while he emptied his slop bucket. They had spoken little but had prodded him with baseball bats and he had been in no doubt that if he had been in any way awkward, they would have been happy to use them differently.

One night, Brother Cedric and another man had visited him and, after cuffing his hands behind him, had beaten him, directing their blows to his body so that the results would not be seen by the priest. A woman had been with them but had waited in the doorway to the cell while they enjoyed their sport. At its conclusion, she had stepped into the cell and kicked him.

'I don't like repeating the language they used, not in front of ladies,' said Ronnie. 'One of them kept saying, don't mark his face, but Cedric – the evil little one – was in two minds whether or not to go the whole hog.' He shook his head. 'And it wasn't nice what they were saying to the woman. I mean they're supposed to be religious aren't they? What they were saying to the woman wasn't very religious.'

Not their problem, Reaper thought. But others in Haven were concerned. At the very least, they said, they should make contact again to confirm the trading deal. The sheep were due to be sheared at the start of summer and they could offer fleeces. They didn't need homespun cloth or blankets because there was still no shortage of woollen goods in shops, stores and warehouses. But trade was one way of making contact and it would be beneficial if they could arrange for someone to train as a blacksmith – and to thereby have a pair of eyes on the inside.

'From what I saw, and from what Ronnie told us, I don't think York is a good place to be,' said Reaper. 'I, for one, would not want to visit there on a daily basis, even if it is to learn how to be a blacksmith. It won't be straightforward and it'll be potentially dangerous.'

Even so, the organising council discussed it with possible candidates and a young man volunteered for the double role of apprentice and spy. Adrian Freeman – 'call me Adie' – was twenty-four. He had been a tyre fitter in a suburb of York and knew the city. In the aftermath of the plague, he had drifted to the coast before finding Haven. He was not academically inclined but he was bright, and he could be relied upon not to ask suspicious questions or to provoke any of the inhabitants. All he had to do was learn a new skill while keeping his eyes and ears open. All that had to be arranged was a way of getting him inside.

Reaper and Sandra returned to York with the Rev Nick Waite, in the hope that one cleric would get on with another, and Cassandra Cairncross, who had an astute mind and was a natural leader. They stopped at the same place as before, across the road from the Indian restaurant, and within sight of the gate in the city walls.

The restaurant caused Reaper to remember nights from long ago, when he went out for a few pints with the lads and they inevitably ended up in a curry house where Charlie Benson would inevitably bring the strong right hand of the law down on a plate of papadums, turning them instantly into crisps. At the time, they thought it was funny. Normal days before the world ended, before his personal tragedy had unfolded. Normal days, when he had been a simple bobby with a simple code to follow: a code of law and order. He still had a simple code to follow; only now it was more deadly.

Days long gone.

He looked at the gate through the binoculars. A woman carrying a pike stepped onto the wall and stared back. She pointed, turned and spoke to someone he couldn't see.

'Now we are here, it does look a little intimidating,' said Nick.

'I'll go, if you like,' said Reaper.

'Not at all. It was just a comment. Cassandra and I will go this time. Beauty and the beast?' He smiled to hide his nerves.

'We'll be all right, Reverend,' said Cassandra.

Reaper had no qualms about the cleric's bravery. He had seen him put his life on the line to save others.

He wore his dog collar and a dark suit on this formal occasion, although normally, he didn't bother. Cassandra, a good-looking woman in her late thirties, wore a modest

Laura Ashley dress and flat shoes so that she wouldn't be taller than her companion.

'Right?' she said.

'Right,' said the Rev Nick.

'We'll be here,' said Reaper.

The two walked forward briskly and Reaper vowed silently that if Brother Cedric took any aggressive action towards his friends, he would gut him with the ten-inch knife that was in the sheath on his leg.

Reaper and Sandra left the car where it was, but moved back out of sight of the guards on the wall. Though it seemed unlikely, there was always the chance that Brother Mark, or some other faction, might send out people to capture them.

They retreated to a block of modern flats that was out of the line of sight of the gatehouse. The way in was in a side street through a metal-framed glass door. There was an entry pad and phone. The door was locked. Reaper tried his boot at the same height as the door handle and it burst in with little resistance. They went upstairs and chose a flat that looked out over Monkgate. It was empty – no bodies – and Sandra cast an eye over the furnishings and decorations.

'It's a rental,' she said.

'What?'

'I'll bet a lot of these flats were holiday lets. Close to the

Minster and city walls. They would have been popular.'

'I suppose they would.'

The lounge and dining area were combined in an L shape. From the window they could see their car on the other side of the street. The guards wouldn't know where they were. There was a bathroom, kitchen and a bedroom with twin beds. Everything was neat and tidy, nothing out of place. If it had been a rental, as Sandra surmised, it had been cleaned and readied for a visitor who had never arrived.

The rooms were not big but were furnished with taste. A sofa and a reclining armchair, a lamp on a coffee table, a standard lamp, a bookcase of paperbacks, a dining table and four chairs, a CD player, and a 32 inch, flat screen instrument of Mammon that could no longer spread the corruption that Brother Abraham despised. Like TVs everywhere, it was stone dead.

Reaper picked up an old copy of the *Yorkshire Post* from the coffee table, laid it on the sofa and sprawled in comfort, the newspaper protecting the cushion at the far end from his booted feet.

'That's daft,' said Sandra.

'What?'

'Protecting the sofa. Who's going to complain? Who's likely to ever come here again?'

'Habit,' he said. 'Besides, it was once somebody's pride and joy.'

She moved a dining chair to the window so that she could look down into the road to keep an eye on their car and watch for the return of Nick and Cassandra. Reaper got up again and inspected the books on the shelves. He picked one and returned to his sprawl.

'What is it?' she said.

'Bernard Cornwell.' She raised an eyebrow that said she hadn't a clue. 'Did you ever watch Sharpe on television? Sean Bean?'

'Good actor,' she said. 'Quite fit for an old bloke.'

Old bloke? Reaper squirmed.

'Well he starred in a TV series set in the Napoleonic Wars.' He held the book up so she could see the cover. 'It was based on these books.'

'So it's a war book.'

'Historical fiction.'

'About war.'

'Yes.'

She watched the street and her silence was a comment. He dealt in war and read about it from choice. He started reading, but found he couldn't be bothered. Lying down full length on the comfortable sofa made him lethargic.

'Give me a call when you want a break,' he said, and closed his eyes.

He had always been a reader, always had a book on the go and a spare as backup. But he hadn't read a book of fiction for years: not since his daughter had been raped and the lives of his family had changed. There had been no incentive, no desire to escape in a book. Escape hadn't been an option, hadn't been allowed. How could he contemplate escape after what his daughter had suffered?

Reaper had learned to live with the guilt of not being there when she had needed him, not being able to save her, despite his status as a policeman. Then her suicide had torn a gaping hole through the pain he had learned to control, so that, afterwards, nothing existed for a long time. He had become a shell, engaging in a sham of living.

His wife, with whom he had grown increasingly estranged, had then been diagnosed with cancer. The sham had gone on as far as the outside world was concerned while, behind closed doors, their antipathy towards each other had developed into a dull, domestic hatred. His wife's fatal illness had simply been another punishment. He felt no guilt when she died. All his guilt concerned his daughter. He had failed to protect her not only from attack, but also the despair that had driven her to take her own life.

No wonder he hadn't read a book of fiction. Escapism hadn't been allowed. The punishment had to be endured without relief. The slaying of his daughter's rapist served both as revenge and as a way out; he had planned the subsequent standoff with an armed response unit in the hope that it would lead to his own death – suicide by police. It didn't happen. They had captured him and put him in a cell. Death hadn't been allowed.

Then the virus had brought the end of the world, as it had been, the end of a world, as it would never be again. For a while, after he found Kate, he had thought the new beginning might give him licence to start life afresh. Put the pain behind him. But Kate had been taken from him and once more he had been left as empty as a crater. It hadn't been allowed.

Protecting Haven was now his life. He enjoyed his interaction with its inhabitants, his friendships and comradeships with Greta, the Special Forces, Pete Mack, Ash. He smiled to himself. He had even been pleased to see Ronnie Ronaldo back in one piece. But Sandra gave the real purpose to his life. He would not let anything happen to her. His born-again daughter.

The Viceroy of India restaurant could invoke memories of normality, could finding a Cornwell novel revive his passion for reading? He'd had shelves of books at home, but nothing highbrow: American thrillers and the complete set of Sharpe novels in paperback. He had intended to read them again at some unspecified period in a future that was forever lost. He didn't think he could be bothered now.

So much had changed. No more pubs, curry restaurants, football or cricket. His weekends off had always included chunks of time doing nothing but watching sport on TV, that intrusion in every living room that Abraham had vilified. He had enjoyed the sport and the time out, but was Abraham right? Before television, blokes actually went to matches, didn't they? They didn't slouch on the sofa, they were part of the spectacle and experience, they interacted with their fellow man. Without a TV set, would he have been more active, taken a different grip on life? Spent more time with his daughter? Repaired the fractures of his marriage before they became terminal?

To be honest, probably not. Retreating into the past, like Abraham and his followers, was not the answer. Smashing television sets before the virus struck would not have been the answer. Weavers had smashed looms in the 19th century and all they had done was give the world a name for those who would oppose progress for no other reason than fear of what it might bring.

Progress was inevitable, always had been, despite the Luddites of the world. Progress had turned cave dwellers into empire builders. Progress had made it inevitable that man would go to the moon. You couldn't have stopped technical advancement. If the world had had a few years more, every home would have had an interactive TV screen the size of the living room wall. Sodom and Gomorrah in surround sound 3D. And progress was essential again *now* if the few who remained were to truly survive. But theirs would be a different kind of progress.

They had to step back and learn traditional skills all over again for when the petrol ran out. That was when the real battle for the future would begin. Communities that lived in shopping malls would be ill-prepared to keep and feed themselves when the last tin had been opened. People still in towns and cities would eventually migrate to the countryside; they would have to when the food ran out. They had to start again as an agrarian society and grow their own crops and raise their own animals.

At least Haven and the other settlements in their loose federation were preparing properly. From that beginning, perhaps humanity would progress in different directions from before. He nudged the book that lay on his chest with a finger. Literature would also be part of the future – had to be – as a way of remembering the past and ensuring the cultural roots of their new society. Who, he wondered, would write new books for this new age? Brother Abraham?

Maybe he would start reading again. Maybe it would be okay to read again.

He smiled as he acknowledged he was making deals with himself. Or was he making deals with a God he didn't believe in? Besides, if he allowed himself to start reading again, what next?

Don't be stupid, Reaper told himself.

He dozed.

Some time later, he sat up and Sandra turned to look at him.

'What?' she said.

'Coffee?' he said.

They had brought coffee and sandwiches. Reaper unpacked the bag and they ate. Afterwards, they switched positions. Sandra picked a book from the shelves and sprawled on the sofa and he took the armchair to keep watch.

'What did you pick?' he said.

'Catherine Cookson.' She held it up for him to see. '*The Parson's Daughter.*'

'Have you read her before?'

'No. To be honest, I haven't read much at all. Not fiction, anyway. Maybe it's time I started.'

He nodded and stared out of the window.

Sandra read the blurb on the back of the book. Did she really want to delve into the 19th century life of Nancy Ann Hazel, 'the young and high-spirited daughter of a country parson'? It was certainly a story that was a world away from now. Maybe the experience would do her good. Get her out of herself. But, like Reaper, she couldn't be bothered and it lay unopened on her stomach and she closed her eyes.

Life went on. It went on at a swifter pace than she had ever known when she was growing up, back in the past. So fast, she couldn't clearly remember what Jamie looked like, any more. Her heart lurched with anguish at her loss and the failure to remember his face, as if she was being unfaithful to his memory.

Why did everything have to be so rushed? How long had they had together? Four months? If she and Jamie had met in the past, they would have gone out together, phoned each other, sent texts, made arrangements, gone clubbing, had weekends away, got to know each other. Except that, back in that world, she never would have met Jamie. Or, if their paths had crossed, they would not have looked at each other in the same way or with the same expectations. They had been from different classes of society, conditioned to respond only to their own kind. It had taken a plague to make everybody equal. It had taken a plague for them to meet and for him to be killed.

How shit was that? You survive the plague and then some sod comes along and shoots you.

She remembered the night he died. Reaper had been away from the village when Muldane's army had attacked. Arif had been on guard duty at the gate. They had slit his throat and were down at the manor house in strength before anyone had time to react. She had been out on patrol with James. They got back, drove down the hill to the manor house, and saw the two bodies on the steps. At first they were just bodies and then she had recognised one to be that of Milo. She had known the second was Jamie, but had at first refused to acknowledge the reality. Then, before she could react, guns were pointing at them.

Why did she surrender? Why didn't she fight? Of course she was shocked, but why didn't she fight, take some of them with her, even if meant her death? At least, she could have joined Jamie. She had pondered her decision many times since and had finally dismissed cowardice or shock. In that split second between deciding to fight or not, she had thought of Reaper. He was still out there and he was invincible and he would come to the rescue. He would make things right and she would be able to take her revenge.

It was a totally irrational thought but it had made her delay any action, surrender her weapons and let whatever was to happen take its course. But she had been right. Reaper had come to the rescue. He always would.

At the beginning, when they first met, she had wondered whether he had sexual desires towards her, despite the age difference – although age difference never seemed to matter to most men; the younger the better, seemed to be their motto. Memories of her captivity in the early days of the plague came in quick, searing flashes, and she forced them away. While her captors were using her, she had retreated inside herself, retreated deep into the back of her mind, so that she was only vaguely aware of whatever they did. But lately, those repressed experiences resurfaced occasionally. Searing flashes that she subdued with other thoughts. Thoughts of Reaper?

It was when he taught her how to shoot that she knew he had no ulterior motives: his body close behind her as he guided her into the correct position, close as lovers. That was when she knew she was safe with him, and that first night they had spent together she had slept in his arms.

She hadn't known her own father. At one time, she had blamed her mother for driving him away, but she had been young and stupid then. Her father had taken his pleasure and disappeared at the thought of responsibility. His departure hadn't mattered. She had grown up in a one-parent world. Most of the kids at her school came from broken marriages or broken relationships. Her situation had not been unique. Besides, her mother had had enough strength for two parents. Her mother had been a survivor, until the SARS virus. Then life had become a lottery.

Sandra hadn't thought about her father for years and she had been quietly content when Reaper had claimed her as his daughter. That contentment had grown into much more in the year since. She could guess his reasons, knew about his real daughter, and wondered, if Emily had lived, whether they might have been friends. Same city, same age. She wondered if her mother would have liked Reaper?

The thought tailed off before it turned into a Catherine Cookson but, still, she smiled. Reaper and her ... they were a team. Best thing since sliced bread – and when would you see that again? They were father and daughter. Born of the plague and bonded forever. No argument. Period.

But things might have been different.

Before the world ended, she had started studying again. She and her mother had laid out the plans that would send her to Tech and take a Foundation Course that would gain her entry to university and raised horizons. And then, who knew? She might have met Jamie, after all, without barriers and it would have been all right for them to fall in love. Sweet Jamie. *God, I wish I could remember your face?* But she remembered his touch, the passion they had shared. She blushed, as she dozed. Would she share passion again? Would that be being unfaithful? Of course not. Life moved on.

But would it move on for Reaper? Without demeaning her own loss, she knew that losing Kate had seriously affected him. Did he think he was too old to find love again? Or did he believe it was God's continuing punishment? He had confessed his feelings of guilt to her ages ago. But surely he'd been punished enough by now.

Come on, God, give him a break, even if he is an atheist.

Dr Greta Malone, she thought. Now she would be perfect. She'd seen the way the doctor had looked at Reaper. It was a shame that he didn't realise what it signified. A woman knew that look. She'd seen Reaper look at Greta, too; secret glances of which the doc was unaware. A woman knew that look, too.

Come on God, you bastard, give him a break.

Nick and Cassandra returned after spending two hours in the city. Reaper saw them approaching the car. They hesitated, and looked around in surprise, because it was empty. He pushed open the window and shouted down.

'We're up here. Everything okay?'

'I suppose so,' Nick said.

Cassandra simply shook her head as if still doubting what she had seen.

Reaper and Sandra packed and went down to join them. They got in the car, made a U turn, and drove back towards Haven. Nick let out a sigh that could have been relief.

'A strange experience,' he said.

'Something is going on there,' Cassandra said. 'And Abraham doesn't know it.'

'Who did you see?' Reaper asked.

Cassandra said, 'Brother Barry, High Chair of the Council.'

'Highchair?'

'He seems to enjoy titles. He was with a fat chap called Morrison. Looked like a pork butcher ... very pompous. He was High Treasurer.'

'Give me strength,' said Reaper.

'Abraham was there as well.'

'What did you think of him?' Reaper said.

The Rev Nick said, 'I liked him. I'm not so sure about his godliness. He seems as if he went to a fancy dress party and someone took him seriously. But he's a likeable chap. I see what you meant about charisma. And he was all in favour of trade.'

Cassandra said, 'He's a good-looking chap and he looks like Christ. But he should remember what happened to the original.'

'You think he's in danger?' Reaper said.

'Not as long as he does as he's told,' she said. 'He's still a figurehead. But you get the sense of unrest inside those walls.'

'Is the trade on?' Sandra said.

'Yes,' said Nick. 'We give them the wool and Adie can learn how to be a blacksmith.'

'When?' said Reaper.

'Adie can go tomorrow. We deliver the wool as soon as it's sheared.'

The Rev Nick accompanied Adie on the first day of his apprenticeship. He negotiated entrance to the city and placed him in the hands of Brother Mark. A Special Forces team escorted them but went in a separate vehicle and stayed out of sight of the walls. The team returned to collect Adie in the evening.

Adie reported that the blacksmith was a fifty-year-old called Joel Hardy, who had worked with horses all his life, had run a forge outside York and also provided a mobile service, shoeing horses over a wide area. The chap was only five eight in height but was powerfully built. Adie said he seemed glad to have the company of someone from outside. Talk was guarded and Joel was always looking to see if anyone was hanging around listening. Joel had taken over the forge of an artist blacksmith, who had specialised in ecclesiastical work.

Once he had been accepted, Adie travelled each day to York by motorcycle. Wool was sheared and delivered.

A wagon stopped outside the Monk Bar and a group of citizens emerged to lift down the bales and carry them within the walls. No words were exchanged except between Brother Mark and the Rev Nick, who had accompanied the delivery.

Chapter 10

REAPER AND SANDRA TOOK TRIPS SOUTH AND SOUTHWEST, along main roads and minor roads, although never beyond Yorkshire's borders. He wanted plenty of notice if any force from Windsor started moving north. They made contacts with other communities and heard rumours that the centre of Leeds had been abandoned after the firestorm that had destroyed much of its centre a year before, the flames feeding upon themselves in a vicious conflagration.

Information about what might be happening further afield was sparse, and Reaper did not want to provoke a situation by motoring down the M62 to investigate the towns that hugged the Pennine hills. The towns would empty soon enough. They had started to empty within their own area, with groups being attracted to the Haven federation. Maybe those who had clung to an urban environment hadn't enjoyed the isolation of winter, maybe they hadn't liked the sight of grass and weeds beginning to grow in the streets or the knowledge that every flat, every house, every building held bodies now decaying into dust.

People came from Driffield, despite there being good farmland around the town. They preferred to go to an established centre where they knew they would get help and guidance. Others came from Pickering, Malton, Skipton, Tadcaster, and many smaller hamlets where a few folk had got together for safety and collective comfort, but now looked towards the promise of a large and organised settlement. The 'Brains Trust' stayed at Scarborough Castle and a small group manned fishing boats in the harbour, but two other groups in the town gave up life as supermarket scavengers and came inland. People came from Dunnington, Stamford Bridge and Haxby, and the suburbs of York.

More villages were cleared and made habitable, fields were worked, resources shared. With Haven at its hub, the federation encompassed twelve villages, twenty-seven farms and two golf courses that had been put to the plough, plus fishing fleets operating from Bridlington, Filey and Scarborough. Their combined population was more than 3,000.

Special Forces toured the whole area. They became de facto police as well as border guardians. Their area of influence covered much of the Wolds and the North Yorkshire Moors. They shared knowledge with their neighbours, but nowhere else seemed to be as well organised. This exchange of intelligence also provided them with an idea of how communities were growing further afield, on the far borders of friendly territories. Knowledge was important if they were to defend themselves against invaders.

As a further precaution, Reaper mapped a route south to be taken once a week. The possibility of a threat from that direction remained at the back of his mind, and he wanted warning if anyone started scouting north or heading their way in strength. The route he chose followed the A64 past York and Tadcaster, eventually joining the M1.

The motorway contoured round the edge of Leeds before heading directly south, cutting a corridor through the countryside past Wakefield, Barnsley, Sheffield, Chesterfield and Mansfield to Nottingham, which Reaper judged was far enough. Here, they would turn off, below the city, and thread their way along the A52, eventually joining the A1 at Barrowby near Grantham. This dual carriage highway would then take them north, skirting Worksop, Doncaster, Pontefract and Castleford, until they completed an elongated oval, and linked again with the A64.

Both highways were self-contained and skimmed conurbations rather than drove through town or city centres. They were highways where Reaper felt they would be reasonably safe. The cross-country roads between the M1 and A1 would be taken carefully. Two teams went for safety: one travelling a hundred yards ahead of the other in case of anything unexpected.

On the first trip, Reaper drove the lead car with Sandra beside him. Keira and Yank were in the second car. They were well down the M1 when they saw the sort of smoke that came from a controlled fire. A sign said that Trowell Services were ahead. As they approached, a homemade sign said: TRADE.

Reaper took the slip road cautiously into the complex of what had been restaurants, bathrooms and petrol pumps. Sandra lowered the window and held the carbine in her arms at the ready. Her seat had been pushed back to allow for such a manoeuvre. A few abandoned vehicles littered the car park. There was no sign of life in the shops or fast food outlets, which were remarkably free of damage. The sign outside said *Costa, Burger King, M&S*. A pedestrian walkway led across the motorway.

'The smoke is on the other side,' she said.

'I'll try the petrol pumps,' Reaper said.

As he turned in the direction of the rows of pumps, they saw another sign that pointed towards a service lane. It said: TRADE. He stopped before entering the pumps and looked back. The second car had stopped at the entrance to the car park and was waiting for his lead.

Sandra said, 'What's that?'

She got out, carbine at the ready, and walked to the pumps. Yet another sign, attached with string, had blown in the wind and had become stuck the wrong way round. She turned it, stood back and pointed so Reaper could see. The sign said: HELP YOURSELF. She got back in the car.

'Do we go across?' she said.

'I think we do.'

He waved Keira and Anna forward. When they were level, he said, 'We'll drive over. Stay here and stay alert.'

The service lane led back the way they had come, to a bridge that crossed the motorway. On the far side, a farm was off to their right along a track. The lane then led down into the service buildings on the northbound side of the highway. They drove against the traffic flow, if there had been any, past more petrol pumps that also had a sign that said HELP YOURSELF. A brazier stood alone, not so much burning as producing the drifting smoke they had seen. On this side, there was also a motel.

They stopped outside the front of the main buildings. The same franchise signs were displayed. The doors were wide open and a man in his sixties walked out into the sunshine. He wore a straw boater and a large moustache as if he'd fallen off a seaside postcard. He was rotund in check trousers, white shirt and a waistcoat.

'Good morning!' he called.

'Good God,' muttered Sandra.

They got out of the car, carbines at the ready, scanning empty vehicles and buildings for possible danger.

'It's all right,' said the jolly man, for he had not yet stopped grinning. 'You're quite safe. I'm Percy Radcliffe.' He turned and shouted. 'Martha! Visitors!'

'I'm Reaper.'

They shook hands and the man's eyebrows went up and his grin froze and he stared at Sandra.

'I'm …' she began.

'The Angel,' he said.

'Pardon?'

'Reaper and the Angel. You have to be. There can't be two Reapers.'

Reaper and Sandra glanced at each other.

'You know us?' said Reaper.

'I've heard about you. Stories are prime currency now we don't have TV and radio.'

'You've heard about us?'

'From travellers. Some who were there, some who just heard the stories.'

'What stories?' said Sandra.

'The stories about the Grim Reaper and the Angel of Death … The Battle of Haven … The Mad Dog Shootout …'

Because they hadn't reacted in the way he expected, Percy Radcliffe now looked distinctly nervous in case he had offended them. Sandra's mouth had fallen open with surprise. A woman came out of the building behind Radcliffe. She looked about the same age, was tall and ungainly and reminded Reaper of someone he couldn't quite place. She was also smiling.

'Welcome,' she said. 'I'm Martha.'

They shook hands with her, too, and this time Reaper said, 'I'm Reaper, this is Sandra.'

'Not *the* Reaper?' she said, and she looked again at Sandra and added, 'And so young.'

'Please, please,' said Radcliffe. 'Come and have a cup of coffee.'

He led the way inside and Reaper and Sandra split and went in different directions. They checked out the building, first and second floors. Sandra went to the pedestrian way across the motorway. Someone was hiding at the far end and she levelled the carbine, only to lower it again when the ducking head re-emerged and she saw it was Keira.

'If that smoke is a barbecue,' shouted Keira, 'Yank wants a double cheeseburger and fries.'

'Yank will be lucky.'

'Are we clear?'

'Give me a minute.'

She went down the stairs and met Reaper by an arcade of dead gaming machines.

'Keira's on the walkway. Are we clear?'

'Clear.'

'I'll tell them to come over.'

She went back up the stairs. Keira was waiting.

'No fries but tell Yank she can have a menu as a souvenir. Come on over.'

Sandra found Reaper seated in what had been the Costa coffee shop. Martha was behind the counter making coffee at a machine that spluttered and gurgled in a way she hadn't heard in more than a year.

'We have a generator,' said Radcliffe. 'I was telling Reaper. And real coffee.'

'What would you like, dear?' said Martha.

'A cappuccino would be wonderful,' she said.

Footsteps heralded the arrival of Yank and Keira, who stopped in surprise at the sight of a fully working coffee machine.

'Jeez,' said Yank. 'Now there's a sight.'

'An American?' said Martha. 'How nice. What will you have ladies?'

'I'll have a three shot Americano with milk,' said Yank.

'You'll be awake all night,' said Keira. 'Could I have a mocha?'

'And an Irish girl? Oh, this is a cosmopolitan morning, Percy.'

When they were all served, Sandra took her drink outside to keep watch, sitting on top of a picnic table with her feet on the bench. The others relaxed and exchanged stories. They told the odd couple about Haven, the place they had only heard of as a myth and a legend. Reaper steered the conversation and there was no further mention of the Grim Reaper and the Angel of Death.

Percy Radcliffe and Martha Brown had met at the services the year before, towards the end of summer. He had been in insurance in Leicester and she had worked in a wool shop in Leeds. He had lost a wife, son and grandson, and she had lost her cat when she left her home in a hurry, driven out by out of control fires and gangs on the rampage. They had arrived at the service station by different routes and within one week of each other.

'People had it before we came,' Radcliffe said. 'They lived here, tried to trade the petrol. There were five of them. Four men and a woman. It led to arguments. I was here three days, sleeping in my car because I had no fuel to go any further, when some travellers shot them. Blasted them with shotguns. The men had fought back and killed one of them. So that was five bodies. The woman went off with those who were left. That's when I put the signs up: Help Yourself. Who needs killing over a gallon of petrol?'

Martha said, 'I arrived the next day. I wasn't going anywhere in particular. I was so desperate, I'd have taken a barn for the winter. But I met Percy. He was burying the dead. Sleeves rolled up and digging graves. I thought that was the mark of a decent man, so I helped him. There was food here. The place was never properly looted. I suppose those passing through would have supplies and assume this place had been stripped. And we went out a few times to stock up. We put the signs up to attract people. That's why we sometimes light the fire. Smoke attracts. We're no threat to anyone and most people on the road these days are just people. The gangs have mainly gone, although you have to be careful.' She smiled, self disparagingly. 'Even I have to be careful.'

'The winter wasn't too bad,' Radcliffe said. 'There's still fuel and we ran the generator when it got very cold. Few people travelled in the winter. People stop, others come to trade. Locals. They tell us what they've got and we match up who has what, with who wants what. It's all very civilised.' He laughed. 'So to speak.'

Yank left the group to relieve Sandra and Reaper asked about local groups. Radcliffe said they were mainly small and peaceful and living on farms and in villages, although there was a larger group based at Nottingham University.

'Maybe fifty or sixty,' he said. 'They've cultivated the land. Dug allotments and have goats and hens. They're trying to make a go of it.'

'You mean professors, students?' Sandra said. Academics to boost Haven's 'Brains Trust', were always in demand.

'No, dear,' said Martha. 'I think they're mainly townies from Nottingham. But they're doing their best.'

'Do you have market days?' Reaper asked.

'Tuesdays and Saturdays,' said Radcliffe. 'Although who can keep track of days? Every three days and four days. And we can make deals for people outside those times, as well, except that people like to socialise. See how the other half are getting on. Swap stories. There's a big demand for stories now there's no TV and radio. Prime currency.'

Reaper asked if they had any news from down south

and the couple exchanged a look before Martha said, 'We don't get many travellers from London, if that's what you mean. I mean, if you wanted to get out of London where would you go? I don't think many would head for the Midlands. They'd go into the Home Counties, or the West Country or the South Coast. And real travellers, I mean those going all the way to Scotland, or even Yorkshire, they would have filled their petrol tanks before they left and wouldn't want to break their journey too soon. No, we get wanderers, rather than travellers. Mind you ...'

Radcliffe said, 'We have heard of a place called Redemption near Windsor. Very organised. Too organised, for some. A sort of government. Lots of soldiers. They say Prince Harry is there, but that just sounds like wishful thinking. They have checkpoints stopping people going in and coming out. I'm not sure whether that's a good thing or bad. The people who told us haven't actually come from there. They've been nearby and picked up the rumours.'

Martha said, 'And then there's that lot from Sheffield. We don't know what to make of them.'

'Who are they?' asked Reaper.

'We've only heard one or two stories. A big group, moving across country. They left Sheffield – everybody seems to be leaving the cities – and seem to be heading vaguely south. Apparently they don't like old folk.' She gave a grin. 'So I don't suppose we'd be popular.'

They promised to call again and made their goodbyes.

The odd couple would do very nicely as an intelligence outpost and, next time they called, they would bring trade goods.

As they rejoined the motorway to drive south, Reaper said, 'Joyce Grenfell.'

'What?' said Sandra.

'That's who Martha reminded me of. The actress, Joyce Grenfell.'

'I've never heard of her.'

'You're too young. Remember the black and white St Trinian's films?'

'Vaguely, from wet Sunday afternoons.'

'She was in those.'

Sandra did not seem impressed.

'What was all that about Reaper and the Angel? The Battle of Haven? The Mad Dog Shootout?'

'It means we have become legend, my little Angel.'

'Don't talk bollocks.'

'Language, Angel.'

'And don't call me Angel. How did that happen?'

'Like the man said, without TV and radio, people are talking to each other again and storytellers are in demand. Someone produced a good story – a battle of good and evil – and it will be passed on, getting bigger and no doubt more gory in the telling. We've had people leave Haven. They probably started it. Or the people who escaped Tyldesley. Some of them went south. Once told, it will just rumble on like Chinese Whispers.'

'Chinese Whispers?'

'A message that gets more distorted the more it's passed on. Like the old story from the First World War. An officer told a private at the front to pass on a message for the generals in the rear. *Send reinforcements, we're going to advance.* By the time it had been passed all the way down the line and reached HQ, miles away from the muck and bullets, it had become, *send three and fourpence, we're going to a dance.'*

Sandra laughed and then the laughter subsided. When she spoke again, her voice was quieter.

'There were a lot of bodies, Reaper.'

'I know.'

'The Angel of Death. I'm not sure I like that.'

He reached out and squeezed her knee.

'We won't tell anybody.'

They saw signs of settlements, as they skirted Nottingham University and took the A52 through the countryside towards Grantham. They didn't stop or make any detours. They could leave that for later trips. But the homemade sign they saw on the A1, on the outskirts of the village of Cromwell, did make them stop: The Tea-Riffic Cafe.

The sign was made from a long piece of hardboard with the words written in red paint. The cafe was a caravan, with plastic seats and tables outside, that was parked on a slim triangle of grass made by the northbound lanes of the A1, and the road that joined it from the village. Two people were sitting outside in the sunshine beneath a green parasol.

Reaper, driving the lead car, slowed from the sixty miles an hour they had been travelling, to almost a walking pace. The two people, a man and a woman, got to their feet, smiles on their faces. The woman waved.

He stopped the car twenty yards short of them in the outside lane and noted in the rear view mirror that Keira and Yank in the second car had stopped 100 yards behind. They surveyed the immediate scene and surroundings. The woman was elderly, grey hair, an apron over a grey dress, sensible flat shoes. She waved again. The man was much younger, maybe still in his twenties, he wore a suit and tie, the three buttons of the jacket buttoned. His smile and demeanour showed no guile and spoke only of innocence. He looked a victim of a different kind, or maybe he was blessed; a human being without blame, guilt or malice.

'Looks clear to me,' Sandra said.

'Let's go see what's on the menu.'

Reaper drove into the nearside lane and stopped a few yards past the tables and chairs. The man remained where he was but the woman followed them. Sandra got out, the carbine at the ready, but the woman was not perturbed. Reaper, slung his carbine over his shoulder and joined them.

'I'm Maisie Day,' said the woman, her eyes sparkling. 'This is Brian.' She turned and saw that the young man hadn't moved and motioned him forward. 'He's not all there,' she said. 'He wasn't all there before the plague, but it didn't help. He's a good lad and wouldn't say boo to a goose. If we had a goose, which we haven't. Never did have, as far as I recall. Anyway, it's good to meet you.' She held out a hand. 'We don't get many customers.'

Sandra shook her hand, while still assessing the situation. Reaper was doing the same.

'I'm Sandra,' she said.

'Reaper,' Reaper said, also shaking hands.

'Now there's a strange name,' Maisie Day said. 'Where have I heard that before?'

Sandra offered her hand to Brian who shook it with a formal flourish and a big grin. He did the same with Reaper.

'Are your friends joining us?' Maisie said. 'We can offer you tea,' and she pointed at the sign, 'which is tea-rific – that was my idea. The leisure industry is reliant on marketing.' She nodded to herself, as if confirming a chapter heading. 'And we have a Dish of the Day. Get it? Maisie Day?' She laughed and Reaper smiled. Sandra went with Brian to the caravan. She glanced inside and looked back at Reaper and confirmed it was clear. 'Which is stew,' Maisie said. 'Which is also terrific.'

'Sounds good, Maisie,' Reaper said, and waved the second car forward.

Keira and Yank stopped the Rover short of the caravan and took a scouting trip round the back. They went up the access road and checked out a house and outbuildings, before joining them and being introduced. Brian beamed at the presence of three attractive young women.

'Brian, put the stove on,' Maisie said, and the young man disappeared into the caravan. 'Please, sit down,' she said.

Sandra had a quiet word with Keira, who went back to the vehicles to stand watch.

Maisie watched her go with a perplexed look.

'You can never be too careful,' Sandra said.

'Of course,' said Maisie.

They sat round a plastic garden table beneath the green parasol.

'Where are you from?' Maisie said. 'Passing through? You're not local, are you? I've met the locals and you're not them. You're much too …' she looked them up and down, searching for the right words '… uniformed. Are you official? From the Government? Have we still got a Government? I heard there was one down near Windsor. Place called Relegation.' She frowned. 'Something like that. But I'm not sure if someone told me or if it's a story I read before the plague.'

Maisie shook her head and said, 'I'm sorry about going on so. We only get a few visitors so I tend to talk a lot. I talk a lot anyway. I talk so much to Brian he quite often goes to sit with the pigs. But I still talk. To myself, quite often. I find I'm a good listener and my mother always told me that a good listener will never be short of friends.' She stopped again and looked round. 'I'm doing it again, aren't I. I'm sorry.'

Her eyes watered as if she were on the verge of crying but she took a deep breath and, when she spoke again, it was much slower and more controlled.

'There's probably a condition to explain why I talk so much. Probably a whole ology to explain it. Probably plague-ology.' Her smile became gentle instead of manic. 'I was a lecturer at Grantham College. Hospitality and Catering. I loved it. I had no family, just the college. I live in the village. After it happened, I went back to the college a few times, but it got dangerous. I met Brian on my way back. He looked lost, poor lamb. I don't know whether he could talk before, but he doesn't now. Not a word.' She shrugged. 'I suppose I've got used to talking for both of us.' Her smile gained strength after her confessional. 'Anyway. Tell me about you.'

Sandra started to tell her about their community and, partway through, Brian came out carrying a tray with five mugs of tea, a jug of milk and bowl of sugar, which he put on the table. He smiled when they thanked him and he took a cup of tea to Keira before going back to the caravan. Sandra completed telling the story of Haven, and Maisie seemed cheered that normality had returned to parts of the country. She also seemed puzzled.

'Haven? I've heard of that, somewhere. Or was it Heaven?' She waved a hand to dismiss her confusion.

'How about you, Maisie?' Reaper said. 'When did you open your café?'

She laughed.

'Yes, I know. Café. It's a bit of madness from a mad old woman in a mad old world.' She smiled. 'Or is that mad new world?' She sipped her tea. 'Three others in the village lived through the plague. Susan was in her twenties. Lived with a chap. She lost him, of course. Arnold is sixty-four and Shirley is fifty-two. We got together afterwards. Never mind the tragedy of what had happened, we were all disappointed about who was left. Susan packed her bags and drove off, don't know where. She didn't say. Which left Arnold and Shirley and me, and I never did like old people.' She grinned. 'Being old myself. So I politely said I preferred to be on my own and they went off to live together at the other end of the village. I mean, we help each other, but we don't socialise. Anyway, I found Brian, so it was all right.

'We have pigs and hens and cows and Arnold's a farmer and he has animals as well. Then there's the fishing – we have specialist lakes here, you know. And Brian's good with the beasts so we were getting by all right, but we needed a little extra. You know, for the soul. Hence,' she held out her hands, 'the cafe. We open it three days a week. A little madness but we have met other people. Not quite like you, but other people. It was quite awful – at the beginning, you know – but it had settled down by the time we opened this. We've had visits from people from Grantham. Nice people. But they don't seem very organised. We do a bit of trading. They bring us tins, we give them eggs. Then there are the travellers as well, some going north, some south. They're as surprised as you were to find us, but they usually stop and have a cup of tea and a chat.'

She shook her head sadly.

'I don't know what they're looking for, these travellers, but they haven't found it yet, and you would think they would have found it by now, wouldn't you? I mean, you found it. Brian and me found it. The folk in Grantham have sort of found it. Even Arnold and Shirley have, and you would never have put them together in a month of Sundays, but it seems to have worked. Amazing how things do, when there's no alternative. But some people just keep on looking. I mean, what's wrong with here? People used to visit. There's a caravan park over the hedge. Anyway, I'll just go and see how Brian is getting on.'

A welcome silence descended in her wake.

They were served lamb stew that had been cooked on a Calor gas stove in the caravan. Maisie said she made a pan of it on the days they opened and, if no one came, they ate it themselves over the following days. The bread that came with it was a day old but had been warmed to make it crisp on the outside and soft in the middle. Sandra ate hers quickly, then went to relieve Keira.

'This really is good,' said Reaper, as they finished.

'You were just hungry,' Maisie said, but obviously pleased by the praise.

The girls confirmed the food was delicious and Maisie Day glowed. Brian sat in a chair at the next table – he had declined an invitation to join them – and was happy to simply be in their presence.

They finished with more tea and Reaper gently prompted Maisie, and they listened as she talked about the area and the tales that travellers had told of where they had been. She had heard of a large group from a city – 'Sheffield, Wakefield, Chesterfield, something field,' she said – who were heading for Skegness. The lady was another intelligence asset, although she was a bit vague, and he felt a brief pang of guilt at classifying her in this way, rather than as the friendly eccentric that she was, but on second thoughts, she would probably have been flattered and called herself 007.

People on the A1, whether travelling north or south, had all seemed to be escaping or abandoning towns or urban areas that, with the passing of time, were becoming derelict and deadly. There were still the inevitable gangs on the prowl, mostly in inner city areas, alongside and sometimes preying on, communities that were trying to make a new start. He didn't ask specific questions. He listened with particular interest to the stories from the south, but she had nothing further to add about the place called Redemption.

As they were preparing to leave, Yank said, 'Maisie, that was great. We must give you something.'

'You have, dear. Conversation. And from an American, too. You don't get many of those to the pound these days. I hope you'll come again.'

'We will,' Reaper said. 'Every week.'

Yank and Keira walked back to their car and Maisie Day pointed at Reaper and said, 'Now I remember. Reaper and the Angel. That was some story. Or did I see it on television?'

Reaper and Sandra got into their car and the two vehicles resumed the journey north.

An odd couple on the M1 and the madness of a cafe on the A1 in post-apocalyptic Britain? The more Reaper thought about it, the more sensible the idea became.

Chapter 11

DUGGLEBY WAS A SMALL HAMLET SOUTH OF MALDON on the way to York. Not on a direct route to the city, but hidden among low fertile lands along country lanes off the beaten track. Farmer Jim Rowley had gathered a dozen travellers and survivors who felt secure with its isolation and who were glad to have an experienced man to guide them in their new life of agriculture. They were making excellent progress and were glad to be linked to the Haven federation.

As Cynthia, an eighteen-year-old escapee from Leeds, told Jenny and Tanya, who called there once a fortnight as part of their duties, 'It's nice to be private, but it's nice to belong.'

Rowley was a bluff man in his forties. Jenny said he had impaired imagination, which had helped him adjust so swiftly to what had happened. In compensation, he was blessed with an extremely practical mind. Rowley's farming techniques could be used as a template for groups starting out on their own. They were planning on sending him small groups who could provide labour whilst getting training on the land.

They never received a warm welcome from Rowley but that was his manner. On this occasion, they sensed something was wrong as soon as they parked in the farmyard. Marje, the elderly lady who ran the kitchen, raised her eyebrows and said, 'Thank God, you've come.'

'What's wrong, Marje?' said Jenny. 'Where's Rowley?'

'He'll be here. He'll have seen you coming. He's been waiting for you these last five days.'

'Why?'

'In the barn. You'll see. Poor lamb.'

The two girls went to the barn, unsure what they might find. Inside, a young man in his early twenties was sitting on the floor in the corner. He was haggard, dishevelled and could have done with a wash. He looked at them anxiously and got to his feet and they saw his wrists were tied and that a length of chain, secured around the rope with a padlock, was attached to an iron ring set in the wall behind him.

His eyes took in their uniform and weapons and recognition flared, as if he had been told to expect them.

'I didn't do it,' he said.

'You didn't do what?' said Jenny.

'What they said I did.'

'And what was that?' she prompted.

'It wasn't rape. It was consensual.'

Both girls took a good look at him. The chain hung from his wrists and went between his legs before it reached the ring in the wall. It rattled when he moved. He was average height and build, ordinary verging on good-looking, Jenny thought, if the mouth had been a bit fuller and the chin a bit stronger. Long dark hair, brown eyes that darted from one to the other, trying to read their conclusions, a shy nervous smile to win their compassion. He didn't realise that he was looking at girls who had been victims themselves. Compassion could be in short supply.

They heard Jim Rowley's quad bike arrive in the yard outside and left the captive to go and talk to the farmer. They exchanged greetings and went back into the farm kitchen. Marje served them with mugs of tea and made herself scarce.

'Tell us what happened, Jim?' Jenny said.

'The lad's been with us seven months. Name of Bobby Simpson. Arrived alone but mucked in with everybody else. Kept his head down and did his share of work. Not the best worker, but he did enough. I got the impression he was waiting for the summer and he'd move on. It would have been best if he had. He'd tried it on with Cynthia but she wasn't interested. There's a chap she's seen at Malton who's taken her fancy. Besides, Simpson is not the wooing kind, if you know what I mean. Not one for romance or small talk. A bit direct.

'Anyway, five days ago he tried to move on, very suddenly.

He came back from the fields early and grabbed his stuff. There was just me and Marje here. You know me, I don't try to keep folk if they don't want to stay but he was behaving funny and his decision was a bit spur of the moment. Late afternoon after a day's work. Why not wait till morning? Then we heard someone shouting from the orchard at the bottom of the ten-acre. That was it. He grabbed my quad bike and tried to get away across the fields. But a quad bike is not as easy to use as it looks. He took a banking, rolled it and came off. The lads brought him back.'

'Why had he run?' asked Tanya.

'Cath Grainger. He raped her in the orchard. Cath is forty, a very nice lady. She was a spinster.' He looked at his boots and his ruddy face reddened a little more. 'I suspect she was also a virgin. She was not exactly worldly wise.'

Jenny said, 'He denies it. Says it was consensual.'

'Course he does. But I saw Cath.'

'Can we see her?'

'I suppose you'll need to, although she's not got over it yet.'

'It will take time,' said Tanya.

'Aye. I reckon a lot of time.'

'Where is she?'

'Upstairs. Marje is with her. She knows you're here and that you'll want to talk to her.'

Jenny said, 'You want us to take care of it?'

'Aye. That's what you do, isn't it? You're the police, aren't you?'

'I suppose we are.' Jenny glanced at Tanya. 'Shall I go?'

Tanya nodded her agreement. The two of them might be threatening. Besides, any victim wanted to confess to as few people as possible. Rowley pointed the way and Jenny found the room on the first floor: a bedroom with a pleasant view of fields and flat countryside. Cath sat in an easy chair by the window. Marje sat on the edge of the bed and looked anxiously at Jenny.

'Can you give us a minute or two, Marje?' she asked.

The elderly woman nodded and left the room. 'Just call,' she said, as she closed the door.

Jenny took her place on the edge of the bed.

Cath was a slim woman with mousey coloured hair tied up in a bun. Her face was thin and her nose too large but it was a pleasant face. A kind face. She looked anxious and her bottom lip trembled. She wore a loose dress that was draped well below her knees. Her lower legs were brown from working in the sun and she wore white plimsolls on her feet.

'Hello, Cath. I'm Jenny.'

She offered her hand and the older woman took it. They didn't shake, simply held hands.

'What will happen to the boy?' she said, in a low rushed voice. 'I don't want him to be hurt. It was probably my fault.' Her voice caught. 'I probably led him on.'

Jenny held Cath's dry hand in both of hers.

'I can't believe that you led him on, Cath. How did you do that?'

'I was wearing shorts. I always did.' She looked into her lap as if ashamed at her wantonness. 'A floppy hat to protect my face but I liked the sun on my legs.' She blushed. 'It was probably my fault.'

'How well did you know Bobby Simpson? Were you friends?'

'Not really friends. I knew him like I know everybody on the farm.' She raised her eyes and her gaze was earnest. 'They are nice people. They really are. Mr Rowley can seem a bit severe but he's a good man at heart. Marje is a dear, and the others are good people.'

'Do you have a particular friend?'

'Not a particular friend. I like Sally, because we are about the same age, but she's not a particular friend.' She firmed her jaw; she was determined to tell the truth. 'I didn't have particular friends before. Just people I knew. Mainly at the church. I looked after my mother, you see. Afterwards, I came here with some people from the church. They went on but I stayed. I like it here. It's peaceful. It's like a family.'

Jenny guessed that Cath had never known a real family. 'Before the virus, did you have a job?'

'I was a primary school teacher.' She smiled. 'For five years. It was a happy time. But then mother became ill and I had to stay at home to look after her.'

'Boyfriend?'

Cath smiled indulgently at Jenny as if she'd asked such a silly question.

'I never had time for a boyfriend, dear.'

'What about Bobby Simpson? Was he a boyfriend?'

'Oh no. He was nothing like that. We hardly ever spoke. The person he was interested in was Cynthia. Everyone knew that. But Cynthia wasn't interested in him. She told him so in no uncertain terms. Mr Rowley doesn't like bad language but Cynthia used some that day in the orchard. I was nearby when she told him off. They didn't know I was there. I heard her slap his face.' She dipped her head again, her cheeks colouring. 'Perhaps I should have slapped his face. Perhaps that would have made him see I didn't want to.'

'Want to what, Cath?'

'Have … sex,' she whispered.

'How did it happen?'

'I was in the orchard. I like the orchard. I was lying down in the shade, reading a book. Bobby sat next to me. He didn't say anything. Just sat there. But he looked at my legs.' She shook her head. 'I shouldn't have been wearing shorts.' Jenny squeezed her hand. 'Then he lay down and started to touch me. I didn't know what to do. I just froze. I suppose he thought that meant I didn't mind, but I did. I just didn't know what to do. Perhaps if I'd slapped his face? Then I suppose it went too far for a slap. I struggled but, well, I suppose if men get to a certain point, they can't help themselves.'

'Cath.' Jenny's voice was low and confidential. 'Did Bobby have sex with you?'

The woman cried and nodded.

'Yes,' she said. 'He did things.'

Jenny hesitated but it had to be asked.

'Did he penetrate you?' she whispered.

'Yes,' came the reply, very small and very soft like a cry of despair lost on the wind.

Jenny knelt on the floor and put her arms around the older woman and they held each other and Cath cried. At last, she took a deep breath and composed herself.

'Don't hurt Bobby,' she said, into Jenny's shoulder. 'It was my fault.'

Jenny sat back on the bed but they still held hands and looked out of the window.

'It's very beautiful here,' Jenny said.

'Yes, it is.'

'I know you probably won't want to leave but, if you did, you could come to Haven. We need a schoolteacher.'

'You do?'

'Fresh start. Mind you, some of those children can be very demanding. It would be a challenge.'

'I suppose it would.' Cath looked out of the window. 'I wonder whatever happened to my children.' She glanced at Jenny and smiled guiltily. 'You think of them that way. You are with them for so long that you think of them as yours.'

'I know,' said Jenny. 'I used to be a teacher, too.'

'Did you?' She assessed her. 'But bigger children, I can tell. Not primary.'

'Yes. Bigger children.'

Jenny smiled but the memories were painful. She still felt that she had let down the three girls who had become her responsibility when the virus had ravaged the public school at which she had been the sole surviving teacher.

'Anyway,' Jenny said. 'It's something to think about. We'll be back in two weeks. You can tell us then if you'd like to come back to teaching.'

She stood up and bent down to kiss Cath on the cheek before she left.

'Thank you,' Cath said. 'And don't hurt Bobby. It was probably my fault.'

'Cath, it wasn't your fault. Believe me, it wasn't your fault. But don't worry. We won't hurt him. We'll just see him on his way.'

When Jenny went downstairs, Marje went back up. Jenny told Rowley that she had offered Cath a teaching post at Haven and he nodded at the sense of the suggestion.

'Fresh start might be best,' he said. 'Everybody likes Cath and no one blames her, but even sympathy can get on your nerves. What will you do with Simpson?'

'We'll take him.'

'You'll deal with him?'

'We'll deal with him,' said Jenny, returning his meaningful look.

They drove through Malton and Pickering and took the Whitby Road across the North Yorkshire Moors. Simpson sat in the rear of the Range Rover, his hands secured behind his back by plastic cuffs. A bag containing his possessions was alongside him.

The journey restored his confidence. He stopped asking where they were taking him, the anxiety left his voice and he became more conversational.

'Two good-looking girls like you. I'll bet you're not short of blokes. But you get out and about, you see. Meet people. I was stuck there, on the farm. You get used to it. Getting up, working, being looked after. It wouldn't have been so bad except the one girl I did fancy was a right stuck up piece. Wouldn't give me the time of day. It was time for me to move on, anyway.'

'What about Cath?' Tanya asked.

'Well, it wasn't serious with Cath. I mean, come on. She was available and I was missing it. Nice lady though, don't get me wrong.'

'She is a nice lady,' said Jenny.

'But not my type. Well, not unless you're desperate and it had been a long time.'

'I suppose that's the problem with being a bloke,' Tanya said. 'Blokes need it more than women. At least, that's what I was told. They'd do it with a hole in the wall if there was nothing else. Is that true?'

Simpson laughed. 'True enough, I suppose. If the hole was padded. With silk panties, say. You haven't got any spare have you?'

They were well onto the moors when Tanya turned the car off the main road and took a narrow lane to nowhere. Two hundred yards and she stopped.

'This will do,' she said.

'What?' Simpson was anxious again. 'You're going to leave me here? It's miles from anywhere.'

'The walk will do you good,' Tanya said.

The girls got out and Jenny opened the rear door so Simpson could climb down. The sun was shining but the air was fresh so high on the moors. Tanya took the Bowie knife from the sheath on her right leg and cut the plastic cord that held his wrists. He rubbed them to help circulation and looked around at the great expanse of nothingness. Jenny dropped his bag on the floor.

'So this is it?' Simpson said. He had regained a little of his cockiness. 'Whitby's that way, I suppose? A long walk to a short pier.' He laughed at his own joke.

Tanya stepped closer to him. He was perhaps an inch taller than her but she held the knife up to his face and he paled at the look in her eyes.

'You don't know how close you are to dead,' she said. 'Cath begged us not to hurt you but I'm tempted.'

A nervous smile flicked across his face as his eyes went from blade to Tanya.

'Told you,' he said. 'Consensual. She wanted it.'

Tanya spat into his face and he didn't raise a hand to wipe it away. She turned the blade and the sun caught the steel and flashed a signal in Jenny's memory. Another blade, three girls she had been unable to protect from the rape and degradation she herself had also suffered. All at the point of a knife like the one that Tanya held in the face of a rapist.

'Walk,' Tanya said.

Simpson picked up his bag and walked across the uneven moorland, heading in the general direction of Whitby and the coast. He turned once, when he was perhaps twenty yards away, and raised a hand in farewell, the grin back on his face.

Jenny, the English rose, raised the carbine to her shoulder, aimed carefully, and shot him in the back. The discharge of the gun echoed across the empty moors. Tanya stared at her partner, partly in shock, partly in understanding.

'He would have done it again,' Jenny said.

Chapter 12

RONNIE RONALDO CONTINUED TO MAKE HIS SOLO scouting expeditions on his Yamaha trail bike. He had been asked to brief Pete Mack in advance and be more specific about his intended destinations and the expected duration of his trips, so that if he went missing again, his colleagues would know where to look. 'Of course', agreed Ronnie. 'Makes sense.' Then, three weeks after his rescue from York, he left early enough one morning to avoid having to tell Pete anything.

'Didn't he give a hint?' Reaper asked.

'The bugger was away before dawn,' said Pete. 'You know Ronnie. Ducking and diving are second nature. He had something on his mind when he got back last night, though. He was on edge. Impatient. Kept smiling to himself. He wouldn't tell me about it. Said he'd heard a rumour that needed checking out. I suppose that's what he's doing now.'

'Where had he been yesterday?' Reaper asked.

'Leeds way. Up the M62.'

They all knew that what Ronnie did was dangerous. He went into uncharted territory with nothing more than his wits and a swift off-the-road bike. He knew the dangers but enjoyed the challenge and he often returned with news of untouched warehouses or industrial complexes to which he would then guide Pete, who went armed and took a Special Forces unit for protection. Reaper hoped that whatever Ronnie had gone to check out was worth it.

He returned at one o'clock in the afternoon. He rode down the hill and into the village square and skidded sideways to a halt, throwing up a cloud of dust. Sandra watched him from the steps of the manor house as he jumped off the machine. His skinny frame in black leathers made him look like a large ant.

'What's the hurry, Ronnie? You're riding like the Pony Express.'

'Where's Reaper?' he said, a gleam of excitement in his eye.

'Inside.'

She took him into the manor house. Reaper was in a small room next to the library. He was studying a map spread on a table.

'You slipped out early, Ronnie,' Reaper said. 'Never told Pete where you were going.'

'It was too daft to tell. I had to go and see.'

'And what did you see?'

He handed a pamphlet to Reaper and waited for a reaction, licking his lips, his head vibrating like a nodding dog, waiting to be asked to tell more, to be coaxed into revealing what he obviously thought was a great discovery. Reaper read the cover of the pamphlet. It said: *What To Do In The Event Of A Nuclear Attack*.

Inside, there were diagrams and instructions about how a family should take cover. It all seemed a little optimistic for those living in a three bedroomed semi-detached expecting to survive an atom bomb. He passed it to Sandra.

'It's probably from the 1960s or 70s when people thought a nuclear war was a possibility,' Reaper said. 'Where did you find it?'

Ronnie licked his lips and shot glances at them both.

'A bunker,' he said. 'Underground. In the Pennines. There was a load of them and other pamphlets and leaflets. These, for instance.'

He handed a single sheet to Reaper that said: *Declaration of Martial Law by the Regional Seat of Government* along with instructions to the civilian population of how they should obey the military authority of the RSG: all curfews, restrictions and rationing. He read the date at the top and passed it to Sandra.

'Last year,' he said. 'What else is in the bunker, Ronnie?'

'Dead bodies, vehicles, food, medical equipment, guns and ammunition.'

'Bodies?'

'They look like they died last year.'

'Who were they?'

He produced four nametags, which he placed on the desk. One was that of a general, another of an air vice marshal, the third said Sir Peter Proberty, all names Reaper had never heard before. The fourth was that of Giles Lambert.

Sandra was at his shoulder. She touched the Lambert nametag. 'Is that …?'

'The Deputy Prime Minister,' said Reaper.

'Good God.'

'It looks like they tried to set up a Regional Government. Move somewhere isolated, lock themselves in, wait till the pandemic was over, then pick up the reins of power.'

Ronnie said, 'There were women there, too, and children. I saw five women and three children.'

'Good grief.' Reaper said, and sat down.

It was a lot to take in. He had read somewhere, years before, that during the Cold War there had been plans to move the seat of Government from London, which had been seen as vulnerable, to a bunker located elsewhere in the country. It seemed they had tried the same thing in the later stages of the plague. It hadn't worked. He wondered if there had been other sites, other bunkers. If there had been, he had no doubt the occupants had all fallen victim to the virus and the forward planning to save the nation had come to nothing.

Sandra said, 'Where is it?'

'High in the hills. Past Leeds along the M62. On the border between Yorkshire and Lancashire. You turn off the motorway, then off the Ripponden road. There's a transport depot cut into the hills. One snow plough and piles of salt for the winter. You get real winters up there.' He said it as if winters elsewhere could not compete. 'There's a hidden entrance at the back.'

'How did you find it?' said Reaper.

'I'm a good listener,' he said. 'Met some people near Bradford. Nice people. They live on a farm. They call it a commune. I've visited a few times to make sure they're all right. They keep to themselves but you never know. Anyway, two of the women had come over the tops from Oldham last year. Gangs were operating over there. They told a strange tale. They were driving on the M62 in the middle of the night, some time in August, and hit a bloke walking down the middle of the motorway. I mean, a Transit can do a lot of damage, and he was badly smacked up.

'They couldn't do a lot for him except make him comfortable. They covered him with blankets and sat with him. Gave him whisky, held his hand. He said his name was Robert. They asked if he lived nearby, if there was anyone they could fetch, but he didn't make a lot of sense. He said, "All gone. They're all gone." The women thought he meant his family. Then the bloke said, "We were the last hope. The last government." And he cried a bit and then said, "Fucking Wombles. We were fucking Wombles." He was in pain, upset. Full of whisky. And knew he was dying. Then he became a bit more like … rational, and said, "We lived under the hill. The last hope. That hill there," and he pointed back from where he'd been walking. Then he stared up at the stars in the sky and said, "Snow plough" and he died. The ladies thought he meant the stars. You know, like Sagittarius, or something.

'Anyway, the commune discussed this tale umpteen times. Not a lot else for them to do during winter. And somebody remembered a vague rumour that there'd been a fall-out shelter under the Pennines, all stocked up with cardboard coffins and tins of baked beans, and they wondered if this is what the bloke meant. And I thought, stranger things have happened. This commune, they're snug and prefer to stay unnoticed. They don't do a lot of travelling, but I thought it would be worth a look. So for a couple of days I scouted the hills round there, where they knocked him down, like. And yesterday, I found the snow plough. I didn't tell Pete because it all sounded so far-fetched until I'd checked it out. But it's there. Ruddy great underground bunker, full of stuff.'

'Ronnie, you're brilliant,' Reaper said.

Ronnie grinned at the praise but, now his story had been told, he looked a little sad.

'Ronnie? What's wrong?' said Sandra.

He took a deep breath then let it out again in a sigh.

'I feel a bit guilty. You know, like it was the commune's discovery but we'll take it.'

Sandra said, 'You could invite the commune to join us.'

'Good idea,' said Reaper. 'What do you think?'

'I think they might.' Ronnie bucked up at the thought of issuing the invitation. 'I never told them about us, like. Wherever I've been, whoever I've talked to, I've kept schtum about Haven. But I think those people might like it here. They're bloody lost souls where they are.'

'Now we have to work out the best way of collecting the supplies,' Reaper said.

'Some of it's already packed,' said Ronnie. 'I think they must have taken it by the lorry load and there are two lorries inside the bunker that were never unloaded. Get them started and we can just drive them away.'

The bunker in the Pennines was momentous news. It gave an insight into what the Government had planned in the final days of the pandemic and, from Ronnie's description of its interior, it contained a great quantity of supplies. The possibilities were discussed that night at a meeting attended by Cassandra, Judith, the Rev Nick, Ashley, Pete Mack, Dr Greta Malone, Sandra and Reaper, where Ronnie told his story all over again.

'I'm not surprised,' said Cassandra. 'I knew there were several bunkers around the country. They were built in the fifties and early sixties but I thought most had been decommissioned. One in stone quarries near Bath was designed as a National Seat of Government and there was another in Wiltshire. Originally, there were five bunkers beneath London itself. But I never heard about the one in the Pennines.'

'How big were they?' asked Nick.

'I'm no expert, but I had some knowledge because of my husband's position in the RAF and because we had a small bunker on the camp itself that was used for storage. My husband also visited RAF Fylingdale – the early warning radar system on the moors above Whitby. The three dishes are above the ground but everything else is underneath, including the Doomsday Room. That's where they watched screens for the first sign of a ballistic missile attack. Rodney said the place had its own underground road system and a generator that was big enough to power a town. The idea of these underground bases piqued my curiosity and I did a little research.

'They could be immense, big enough to house as many as 4,000 people. They had medical centres, hospital wards, canteens. They stocked them with libraries of specially selected books to use as a data base to get the country back on its feet afterwards. There were dormitories, communication centres. They filled acres of space beneath the ground.'

Ronnie said, 'This one's not that big. I looked at the dormitories. I don't think it would have taken more than 500 people.'

Nick asked Cassandra, 'Were there many of these bunkers?'

'The well known ones, that I mentioned, but I suppose it's inevitable there would be others that weren't common knowledge. The threat of nuclear attack didn't seem quite so relevant by the 1980s and they were expensive to maintain. Most were decommissioned in the eighties and nineties and some were declassified, but I suppose some remained on the secret list, just in case. Like this one.'

Reaper said, 'Maybe the Pennine bunker wasn't the only one that was re-activated.'

'Possibly,' said Cassandra. 'But they couldn't hide from the virus like they thought they could hide from nuclear fall-out.'

'How long could they survive underground?' asked Reaper.

'The usual time period they planned for in case of nuclear attack was three months. By then, they expected the radiation would have fallen to a safe level.'

'So we might assume that this chap, Robert, lived for three months in the bunker. Surrounded by dead people,' said Reaper.

Ronnie added, 'And then, when he stepped outside, he was knocked down by a Transit. Hardly seems fair, does it?'

They visited the bunker in strength to strip it of its supplies.

If possible, they wanted to do the job in one trip. The location was isolated but they would be seen en route and might be spotted at the site. This possibility would increase if they made several collections, which could then attract other scavengers and Reaper was determined not to share what Ronnie had discovered.

This assumption of ownership did not sit well with the Rev Nick, who attempted a tentative argument that everyone had equal claims on anything left behind, but it was only half-hearted opposition. He realised that whatever they took would be put to the best use possible by the citizens of the federation.

Ronnie led the convoy and took point on his Yamaha to ensure the roads were safe, travelling well in advance of the following vehicles. Sandra drove the first, a Special Forces Range Rover, in which she was partnered by Keira. This was followed by a military Land Rover with roll bars and a heavy machine gun on a weapons mount on the front passenger side, that was driven by Haven's chief mechanic, Gavin Price. The gun was manned by Leading Aircraftman Clifford 'Smiffy' Smith, a black RAF ex-serviceman. Two lorries followed, Pete Mack in the first with a co-driver, and two men in the back. A driver and co-driver manned the second lorry, again with two men in the back. A Range Rover driven by Kev Andrews, with fifteen-year-old James Marshall alongside him, was tail end Charlie. Reaper, with Yank in the shotgun seat, and Dr Greta Malone and the

Rev Nick sitting behind them, was in a third Special Forces vehicle. He had licence to rove alongside the convoy. Everyone was armed, except for Nick and Dr Malone. 'Blame the Hippocratic oath,' she'd said.

Tanya and Jenny had been left behind at Haven, along with Ashley, their head of militia, as home security.

The journey was uneventful, although, twice, groups watched them go past from the fields at the side of the motorway. Reaper hoped they would be intimidated by their size and show of weapons. They went south of Leeds and along the M62, deeper into the territory Reaper had been avoiding. Signs for Bradford and Huddersfield went by and they left conurbations behind as they climbed into the high moorlands. A long swooping stretch took them down a valley and past a reservoir, up the other side and onto the tops, so that it seemed as if they were driving across the roof of the world.

Here, the two parts of the motorway split apart, where the planners had followed contours for ease of road building, so that the three-lanes of the western highway ran at a higher level and separate from the eastern highway. It looked as if the moors had bulged and pushed them apart. A lone farmhouse sat incongruously in the middle of this split. What a place to have lived, thought Reaper, surrounded by clouds and two streams of traffic heading non-stop across a magnificent emptiness.

Down to their right, below the farmhouse and the

highway going east, was a reservoir and, beyond that, according to his map, the road to Ripponden. At a junction at the highest point on the moorland, Ronnie was waiting for them. He led the way onto the Ripponden road, then turned off again.

The yard, where the snow plough had been left, was too small to accommodate all their vehicles and Reaper worried that they would be seen, but Ronnie opened the double doors of an empty vehicle storage shed and one of the lorries nosed inside. Ronnie disappeared through a door at the back carrying a camping lantern and, a few minutes later, with the creaking and grinding of old machinery, part of the rear wall of the shed slid sideways, with Ronnie pushing it manually. The dim glow of the lantern revealed a hollowed out cave with a few old spades and pickaxes leaning against the wall, a small stack of firewood, a sack of coal, a brazier, and a camp bed upon which was a rolled sleeping bag.

At the back of the cave were steel doors and a sign that said: *Danger. Keep Out. Emergency Reservoir Access. Authorised Personnel Only.*

Ronnie grinned at Reaper and held his hand out to indicate the steel doors, as if he was a magician about to perform a trick. He walked up to them, placed both hands flat on the steel and pushed. The doors opened.

'That bloke Robert. He never locked it when he left,' he said.

He pushed one door wide and Reaper pushed the

other. The lamp Ronnie had brought didn't penetrate the darkness.

Reaper shouted back to the lorry driver, 'Headlights!' and a moment later, the twin beams dispelled the shadows and showed the start of a concrete road that led downwards into the hill. Suddenly, the headlights were unnecessary as strip lights in the ceiling came on. Ronnie reappeared. 'The generators are still working,' he said. 'There's a car park and turning area down the slope. There's space for the lorries.'

Ronnie climbed into the cab of the first lorry, which led the way down the slope, the second following. There was now space to get the three Range Rovers and the Land Rover out of sight, parked in the shed and at the entrance to the bunker. They closed the shed doors. Kev and James remained outside, taking guard duty.

Reaper and the others walked down the road, which was wide enough for one lorry, for about fifty paces before it levelled into the promised parking space. Two other lorries were already there, as Ronnie had said, their rear ends at what appeared to be a loading bay. There was enough space for the two lorries they had brought, but they wouldn't be able to turn until the others were moved.

Deep alcoves were cut in the walls, each containing a vehicle. The choice of the country's last government had been Range Rovers: comfortable and all purpose. There were six of them. Two narrower roads led off from the loading bay. Each was sign posted: *First Avenue*, and *Second Avenue*. Beneath each was a list of destinations.

First Avenue led to *Communications, Radiation Monitoring, Map Room, Cabinet Room, Offices, Armoury, Canteen, Barracks*. Second Avenue led to *Civilian Living Quarters, Dormitories A and B, Canteen, Medical, Library*.

What looked like six dodgem cars were lined up. Two were four-seaters, the other four had two front seats and rear space for cargo.

'They're electric,' Ronnie said. He pointed to the cables that connected each to a wall socket. 'I plugged them in yesterday, see if they would charge up.'

'How far do the tunnels go?' asked Reaper.

'Not far. It's walkable. But you'll need the dodgems for moving supplies. Most of the bodies are in bed. About a hundred squaddies. Two shot themselves. A few senior officers and about sixty civilians, including medics.'

They had all been excited about getting here and exploring this realm beneath the ground but, as Ronnie had given the figures, Reaper realised they were in a mausoleum. This was the last resting place of up to two hundred people who had travelled here in hope and died in despair. The others in the group caught his mood and his gaze found the Rev Nick.

The cleric said, 'We've all experienced death in many forms over the last year. We have seen that life is precious and yet it can be snatched away so swiftly, so cruelly. What we are standing in now is a grave. Let us tread carefully and let us be respectful to the memories of those who died here.'

He dipped his head and held his hands together and they all acknowledged a long moment's silence.

Reaper broke it.

He said, 'Pete, find out what's in the trucks. We'll split into two groups and take an avenue each.'

Greta went with Sandra to the medical centre and others inspected the civilian quarters. Reaper and Smiffy took another group down the military and office wing. Most of the soldiers were, as Ronnie had said, in their bunks in the barracks. One had shot himself in the showers.

Smiffy looked at their uniform badges.

'Paras,' he said.

The armoury had 120 Heckler and Koch L85 rifles with optical sites and four that were slightly different.

Smiffy picked one up and inspected it.

'Long range sniper rifle. Five round magazine, folding stock, bipod to hold it steady and a range of about 1,000 metres. This thing on the end is a sound suppressor. It also reduces the flash of the shot. The sight is brilliant.' He squinted at it. 'Twenty-five times magnification. Even I could hit a barn door with one of these.'

Reaper picked up an item he didn't recognise.

'Grenade launcher,' said Smiffy. 'They fit under the L85.' He pointed at other equipment. 'Mortars, General Purpose Machine Gun, Light Machine Gun, Combat Shotgun,

Combat Body Armour, night sights.' He pointed at but did not explain what the last item was; Reaper knew a helmet when he saw one. 'They've got top quality gear. Loads of ammunition, too.'

A hundred and twenty combat rifles, twelve grenade launchers, four mortars, two heavy GP machine guns, six Light Machine Guns and twelve shotguns. In the barracks, the men had Sig 226 handguns in holsters, hanging from their bunks or in their lockers.

Smiffy called and Reaper joined him in a side room.

'Clansman communications,' he said. 'It's a combat net radio system. I thought they'd been replaced by a newer version. All singing and dancing, like.'

'I didn't know you were an expert, Smiffy.'

'I'm not. Had a mate who was in Signals. The new sort could send everything from your Afghan holiday snaps to mucky movies. Maybe when the world went tits up, the Paras went back to basics.' He pointed at hand-held receivers. 'Manpack radios, range about 500 meters.' He pointed again. 'Vehicle mounted radio. Only one of them.' He looked at Reaper. 'I wonder if those Rovers at the entrance have them? Did you notice whiplash aerials? Maybe they planned on having one for base HQ and the others for mobile units? Range about thirty kilometres. Radio transmission or morse code.'

'You may just have got yourself a job as a Radio Operator.'

'Not me. About all I can do is plug the headsets in.'

Pete Mack arrived outside the barracks in one of the dodgems, the Rev Nick alongside him.

'One truck contains nothing but ammo. The other is full of books.'

'Books?' Reaper said, and wondered whether they should unload it and use it for something more useful.

'The books are excellent,' said Nick. 'Remember what Cassandra said. They compiled a library of books that could be used to start again? They're *those* sort of books. We need them, Reaper.'

'Okay. We'll take them. Let's start moving the guns from here. And the radio equipment.' He looked at Smiffy. 'Let's have a look at the communications room.'

The bank of radio equipment was impressive and daunting. Reaper sat in a chair before a bank of dials and knobs. A headset lay on the desk, its cable snaking away to a jackplug connection. He flicked switches and dials lit up. He held the headset to one ear and heard static. He handed it to Smiffy.

'Put them on and try the dials. See if you hear anything other than static.'

Smiffy sat at the desk, put on the headphones and moved the dials. Reaper left him to it.

Pete started organising and Reaper inspected the bedrooms used by the officers: a general, a wing commander, a major, a captain and three lieutenants. All were in uniform, most of them lying on their beds. The major was sitting in an armchair with a glass still in his hand and a whisky bottle by his feet.

He went in the canteen, kitchens and storerooms. They were well stocked with tins and packets of food and cases of lager. The walk-in refrigerators were still working. Inside were steaks, beef roasting joints, lamb and pork chops, chickens, sacks of frozen chips and vegetables. He moved on, inspected empty offices and a cabinet room with two bodies slumped in chairs and another face down on a rather fine Oriental rug.

Back at the loading bay, he checked the Range Rovers. All six had whiplash aerials and were fitted with Clansman radios. They were ready and waiting for Special Forces to take them.

Reaper was tired even though he'd only made a tour of inspection. He had been excited when he had been told of the bunker, had looked forward to seeing it and acquiring the riches it contained, but it really was a tomb and the feeling of so many lost souls trapped beneath the moors was oppressive. Of course, it was all in his mind. But he still felt it.

Pete Mack was efficiently allocating space and dictating where items went, so Reaper walked down Second Avenue to the medical centre. Here, Greta was giving the orders.

'We've got a mobile operating theatre,' she told him, 'and all the gubbins that goes with it.'

'Gubbins?' he said. 'That's a medical term, is it?'

'It'll do for you.'

'I'll leave you to it.'

On the way back, he saw Sandra step out of a doorway shaking her head. She was followed by Ronnie dragging a large steel box that was obviously heavy. She made no attempt to help him.

'What have you got?' Reaper said.

'Ronnie's found gold,' said Sandra.

'I'm taking it back for Judith,' he said. 'For the bank.'

'Can I see?' asked Reaper.

Ronnie opened the lid of the box. It was full of one ounce gold Kruger Rand coins and looked like pirate treasure.

'Jesus, Ronnie. It's a lottery win.'

'If we had a lottery,' said Sandra.

'And if there was somewhere to spend it,' said Ronnie. 'But there will be. I talked to Judith. Some time in the future, people will use money again. Bound to happen and probably sooner than later. And these Kruger coins are the best, so when we do have money again, we'll be well set up.'

Sandra looked at Reaper.

'Do we take it?' she said.

'We take it,' he smiled. Judith had told him about the Bank. 'Well done, Ronnie.'

They loaded everything they deemed essential onto the two spare lorries. Gavin had located the bunker's fuel tanks. The generators had been running for a year, yet were still half full. But, as Ronnie had reported, everything apart from the refrigerators had been switched off when he found the place, presumably by the unfortunate survivor known only as Robert.

Reaper checked with Smiffy but he hadn't heard anyone broadcasting radio messages.

'Just static,' Smiffy said. 'The airwaves are dead.'

Before they left, they defrosted steaks in the microwaves in the civilian canteen, and cooked steak and chips. With it, they drank cans of lager, or wine, from the Deputy Prime Minister's private stock. Halfway through, Reaper said he would go outside and relieve James and Kev, so they, too, could enjoy the bounty they had discovered.

'I'll go with you,' said Greta. 'I could do with some air.'

'You don't have a gun,' he said.

'I'll be the one that runs for help. Not that you ever need any.'

He raised an eyebrow at the remark and Sandra said, 'Oo-ooh.'

Greta and Reaper laughed and left the canteen. They walked up Second Avenue.

'This is a strange place,' she said.

'It's a sad place.'

'Not somewhere I would have wanted to be at the end.'

'But you're a doctor. You knew what the end would be. Presumably, they thought they had a chance.'

They reached the loading area and Reaper looked back down both avenues from their apex.

'What a strange bloody world.'

'In the days of The Bomb, the Government felt places like this were necessary.'

'This time, we'll make sure we don't build another bomb.'

They turned and walked up the slope and, when she stumbled, he held her arm briefly to steady her, then relinquished his touch as if her skin was fire. Neither spoke, both aware of the contact, and they went out into the shed, past the Range Rovers, and pushed open the front door just enough to give them egress to step out into moorland air that tasted so very fresh.

For a moment, they stood side by side, simply enjoying the outdoors after the hours beneath ground with the dead.

'Yo!' shouted James.

He was on a hillside that gave views of the approach road in front and the hills behind them.

Reaper said, 'You're relieved. The job's almost done. Get down below and grab some grub. Steak and chips and lager and wine. Well, lager for Kev.'

'Righto, me hearty!'

'You're still too young, aren't you James?'

'Probably,' said James. 'But I could manage a glass of red.'

The landscape of the Pennines was totally different to the gentle hills and pastureland of Haven. Greta suspected it would have had an alien feel, even before the pandemic. This other worldliness was now underlined by the total lack of traffic on the double fringes of motorway that cut across the high moorland, as if left there as decoration by a long dead giant. Sunshine reflected from the water of the reservoir and a few fluffy white clouds emphasised the blue of the clear sky, but the air still had an edge to it.

They sat on a hillock and she stared upwards.

'No vapour trails,' she said.

Reaper followed her gaze but said nothing.

'Even on the most perfect day, you got vapour trails,' Greta said. 'Somebody going somewhere. Families to Majorca. Businessmen to Stockholm. Superstars to LA.'

'It'll be a long time before aircraft fly again,' Reaper said. 'If they ever do. Maybe we'll have airships next time round.'

They sat in silence for a while, looking into nowhere, rather than at each other. Greta began to think it had been a bad idea to come outside with him. His feelings seemed sealed. Everything about him was surface; observation, reaction, response. No pro-action, as far as she was concerned. No hint at what he might be thinking. About her.

She had grown up in Bromley with two brothers so she knew about the silences of men. Give them an emotional issue to deal with and they would opt for the pub. Maybe, if they were pushed into a corner by a girlfriend, they might buy a bunch of flowers and hope that would save them having to say anything.

Greta had had her share of boyfriends and one serious partner. When she met Andy, they hadn't needed words. A look or touch had been enough and the sex had been great. They hadn't even spoken a great deal when they split up. There had been no deep discussions just a brief row. The excitement had gradually seeped away and they hadn't been ready to settle for a comfort zone and call it marriage. Besides, he'd been seeing someone on the side and Greta found out. The betrayal had been inevitable; if he hadn't found someone, she would have, but because the infidelity was his, she had the moral ground from which to pick a fight. Even then, just words. No deep insight, no confessions. Just a parting that had taken her to Yorkshire. And the pandemic.

Greta had been in the middle of it at Scarborough General Hospital. She had been unable to lock herself away in a room until it was all over. She had been surrounded by the dying and the dead. The hopeful and the desperate. The hope had died in their eyes long before their bodies followed. She had been their last hope and she still felt an irrational sense of failure. At the end, she had contemplated suicide. A swift and painless exit from what was left of the world. She had the necessary medication in her bag when she had driven to the harbour. For one last time, she wanted clean air and horizons. Sitting here on the moors reminded her of the occasion not much more than a year ago. Had it only been a year?

She had sat there for an hour, staring at sea and sky, in contemplation of her lost family: father a surgeon; mother a teacher; one brother an officer in the army; the other an economist at Tory Party headquarters. They had been at the pinnacle of middle class success. And for what? For a mutant virus from the depths of China to kill them all. As she was on the point of taking the pills, Richard Ferguson turned up and introduced himself. Intense and full of purpose. There was much to do, the physicist said. Society to rebuild. Would she help?

Why not? She had been enthused by his determination and guilty at what she had contemplated. Later, she realised his enthusiasm was more about the concept and challenge of survival rather than people. Later still, it dawned on her that he was attracted to her but, like many men, he was tongue-tied and didn't fully recognise his own desires. The fact that he never asked made it easier to avoid turning him down. Her move to Haven to be at the centre of the community made logistical sense. But it also left Ferguson behind, worthy man though he was, and allowed her to have a closer look at the intriguing Reaper. What she had seen, she liked.

'Do you still think of Kate?' she said. He didn't answer straight away but turned to look her in the face. 'I'm sorry,' she said. 'If you don't want to talk about it ...'

'It's all right. I don't mind. Yes, I still think of Kate. I loved her.'

His eyes remained fixed on hers and she licked her lips, unsure what to say, as if the next words might be crucial, might hurt him or damage anything that might develop between them.

'I never had anybody like that,' she said.

'I was lucky. For a few months, I was lucky.'

'Do you think you might fall in love again?'

He said nothing for a long time, but his eyes remained locked on hers. Eventually, he said, 'Kate made the first move. I never would have. She said my problem was that I carried too much guilt. She was probably right. I carry even more now. Not just for my family, but for her, too. Why did she die and I survive? Again? All that guilt doesn't leave a lot of room for other feelings.'

She touched the back of his hand and he didn't pull away.

'We all feel guilty, in one way or another. I feel guilt because I survived, because people died that I couldn't save, and because I almost killed myself, when it was over. I'd seen so much, I'd stopped feeling. If the Prof hadn't happened by, I would have, too.'

'I always thought you and Richard would become an item.'

She shook her head. 'He might have thought that, but it takes two to tango and I don't think he'd make a very good dancer.' Reaper smiled at her poor joke. 'Besides, I had my eye on somebody else.'

Reaper turned his hand so that their palms met and their fingers entwined. 'Kate said we should enjoy the moments we can,' he said. 'I know she was right, but it's difficult. Besides, I'm not a very pleasant person.'

'I don't think pleasant is a word that fits you in any capacity, Reaper.' She smiled, almost sadly. 'But I'd like to share moments with you.'

He nodded his head in what might have been agreement and then turned away to look at the valley before them. They still held hands and she leant against him and rested her head on his shoulder.

Chapter 13

THE SPECIAL FORCES TRIED OUT THE NEW WEAPONS that had been acquired. The L85 military rifles had a slightly longer barrel than the G36 police carbine they already carried, but could be used for automatic fire. The G36 had been regulated to fire only single shots. One member of each team switched to the L85, and each team had a combat shotgun, with a seven-cartridge magazine of twelve-gauge. James Marshall, who was their best shot, also took one of the sniper rifles.

Each team had a new vehicle fitted with a radio and the spare was used as a base radio in the Manor House. The two spare radio-equipped vehicles were taken to Scarborough and Bridlington, which were just about on the range limit and gave them permanent contact. The radio batteries were charged by generator. The Prof had gone ahead with developing wind and solar power and the Brains Trust had devised a way of storing the resultant electricity. It was early days, but the next winter would not be cold and dark and the Manpak batteries could be recharged without problem when necessary.

Ronnie returned to the commune that had provided the information about the bunker and they agreed to move. They arrived in three camper vans that had been painted in psychedelic colours and designs. They were a sad-looking lot who seemed to have attempted to recreate the peace, love and happiness of the hippy seventies, but without the flair. There were twenty-seven of them of various ages: men, women and children. They were bedraggled and looked in need of a good meal but Reaper was pleased at the racial mix.

Three Asians were among the group, two adults and a child. The adults were in mixed race partnerships and the child was being cared for by a white woman. Haven was, he was pleased to note, colour blind. It had a policy of equality and religious tolerance that he knew might not always be found elsewhere. Reaper also noticed that the woman looking after the child seemed to have a particular rapport with Ronnie.

Pete Mack made another foray to the oil terminal at Immingham and returned with two of the group who were holding the depot. Charlie Dyer and Susan Watson travelled in their own vehicle and met the committee and other members of the community. They had had enough of isolation and were looking to move somewhere that promised a better future. They had eight tankers of fuel to bring with them and twenty-four other members: eighteen men and six women, one of whom was seven months pregnant. Eight tankers of fuel, they thought, might help them broker a deal, but the Rev Nick explained that no one got special treatment in Haven. What they would get was housing, farmland, animals and help in settling into the only way of life that made sense. That and neighbours and a better aspect than the docklands they presently inhabited.

They were shown homes in a nearby village and met the people already settled there, and a vacant farm that was ready for occupation. Charlie and Susan were impressed by what they saw and the progress made by Haven. They said they would urge their friends to make the move and left with messages of goodwill and boxes of fresh supplies on the back seat of their car. Pete Mack would visit them again in three days.

After they had gone, Reaper sat with the Prof and Alan White, an industrial chemist and another member of the Brains Trust, on the benches outside the Farmer's Boy. They drank coffee. Alcohol was still only served one night a week, although there was nothing to stop those who wanted to, collecting bottles and cans when they went foraging on their own, in the nearby towns. Pickings, however, were getting thin on the ground.

As well as wind and sun power, the Trust was pursuing the use of fast growing crops such as wattle for fuel. Sugar cane, if grown in sufficient quantities, could produce alcohol and ethanol and had been successfully used in Brazil as an alternative to petrol. They were looking at waterpower, the possibility of solar towers, the uses of steam power, and wood fuel for cars, which had been widely used across Europe during the Second World War. The Prof was also planning experiments with hot air balloons.

While the speculation seemed impressive, Reaper was withholding judgement. A lot would depend on what crops were suitable for the Yorkshire climate and whether the sun would shine enough to make the more ambitious plans viable. Winter was full of long dark nights and short grey days. The grand ideas they started with might not work but, from them, he was sure, would come alternative improvements in their standard of life.

'The petrol will buy us more time, I suppose,' said Reaper. 'The same with guns and ammunition. We need it as long as others have it. But eventually, we'll be back to bows and arrows.'

'We could make gunpowder,' said the Prof.

'That's a comforting thought,' said Reaper. 'I was hoping science might just die.'

He stated his hope as a humorous provocation.

Alan said, 'You'll always have alchemists. Human nature. Someone will always be trying to turn lead into gold, figuratively speaking. Before you know it, we'll be back in the same old rat race.'

'That's what worries me,' said Reaper. 'Ambition.'

The Prof gave him a strange look. 'Nothing wrong with

ambition, man. We reached for the moon and got there. We can do it again.'

'It's all very well for men of science to devise plans and for men of power to put them into operation, but who does the work? At the moment we're existing, but add ambition and we'll be back to serfs and slavery.'

'Rubbish,' said the Prof.

Alan said, 'No, he's talking sense. I've been thinking along the same lines. There's a lot we have to re-invent, a lot of skills we have to learn all over again, and there's not enough people to do it all at once. We don't have nuclear power, electricity or a gas supply. We don't even have coal. It needs to be dug out of the ground, and I can't see anybody volunteering to do that, when they can have a log fire and live off the land. For an industrial revolution, you need people.' He gave each man a stare to emphasise his words. 'You actually need poor people, an underclass, to do the digging and mining necessary to build a civilisation like the old one.'

'That's the point,' said Reaper. 'Do we want a civilisation like the old one? This is a fresh start.'

'It won't be like the old one,' the Prof said. 'We will learn from mistakes and, over the generations, we'll build a better society. But we will need men of science to lead the way. We can't remain farmers for all eternity.'

Reaper said, 'But these grand plans to re-invent the world. They need a hierarchy. There will be those at the top who are in charge, the clever sods who do the planning, the artisans with skill, and then the rest of us, the poor bloody peasants, who will be expected to do the work.'

Alan nodded. 'Reaper's right. At the moment, we're living in a post-apocalyptic survival mode. We are grateful at the chance to help each other. We live in a mutual self-help community. It's the closest we'll get to a utopian state. This is what Karl Marx believed to be socialism. But it can't last. Man's nature will not let it last. Haven is, at the moment, run by an unelected committee. It's a committee that is scrupulously fair but, before long, there will have to be elections. Newcomers to Haven will demand their say in the way it's run. Eventually, there will be elections and we'll be ruled by politicians.

'This may start as a democracy, but I have a nasty feeling that there will come a time when hard decisions have to be made, perhaps about the division of labour, and we will end up with a dictatorship. We will go back to feudalism. When that happens, let's hope we have a benign ruler.'

The Prof shook his head as if the arguments were specious. 'Of course, certain people will rise to leadership,' he said. 'It's natural selection. And we will need strong leadership. But surely this is years away. It's a process that will evolve naturally. We are getting along quite all right as we are now.'

'But for how long?' said Alan. 'Haven will, probably quite soon, be ruled by politicians: men who will not necessarily be motivated by the common good. How many politicians do you remember who were truly altruistic? Most had large egos and a desire for power. Our new politicians will be the same. They'll impose laws and make decisions about the way the rest of us live. Eventually, somebody will re-invent money and work out how much a labourer in the field is worth, compared to a doctor or an engineer – or someone who fits solar panels. We will have rich and poor, a society divided by wealth, only this time without a National Health Service or old age pensions. Maybe we'll have a workhouse. We are heading towards the Middle Ages without a safety net.' He smiled and shook his head. 'I'm sorry. I didn't mean to sound so pessimistic.' He sipped the coffee, which had gone cold, and held up the cup. 'I suppose we should make the most of what we have, while we have it.'

'You've thought this through, haven't you?' said Reaper.

'I'm sure others have, as well. It's only a matter of time.'

'I don't think many others have thought about it,' said Reaper. 'But you're right. This is the honeymoon period. And people never learn from history.'

The Prof had become less adversarial. 'I have to confess, my thoughts had not gone in this direction.' He looked bemused and cross with himself. 'I should have. It's a logical process. But I've been too busy doing things. I'm ashamed to say that I've been enjoying myself far more than I ever did in academia.'

Alan said, 'Feudalism is inevitable but it will be called progress. In a thousand years, historians will describe what we are going through as a marvellous example of man's ability to recover from adversity. Ours will be the first step on the way to New Britain or New England or New Albion, or whatever they call it. Ours will be the first building block of a new society. They will applaud it from a distance of a thousand years. They won't have to live through it, like the poor bloody sods in history. We only abolished slavery in 1833. They had it in America until 1865. In other parts of the world, it never ended. I fear that, before long, it will be back, under another guise.'

The day Pete Mack brought word that the people in Hull wanted to join them, Adie Freeman, their apprentice blacksmith, returned from York to say that Brother Abraham wanted to see Reaper. Adie's reports from the city had been increasingly gloomy, although his only source of information was Joel Hardy, the man who was teaching him his trade, and his own impressions on the short walk from the Monkbar to the smithy.

'Something is going on,' said Adie. 'But Joel won't talk about it and I'm always followed. Not that anyone else would speak to me. People avoid me. It was Brother Mark who told me Abraham wanted to see you. He gave me the message at the barrier, when I was leaving. Almost on the quiet as if he didn't want anyone else to know. He said it was urgent.'

'Bad timing,' said Reaper. 'He'll have to wait.'

'Don't be stupid,' Sandra told him. 'You go to York. We can manage the run from Immingham.'

She was right, of course: no one would have prior knowledge of the run and the show of force they provided would discourage any interference. Intelligence told them there were no groups en route that were capable of mounting an attack, even at the sight of eight petrol tankers. Besides, it would be good for him to let someone else lead for a change.

The next morning, he went to York in a Range Rover driven by Yank. Adie went under his own steam, astride his motorcycle. They parked both vehicles on Monkgate, but out of sight of the castle walls. Reaper took Yank up to the first floor flat. It was as good a place as any for her to wait for his return. He left his armaments with her but, as before, he hung on to his knives. Then he and Adie walked up the middle of the road to the barricaded entrance to the city. Cedric, the small man in black, was not in sight.

Brother Mark met them and, while Adie made his own way to the blacksmith shop, presumably followed as usual, Reaper was escorted to the Holy Trinity Church in its secluded churchyard setting. A middle-aged man and a large woman of exceptional ugliness sat on the bench in the sunshine. The man had a knife at his waist and a cricket bat alongside him. She had a baseball bat. The man got to his feet and Brother Mark exchanged words with him and then indicated that Reaper should go inside alone.

Incense had been burning and had perfumed the air. Abraham was at the front of the church, sprawled on a chaise longue before the altar. Had illusions of grandeur tipped the balance of his delusion? Was he now a god, rather than God's messenger?

'Brother Reaper.' Abraham got up from the couch and walked down the central nave to greet him. 'Thank you for coming.' Abraham embraced him like an old friend. 'Please.' He indicated a box pew in the central nave that had been converted for comfort rather than worship. 'Have a seat.'

Two benches occupied the confines of the pew; they faced each other and were loaded with cushions, so there was little room to put your feet. They reclined rather than sat, as if potentates or at a Roman dinner party.

'You are well?' asked Abraham.

'Thank you, yes.'

'Brother Adrian is happy at his toils?'

'Adie is enjoying the work.'

'Good, good.' Abraham steepled his fingers.

'Why did you want to see me?' asked Reaper.

The monk glanced down the church, as if ensuring they were alone.

'Perhaps you would pray with me, Brother Reaper?'

He turned so that he sat and put his feet on the floor and pressed his palms together. If Reaper did the same, because of the constriction of the cushions and space, they would be sitting side by side, but facing in opposite directions. Abraham nodded to encourage him to adopt the pose and he did so because of the look of concern in the monk's eyes.

Reaper clasped his hands in front of him, rather than hold them in the universal posture of prayer, but dipped his head so that he would hear whatever the man wanted to whisper.

'These are troubled times, Reaper. This dominion of God is coming apart at the seams. I'm a prisoner. A figurehead to give authority to Brother Barry. The man is mad, a conclusion you may find strange coming from myself. I'm sure you have doubted my sanity ever since we met. But I didn't set out to hurt anyone. Foster's different. He's taken complete power. He now calls himself the High Sheriff of York and he has enough cronies to impose his authority. Men and women who enjoy giving physical pain to any who refuse to obey. Men and women who will kill at his order.'

'Don't the people still believe in you? Have you tried to oppose him?'

'I threatened to. He had me whipped on the high altar at the Minster. Told the congregation I had begged for punishment, that I was still attempting to rid myself of sin. It was very persuasive claptrap with me prostrate and being beaten. Said I had set an example, that others found wanting or in commission of sin, could hardly expect less. He called the whip the kiss of God.'

'Couldn't you do anything?'

'He threatened Mary and Rebecca. He plans to take them for his own. He wants me to marry them at the Minster on Sunday and confirm him as High Sheriff. He wants them both as his brides. All those years playing mind games have sent him over the brink, Reaper. And God forgive me, but I gave him the perfect opportunity to play his games for real.'

'What about Mark?'

'Mark remains faithful. They keep us apart. But I managed to slip a message to him yesterday, asking you to visit. Foster doesn't know, so we haven't much time. This whole sorry mess is going to fall apart before long. We have been living on foodstuffs looted from supermarkets. The way we are attempting to live is unsustainable. I know that now, and Foster will make the collapse happen quicker.'

Reaper considered returning with a full complement of Special Forces and taking the city, removing Foster and his followers, and letting the people choose their own future, but he immediately saw problems. Would he be right in leading his people into a battle that could bring casualties to them and casualties to innocent people who had been conditioned to defend the city for God? Was it right to interfere in another community's way of life? Wasn't that how wars started? With unprovoked aggression?

Abraham read his mind. 'I'm not asking you to invade, Reaper. That would be against the tenets of God and yourself, for you are a man of principle. Besides, Foster has guns. They are not on show but I know he has them. What

I am asking is that you save Mary and Rebecca. I fear for them and they do not deserve rape and degradation simply for being misguided enough to follow me. Brother Mark will have them at the Monkbar tonight. I can't give you a time. But as soon as it is dark enough, he will send them through the gate. Can you be waiting to take them to safety?'

'I'll be there,' said Reaper. 'What about you?'

'I shall continue to play my role. These are my people, after all, and perhaps I can be of use to them, despite Foster. And now, Brother Reaper, I urge you to go as swiftly as possible, before Foster discovers your presence.' Abraham placed a hand on Reaper's lowered head and said, 'Thank you, brother. I shall pray for us both and for my people. Go now.'

Reaper left him. He wondered if the girls were in the church or under guard somewhere else. Brother Mark waited outside. He looked nervous. The man and the woman were now sprawled on the grass. When he emerged, Mark turned and led the way down the path and through the curved arch in the high stone wall that took them back into Goodramgate. He set a quick pace. Perhaps he, too, was nervous of discovery. They saw few people and they didn't speak. The woman carrying a pike walked the wall alongside the gate and kept watch.

At the exit, by the stacked aluminium barrels, they were

out of sight. Reaper held his hand out and, after a moment's hesitation, the monk took it and they shook. His grip was fiercely firm. No words, but a nod of acknowledgement. Reaper left with a cold shiver in his spine as he walked that first lonely fifty paces down the road, half expecting to feel a crossbow bolt thudding into his back to speed him into eternity.

Yank saw him from the window and brought down his weapons.

'That didn't take long,' she said.

He looked back at the city as he fastened the gunbelt and hoped Adie would be okay.

'What did he want?'

'Salvation,' he said.

If not for him, then at least for the two members of his holy trinity.

They were halfway back to Haven when they saw the boiling black clouds on the horizon in the direction of Immingham.

Chapter 14

SANDRA TEAMED UP WITH KEIRA FOR THE DRIVE to Immingham. They planned a similar convoy to the one that had visited the bunker in the Pennines. Kev and James, Tanya and Jenny, in their Range Rovers, plus Gavin driving the military Land Rover with Smiffy behind the mounted machinegun, and Pete Mack sitting in back. Ronnie rode point as before on his Yamaha.

They met opposition as they approached the suspension bridge across the Humber. Sandra was in the lead car as they approached the Boothferry roundabout on the A164, when they heard shots ahead. The road to the bridge became a dual carriageway with steel barriers down the centre. Keira was driving and Sandra lowered the window and raised the carbine. They took the slight curve and the tollbooths came in sight but there was no sign of Ronnie. All twelve of the booths – six to serve in each direction – had been blocked by vehicles. More shots, as rifle fire scorched the tarmac and pinged off the bonnet of the car. A bullet put a hole through the windscreen, which starred but didn't break. There were trees on their left and nowhere to go. She saw Ronnie's Yamaha on its side in the undergrowth.

'Jasus,' said Keira, and pulled the wheel right, through a narrow gap as the steel barriers ended. The vehicle bounced across the central reservation, the tyres screeching, and she drove it across a turfed area and down a steeply inclined service road.

'Keep going. See if we can get behind them,' said Sandra.

They turned left at a T junction between trees and left again into an empty car park at the side of the highway. Signs for the Humber Bridge Tourist Information Centre pointed into another empty car park. Kev and James were right behind them. The gunfire came from above them on their left. Gavin must have stayed on the road. They could hear the reassuring sound of the machinegun being fired by Smiffy. Presumably, Tanya and Jenny had also stayed on the other side of the road.

'Stop,' she said, and Keira braked. Kev stopped alongside and Sandra said, 'Up the hill through the trees. Take them from the flank but keep your heads down. You don't want to get shot by Smiffy. We'll get behind them.'

Kev drove the car towards the steep banking and tree line.

Lavatories, kiosks and the Tourist Information Centre were to the right of Sandra and Keira. A metal fence separated the car park they were in, from another one. Sandra pointed and Keira drove at a padlocked gate and crashed though. It made sense that access roads would lead here from both carriageways across the Humber to the tourist centre.

Keira drove the car out of the car park and the road began to turn and they could see the tall twin towers of the bridge ahead. The road went beneath the highway and curved back on itself. They emerged a hundred yards on the other side of the tollbooths. A red BMW with two people aboard, went past them heading across the water. Resistance had ceased. Smiffy's machinegun had proved too powerful. Sandra let the Beamer go. It was against her nature to shoot for the sake of it and they were no longer being threatened. The span of the bridge arced upwards towards its centre, so they could not see the other side. She pointed and Keira drove to the booths. Sandra got out and went to the nearest.

'Smiffy,' she shouted. 'It's all clear. They've gone. Any casualties?'

'We're fine.'

'Seen Ronnie?'

'I'm all right, boss. Just bruises.'

'James?'

'No problems.'

James and Kev came out of the treeline, guns held at the ready.

'Right,' said Sandra. 'Let's move one of these cars so we can get through.'

'The Land Rover will do it,' said Gavin.

Keira checked the booths, blockages and undergrowth at her side of the road, while James and Kev did the same on the other side. Sandra opened a Transit, made sure it was empty and that the gear lever was in neutral, and released the handbrake. She jumped down and Gavin drove the Land Rover forward and began shunting it out of the way.

'Another lane clear that side,' she shouted, and Kev released the brake on a Mondeo, and he and James pushed it clear and to the side of the road. The ambush was amateur. But it wasn't an ambush, she realised. It was a delaying tactic. 'James, Kev. Get your car. We need to get going.'

Which was when the explosion at Immingham shook the air with such force that the ground shook and they forgot to breath. They crouched protectively in shock.

'They've blown the oil refinery,' said Pete Mack.

More explosions followed and black clouds coiled angrily into the sky.

Sandra said, 'We'll go forward. But slowly. Gavin, you and Smiffy take the other side.' She indicated the other side of the dual carriageway that would, in former times, have been for oncoming traffic. 'James, Kev, with me, but leave space behind us. Jenny, behind Smiffy. We may need to come back in a hurry, so plenty of space. Ronnie, you stay well back.'

They set off along both sides of the carriageway that were each two lanes wide. Once they were on the bridge, the lanes became narrow and claustrophobic. A three-point turn would be tight. They might have to reverse all the way back, which would not be good if they were in a hurry. More explosions, but these were nearer, and gunfire in the distance from the far side, which they still could not see.

They crested the top of the bridge. The suspended highway curved elegantly and dipped towards the far side of the Humber. When it reached land it became a full dual carriageway again that climbed into low hills.

Two tankers were burning on the far slopes and then they saw the rolling battle that was being fought below them. Sandra touched Keira and she stopped the car. Their vehicles in the other lane also stopped. A tanker was climbing the bridge towards them in their lane. Sandra got out and used binoculars.

'They've shot out its tyres,' she shouted to Keira.

Another tanker was following. On the far side, a car skidded, straightened, and came towards them fast. A blue Jaguar. Men appeared on foot in the road, firing after it. Then they moved aside as a blue 4x4 set off in pursuit. It had a full four-door cabin and one man standing in a truck bed at the back. The man in back was leaning over the roof and firing automatic bursts at the Jaguar. Sandra trained the binoculars on the car. It contained women.

'Let the Jag through,' she shouted to Smiffy.

She leant on the central barrier and raised the military rifle she carried, and fired a burst into the road ahead of the pursuing vehicle. The warning was clear. The vehicle slowed and then stopped.

James said, 'Do you want me to put him down?'

She glanced behind her. The youth was ten paces away, his carbine to his shoulder. He meant the man standing in the back of the now stationery truck who was still pointing his gun at the Jaguar, which was close to Smiffy in the Land Rover. The man fired and the Jaguar swerved, lost speed but continued coming.

'Put him down!' said Sandra.

One sharp crack and the man tumbled backwards. The car was too big to turn and began to reverse. The Jaguar passed the Land Rover and headed slowly over the crest of the bridge towards the tollbooths.

'Jenny!' she shouted. 'Go see who they are!' She looked back at James. 'Good shot! You and Kev go back to the booths. Make a defensive position in case anyone comes after us.'

More explosions from the far side of the bridge. More gunfire. Sandra used the binoculars again. The two tankers had stopped, a man jumped from one and was shot. He rolled, but lit a Molotov cocktail and threw it at the tanker. The bottle exploded and then so did the tanker. The bridge shook, and she crouched against the central reservation.

'Turn around!' she shouted back to Keira. The other tanker exploded and she imagined the bridge breaking, the concrete and steel cable falling into the water far below, along with her and the Range Rover. 'Let's get out of here, Gavin!' she shouted.

They re-grouped at the tollbooths. Once Sandra and Keira were through, they pushed the blocking vehicles back into position. Smiffy took the machinegun from the mount of the Land Rover and placed it on the bonnet of one of the barrier cars. Kev and James also took up positions to keep watch in case anyone attacked.

Susan Watson and three women, one of them pregnant, got out of the Jaguar. All were upset, one of them crying hysterically, but none of them were wounded. Sandra went straight to Susan Watson.

'What happened?' she said.

'John Steel,' Susan said. 'He's from Sheffield. He wanted the fuel. We heard he was coming, so we couldn't wait for you. We thought if we could beat him to the bridge, we could hold it until you got here.'

'How many people has he got?'

'Right now? Not many. But they say he has about four hundred men, mostly armed, and about three hundred women. They don't accept the old or children.'

'How did you know he was coming?'

'He sent people to talk to us, like you did. It was pretty much an ultimatum. Join us, or we'll take it. We have ...' She glanced across the bridge at the smoke and the occasional explosion and started again. 'We *had*, three old people and Glenys, who's pregnant. Steel wouldn't have taken them. Besides, when we saw what you offered, there was only one choice.'

'Why didn't you tell us about Steel?'

'Charlie said if you knew, you might not let us come.'

'How did he know you were leaving?'

'Two of our lot didn't want to go to Haven. Young blokes. They thought Steel offered better opportunities. They went missing during the night. I guess they went and told him we were leaving.'

'Did everybody come?'

'Yes. Two of the women were in the cabs with their men. Charlie stayed till the last. He set charges to blow the place.' She took another deep breath to retain her composure. 'I don't suppose he made it.'

Sandra was angry that Charlie Dyer and Susan hadn't told them the full story when they had visited Haven, but she also realised that the woman had just lost most of her friends and, probably, a loved one.

'Did you have a man?' she said, and Susan nodded. 'Was he in the convoy or with Charlie?'

'He was in the lead tanker.'

The one Sandra had watched through binoculars. The driver had been shot as he jumped from the cab. Probably his last act had been to throw the Molotov cocktail.

Susan said, 'I don't know what's happened to him.'

Sandra swung the rifle on its strap into the small of her back and took a step closer to the older woman and put an arm around her.

'He didn't make it,' she said, and Susan finally started to cry.

The Jaguar was drivable despite having bullet holes in it. Keira kicked out the shattered windscreen in her Range Rover. The front was battered from ram-raiding the gate but it was still roadworthy enough to get them home, where the vehicle could be replaced. They formed up for the return trip, while maintaining a watch on the bridge.

'It doesn't look like they're coming,' said Pete Mack, hefting a carbine at the barricade.

As if on cue, a dark green vehicle appeared on the crest and approached slowly. They watched it through binoculars. Something flapped from a tall aerial at the back.

'White flag,' said James.

'What the hell is that thing?' said Sandra, meaning the vehicle.

'It's a Hummer,' said Gavin. 'With a steel sheet welded to the front. Impressive. No wonder they wanted the petrol. A Hummer does about twelve miles to the gallon.'

'No one fires,' shouted Sandra. 'Stay alert.'

The Hummer stopped sixty yards away and a large man in military fatigues got out of the passenger side. His head looked as if it had burst in the sun, and was surrounded by a halo of wild curly hair and bushy beard that were bright ginger. He wore a side arm but carried no other weapon.

'Hello, Haven!' he shouted.

Sandra handed her L85 to Pete Mack and climbed onto the roof of a car alongside Smiffy.

'Who are you?' she shouted back.

'John Steel,' said the giant. 'I take it you are the Angel?'

'That's me.'

'We've heard about you. The Reaper and his Angel of Death!' He laughed, a deep, rumbling sound. 'You don't look much!'

'You want to find out?' Her voice was controlled but challenging.

'Not today. We've got to bury our dead today. Or maybe tip them in the Humber.'

'So what do you want?'

'To see my enemy, face to face.'

'Are we your enemy?'

'I think so.'

'Why? It's a big country. Few people. You can go anywhere.'

'I've heard good things about Haven.'

'So why not build your own?'

'Why bother when I can take yours?'

'Easier said than done.'

'You're farmers. Not even Reaper and his Angel can stop an army.'

'Don't bet on it.'

'There's someone else on the bridge,' James said, in a voice low enough not to carry to John Steel. He was lying

247

full length on top of a furniture van. He had switched from carbine to sniper rifle. 'Cycle lane.'

Sandra moved her eyes without moving her head. She felt suddenly vulnerable. She couldn't see anyone.

'There's always surrender,' John Steel said.

'We wouldn't know what to do with you,' she said 'A lot easier if you stay away.'

Steel laughed again and Sandra said, more quietly, 'James. If you see a threat, take it down. Tanya, if this goes pear shaped, take Steel.'

'You and Reaper could just walk away. Be sheriffs in another town.'

'What about Haven?'

'Haven would work for me. But at least the people would have their lives.'

'I don't think so, Steel. I think we're finished here. Tell your gunman in the cycle lane to go home. And do the same yourself.'

Steel's expression changed. He punched the air and ducked and shots were fired too quick to be counted.

'Got him,' James said.

Sandra was aware that a bullet had gone high and wide above her head. Tanya had also fired but Steel was out of sight and the steel panel on the front of the Hummer began to rise, like the blade of a snowplough. A burst from Smiffy's machinegun clanged against it. Smiffy changed his trajectory and aimed below the steel, hoping for a ricochet

against the tyres. Others also fired, along the barrier. The
Hummer reversed at speed.

'Let it go!' said Sandra.

Pete Mack left his firing position behind a car and
looked up at her.

'Don't you think you should come down from there
now? If they have anybody else out there, you make a
pretty good target. Even for an angel.'

He grinned and she blushed and realised she hadn't
flinched when the shot was fired. She had been determined
not to show fear but making herself a sitting duck was
taking bravery or foolhardiness a tad too far. She climbed
down and jumped the last bit, into Pete's arms.

'Looks like we've got another war,' he said.

Reaper made radio contact as soon as he was in range
and was reassured by Pete that they were all safe and the
situation was under control. They kept watch but, from
what Susan told them, it seemed unlikely that Steel would
launch a full-scale attack.

'His convoy is too big,' she said. 'They say it's like a
travelling circus. Trucks, caravans, tents. He started in Sheffield,
gathering hard men. He didn't kill anyone for the fun of it. If
people got out of his way, he let them go, but he took whatever
he wanted. If anyone objected, he killed them. He moved out
of Sheffield late spring. It's not so good in the cities any more.
That's what his people said, the ones who came to talk to us.

'Steel isn't his real name. Apparently, he ran a nightclub, before the plague. He was a hard man himself, and a wrestler for a short time. Called himself the Man of Steel, as in Sheffield, steel city. He liked to be with the bouncers on the door. First there if there was trouble. Generous with his fists. That's how one of his blokes described him. Anyway, they began to move a couple of months ago. They stopped at Rotherham, then Doncaster. Recruited more people and, if anyone had any hoards, he took them. At Doncaster they faced another hard gang. It could have been a bloodbath but Steel and his second in command challenged the two leaders of the gang. Just the four of them. Knives, axes whatever, but no guns. Steel and his mate won and the gang joined him.

'Then he went east to Gainsborough, down to Lincoln, and up to Market Rasen. That's when he first sent people to talk to us. When he was in Market Rasen. Well, not so much talk as tell us he was coming to take over the refinery. We could look after it for him but we should now consider it to be his. Last week, he moved the whole caravan to Cleethorpes. A summer holiday at the seaside, they said. I think that's where they planned to stay but they heard about Haven. They'd heard whispers before, asked us if we knew about you. This land of milk and honey, somewhere in the north. We said no. We hadn't heard about you. But somebody in Cleethorpes must have told him because he'd decided. Steel came to see us himself five days ago and he told us. "A good place to spend winter. And who knows," he said. "Maybe a good place to settle."'

Sandra said, 'His main force is still in Cleethorpes?'

'It has to be. The two who left us only gave him short notice about what we were up to. We almost made it. Another half hour and we would have been across the bridge and we could have held him off. We had a load of home made bombs, explosives. We could have kept him away until you got here.'

'From the sounds we heard across the river, a lot of those bombs were used.'

'Nothing to lose by then,' she said. 'He wouldn't have said, nice try but hard luck. He'd have killed everybody. I suppose they're all dead now.'

It was probably no comfort to Susan Watson, but those who had died had probably inflicted enough damage on Steel's flying column to make any imminent attack unlikely. A full-scale attack would take days to organise if his army was enjoying a break at the seaside. Besides, he would be unlikely to be in a rush. He was clever enough to move across country, enlarging his following. He would be astute enough to send out scouts first and gather intelligence.

Sandra sent the Jaguar with the four women ahead, escorted by Jenny and Tanya. The rest of them waited at the bridge, in case Steel tried the unexpected. While they remained on watch, Smiffy mounted the machinegun on a rear swivel of the military Land Rover. For the return journey, he would cover their back as tail end Charlie.

Intelligence would be key to any outcome and Sandra took Ronnie to one side.

'We need someone to stay behind,' she said. 'Stay hidden but keep watch. We need to know when they cross and in what strength. It's less than two hours easy motoring to Haven. We need advance warning.'

'No problem,' he said.

While they were talking, Kev joined them.

'Hey-ho, me hearty. This may sound stupid, but I'd like to volunteer.'

'What for?'

'To go across the river. Go to Cleethorpes and find out what's happening. Join Steel's army. If I can find a bike, I can go the long way round.'

'Someone on the inside would be good,' she said. 'But any newcomers will be suspect. He'll expect a spy. It's a hell of a risk.'

'So's life.'

'If Steel susses where you're from, you'll be dead.'

'So? Live fast, die young and leave a beautiful corpse.'

'Young?' she said. 'Beautiful?'

'One out of three isn't bad.'

They grinned, acknowledging the risk, but realising it would be of great help to the cause of survival.

Sandra said, 'You'll need different clothes.'

'I'll get them on the way.'

'What about a bike?'

'No problem. We're only a few miles from Hull. Ronnie can drop me at a dealership then come back here.'

'Then take care, Kev!'

He removed all his weapons but his knife and put them in the back of one of the cars. If he was going to try to mingle, he couldn't look like a warrior. He waved to them. 'Wish me luck, me hearties!' They wished him luck and Ronnie took him into Hull.

They stayed at the barricade another hour, until Ronnie returned solo. They had packaged all the spare water and combat rations for him.

'They'll probably come across the bridge and make it secure,' she said, 'so be careful.'

'There's a clump of trees in the middle of the Boothferry roundabout. That's the obvious place to keep watch,' he said, 'so I won't be there. I'll be in the trees on the far side of the roundabout.'

Sandra said, 'We'll leave one of the radio cars at Beverley. If they cross in force, radio from there. If we need to contact you, we'll get close enough to use the PR.'

He rode away and, soon after, she gave the order. They mounted up and prepared to go home and plan for war as Reaper and Yank pulled up.

'We met the others on the road,' he said to Sandra. 'What's happening?'

He was on edge and she took him to one side, away from the others, and told him all that had occurred. 'It seems like those rumours of a group from Sheffield were true,' she said. 'Only they didn't go south.' When she had finished he put a hand on her shoulder. It was shaking.

'When I saw that smoke, I thought I'd lost you.'

'I can cope, Reaper.' She saw that the words stung him. That he might not be indispensable. She smiled to soften them. 'You taught me well. And you can't be everywhere at once. Anyway, what's happening at York?'

'Chaos. Like we predicted. And it's come at precisely the wrong time. We'd better get back. There's a lot to do.'

Yank shouted across from the group, where she had been exchanging information.

'Hey, Sandra ... I like the new name!'

Reaper glanced between them and said, 'What new name?'

Sandra said, 'John Steel has heard of us. The Grim Reaper and the Angel of Death? He thought it was funny. Said this time, we had no chance.'

Chapter 15

A CROWD FILLED THE SQUARE IN FRONT OF THE MANOR house when they got back. Word had spread with the arrival of the newcomers. The dark clouds on the horizon from the explosions at Immingham seemed to portend doom. Reaper had radio messages sent to Bridlington and Scarborough and arranged for messengers to visit all the other settlements of the federation to warn them of the invading army.

He explained what was happening at an impromptu open-air gathering. At the more private meeting that followed, he asked if any newcomers had arrived. Steel would want to infiltrate, just as they were attempting to do with Kev. They should all be alert to the possibility of spies in their midst.

Sandra sat on one side of Reaper; Greta on the other.

'Immingham has probably forced his hand,' he said. 'He was probably going to lay low and send people in, to work out our strengths and weaknesses. Now we know his intentions, but that doesn't mean he'll move quickly. He has to prepare. Hopefully, he'll underestimate us.'

'A force of four hundred armed men is a lot,' said the Rev Nick.

'You can always surrender,' said Reaper.

Sandra said, 'He offered terms. You work for him. That's it.'

'It's hard enough working for ourselves,' said Cassandra. 'Living off the land is always hard work.'

'It will get better,' said Nick.

'Not if Steel takes over,' said Reaper. 'But it's up to you. He's already given amnesty to Sandra and me.'

'Amnesty?' said Nick.

Sandra said, 'At the bridge, he said we could walk away. It's just Haven he wants.'

'And will you?' said Nick. 'Walk away.'

'Not unless you tell us to,' she said.

'So you're staying,' said Pete Mack. 'So let's stop talking bollocks and get on with planning what we're going to do.'

Ashley said, 'We have a hundred militia. We have good weapons. If it was a case of defending the manor house, we could do a good job. But it isn't. There are farms and villages, the fishing fleets. We can't defend all those. Neither can the people there. Steel can take us piecemeal unless we take him on in open battle. That may be our only option but I don't recommend it.'

'Neither do I,' said Reaper. 'When our most valuable

commodity is at risk.'

'What?' said Pete.

'People. We can't afford to lose any more. And I don't want to kill any more of Steel's army than necessary. We may need them, when it's over.'

'What have you got in mind, Reaper?' said Ashley.

'Remove the head of the snake. Remove the venom. Remove those leaders among the enemy who want to kill. Then convert the others to a more peaceful way of life.'

'Well, that's an easy solution,' said the Rev Nick, sitting back in exasperation.

Reaper was unperturbed by the cleric's attitude. 'They say he has more than seven hundred followers. These were ordinary people before the plague. I'll bet they would like to be ordinary people again. Most of them are not killers. Most of them would probably love the chance to have what we have. A future. Peace. Good neighbours. They've been blinkered by a bully. Steel, and all those like him, need to be killed. Not in battle but quietly, so that nobody else dies. A knife in the back will do.'

The Rev Nick shook his head. 'This is all before we even attempt to negotiate. This man isn't like Muldane. He doesn't rape and enslave. We could negotiate. You are so certain when it comes to life and death, Reaper. Who made you God?'

'Maybe God did,' said Reaper, and he glanced at Sandra with a smile. 'And he gave me a guardian angel.'

'The Angel of Death.' Nick intoned the title with great

sadness and shook his head again. He said to Sandra, 'Is that how you want to be known?'

'I don't care what they call me. We're all here because of Reaper. We've fought together – all of us – to keep this place going. But what some of you still don't realise is that you can't wait and let the other bloke have first swing. Steel doesn't want to negotiate. He wants to rule. Reaper's right, most people have ordinary hopes and dreams. A life, a partner, a future. But there are some bastards out there who are natural born killers and the plague gave them the chance to go and murder and rape and pillage. Well, the plague also freed us from convention. Me and Reaper, we kill because it's necessary. I've tasted blood. Literally. And it doesn't scare me any more. So yes, call me the Angel of Death. Shout it loud. Maybe it'll scare some of those bastards out there that need killing.'

Her speech surprised Reaper. It surprised her. He reached across and gripped her hand briefly then turned to face the others, but her words had already left them all slightly stunned.

'Whatever you two decide,' Ashley said. 'I'm in.'

'Me, too,' said Pete Mack. 'Goes without saying.'

'There are no other options but resistance,' said Cassandra.

'I'm in total agreement,' Judith added.

Greta smiled around the group and said, 'There can be no argument.'

The Rev Nick let out a sigh that seemed to deflate his whole body and make him seem smaller. 'I know,' he said, in a small voice. 'I know there's no other way. I just wish there was.'

'What now, Reaper?' said Pete Mack.

'We send out scouts, arm the militia, hope Kev can discover the secret of a negotiated peace, or find a way to kill the bastards at the top, and wait for Ronnie to tell us when they're coming. In the meantime, I have to go to York.'

Two teams went to the city: Reaper and Sandra, and Keira and Yank. They wore dark blue sweatshirts to cover their arms and leather gloves to hide their hands. They parked the cars well short of the castle walls and went to the apartment. They pulled the curtains closed, heavy velvet drapes that were lined. They lit a lamp and made themselves comfortable. After a while, Keira took a peek outside.

'It's getting dark.'

They were applying camouflage face paint.

'It's the first time I've used makeup in ages,' said Keira.

'All you need is a touch of Chanel and you're ready for the ball,' said Yank.

Sandra looked at Reaper's face and said, 'It suits you.'

'Does it make me look like Sylvester Stallone?' he said.

'More Ronald McDonald,' said Yank.

'Thanks.'

Keira held up a bottle of water. 'Anyone?' she said.

'No thanks,' said Sandra. 'It might make me want to pee.'

'Do what I do,' said Yank.

'What's that?' asked Sandra.

'Pee.'

They left the apartment and moved silently in the shadows of a deepening night. A torch blazed on top of the castle wall next to the Monkbar, which made the darkness beyond its reach denser than the night. Sandra went past the Viceroy of India restaurant, back to the walls and window, slipping into doorways, weapon held upright but at the ready. When she reached a point with a clear view of the gatehouse, she crouched on the pavement and squinted through the night sight on the L85 rifle. Reaper went across the street with Keira and Yank and slipped into the bushes and undergrowth at the corner of the junction. The two girls adopted support positions and Reaper crossed the road, using the buildings outside the Monkbar to shield him.

A second hand shop was on the corner and he eased himself against the window and peeked round. He could see across the top of the parked cars that blocked the entrances but nobody moved inside the walls at ground level. The beer barrel chicane through which the girls, Mary and Rebecca, were supposed to emerge, was only a few yards away. It was dark enough. Now all they had to do was wait.

Waiting was the worst part; the time when the mind played tricks and ran alternative scenarios to make you doubt what you were doing. Was that noise down the road behind him a rat or Brother Cedric sneaking closer with his crossbow? But then, when Reaper came to think of it, there wasn't much of a difference, and he was probably being unkind to rats. Cedric was one of those people to whom evil came naturally, and no one would tell Reaper they didn't exist. He believed in good and evil, whether through nurture or nature. For Brother Abraham, good and evil defined his belief in God. Was Reaper close to conversion?

Almost an hour passed. The shop window was full of distractions. *We buy and sell and part exchange*, said the sign. Laptops, CD players, hi-fi systems – if that was what people still called them – and musical instruments. He couldn't see a lot of use for much of the stuff in the window apart from the accordion. Did that qualify as a musical instrument? What was it someone once told him when he was giving an example of an oxymoron? That was it: accordion music. Accordion? Music? He almost laughed but someone walked from the tower above the gate, across the open stretch of wall, farted loudly and walked back.

The moon shone fitfully between sluggish clouds. He stared across the road, but Sandra had melded into the background and he couldn't spot her. A scuttling sound echoed inside the city. This time it probably was rats. A dog barked and others took up the cry. They sounded like a pack. Wild dogs on the scavenge. Well … maybe they'd eat the rats.

From the other side of the gatehouse he heard soft footfalls and he risked looking around the corner. A white face showed at the chicane of metal barrels. Reaper left his cover and lightly ran the ten yards towards the chicane, dodging the rear end of a blocking car. Brother Mark was leaning out, staring into the darkness. Reaper suddenly thought it could be a trap, but he was too far committed to back away. Besides, if it wasn't a trap, the safety of two girls could hang in the balance.

He stopped short of the chicane and Mark, suddenly aware of his presence, almost flinched at his closeness. The monk raised a finger to his lips and went back between the barrels. The two girls slipped out a second later. They wore dark monk's habits with the hoods up. Brother Mark did not reappear. Reaper held his gun at the ready and scanned the tower and the castle wall. He pointed and the girls followed his direction and moved quickly past him, towards the safety of the corner. Perhaps he was taking up too much room, or perhaps they shouldn't have been running hand in hand, but they were too close to the blocking car and one of them banged into it and cried out, a small cry, but loud in the stillness of the night. Both girls stopped. He heard footsteps on the walkway above them.

'Move,' he urged, and the first girl ran, but across the road instead of round the corner. Perhaps she panicked, perhaps she believed the darkness would hide her, but the moon chose that moment to come out from behind a cloud.

'Escape!' someone shouted, and Reaper heard the distinctive sound of a crossbow being fired.

The running figure was flung forward and Sandra opened fire in short bursts. Single shots came from further across the road as the back-up team offered covering fire designed to keep the defenders hiding behind the walls. Reaper grabbed the second girl, dragged her round the corner and pushed her in the direction of the undergrowth across the road. 'Run!' he hissed. She ran.

Sandra and the back-up team kept firing as Reaper shouldered his weapon and ran into the moonlit roadway to the fallen girl. A crossbow bolt was deep in her back. He partly rolled her and picked her up in his arms as another bolt whisked past his head to clip the roadway in front of him. The moon went back behind a cloud and, for a moment, he felt enclosed by the night, but then someone threw a torch from the battlements and it hit the ground near him, sending a shower of sparks and casting him in its glow. The girls intensified their pattern of fire but, as he moved, he heard another bolt skid across the tarmac.

He kept running with the girl in his arms. He was soon out of crossbow range but he remembered what Abraham had said: Barry Foster had access to guns. He kept moving until the curve of the road took him out of the line of fire. He was outside the flats. Keira joined him from across the road; the other girl was with her.

'Yank is across the road, keeping watch,' Keira said.

'Inside,' Reaper said.

Keira opened the doors and he carried the wounded girl upstairs and lay her face down on the sofa. Even though he had run a good distance, she had been light in his arms. He wondered which one it was. Keira turned on the lamp and the second girl hovered in the doorway.

'Is she all right?'

The girl in the doorway was Mary, the plainer of the two. He put a finger to the neck of Rebecca. There was no pulse. The bolt was solid aluminium, green feathers at the end of the eight inches that protruded from her back. Maybe another eight inside her. From the angle, it could have gone straight into her heart. Reaper felt sick and angry. How many more victims would he see die? He had the urge to go straight back and find Cedric and hang the little bastard from the battlements. He controlled his emotions.

'Is she ...?' the girl in the doorway repeated.

'She's dead,' said Reaper. He pushed the cowl from her face. Her eyes were closed, her lips parted. She could have been asleep. She was still beautiful. And forever young. 'We'll take her home.'

He didn't attempt to remove the bolt. Just picked her up in his arms once more. Strange that now he knew she was dead she felt heavier. They met Sandra on the stairs, the question in her eyes. He shook his head.

'Fuck,' she said, quietly.

They went carefully but no one followed. A whistle and Yank appeared out of the darkness. Mary insisted on riding with her dead friend. She sat in the back of a Range Rover and Rebecca was laid sideways so that her head was in Mary's lap and they drove home in silence.

Dr Greta Malone removed the bolt and left Cassandra and two other ladies who were roused from their beds, to prepare the girl's body for burial. She found Reaper and Sandra sitting on either side of a table outside the Farmer's Boy, sharing a bottle of wine in the darkness.

'I'm sorry,' she said, sitting on the bench next to Reaper.

'So am I,' he said.

Sandra got up and Greta widened her eyes.

'Nothing personal,' Sandra said. 'I'm going to bed.' She walked around the table and kissed Reaper on the head. 'Night,' she said to them both, and went across the village square to the manor house.

'It doesn't get any easier, does it?' Greta said. She reached across the table for the glass left by Sandra and poured wine.

Reaper said, 'We would have got away safely but Mary cut her leg. Something broken on the back of a car. She didn't see it in the dark and the shock made her cry out. Then Rebecca ran the wrong way. She was a beautiful girl. Well, you know she was beautiful. You saw her.'

'She was beautiful,' Greta agreed. She sipped the wine.

Reaper said, 'Not that it matters. Just another life. Another wasted.'

She put her hand on his on the table. He didn't object. 'You've seen too much. We've all seen too much,' she said.

'Mary blames herself. When is it going to end?'

They sat for a long time without speaking, each lost in themselves but taking strength from being lost together.

Jenny and Tanya left at dawn to patrol south to the Humber and use a personal radio to check in with Ronnie. Cassandra debriefed Mary. At her insistence, Reaper was absent, but Sandra, without weapons and in a dress, sat in on the interview. The girl's emotions were still fragile and Cassandra felt coaxing information would be better achieved by a feminine approach.

Adie didn't return to the city. He knew it would no longer be safe, but he worried about the blacksmith, Joel Hardy, and the ordinary folk of York he had seen in the streets. He had been unable to speak to them but he had sensed their depression and fear.

A man arrived at Haven in a VW camper van with a sink and cooker in the back and rear seats that had been folded into a bed. He was alone. He said he was Arnie and had come from the Manchester area. Reaper glanced over his vehicle with interest.

'I haven't seen one like this before. Most people tend to choose something bigger. I did myself, at the beginning.'

'They're good vehicles and grand for a bloke on his own.' Arnie smirked and added, 'Enough room for two, if you get lucky.'

Arnie was in his early forties, medium height and build, dressed in jeans and a designer sweatshirt. He had a growth of stubble on his face, a shaven head and a face that was unremarkable until he smiled and showed the gap where his front teeth should have been. His lack of teeth didn't stop him suffering from halitosis. Reaper suspected that if Arnie had got lucky on his travels, he would have had to use considerable persuasion. He wore Timberland safety boots with steel toecaps, excellent fighting boots; not a factor that was too suspicious on its own – everyone needed protection, but Reaper suspected him anyway. In the back of his camper van was a shotgun, a large kitchen knife with the handle taped for a better grip, and a claw hammer.

Pete Mack took Arnie under his wing and became his best pal, to monitor what he did and the questions he asked, and to feed him false information. At noon, two women arrived in a Volvo estate with bedrolls and a camping stove in the back and asked for sanctuary. Judith and Cassandra dealt with them. They said they were Shirley and Myra, they were middle-aged, travel worn and innocuous looking, but then looks could be deceptive. They were also treated as potential spies.

Sandra, back in her fatigues, body armour and weapons, reported what they had learned from Mary, which did not add much to what Abraham had told Reaper the previous day. Abraham was still a prisoner in the Holy Trinity Church. Mary and Rebecca had been held in the Treasurer's House on the other side of the Minster. Foster had made it his home and headquarters. He had been attracted to it, she said, because it had been the medieval home of the treasurer of the Minster and was supposed to be haunted. A Roman road ran through its cellars and legionaries had, allegedly, been seen marching along it. Reaper wondered whether Foster actually believed the rubbish he spouted. If he did, it made his megalomania easier to understand.

Abraham had told him York contained 182 men, women and children. Mary said Foster had first imposed a curfew and put armed guards on the streets that were inhabited. Some of these guards had guns; some had crossbows. He had turned the area around The Shambles into a ghetto from which no one could leave without permission. The changes had happened swiftly, over the last few nights. Then, last night, he'd gone further and moved everyone into the Minster for their safety. God would protect them against the baleful influences of outside, he'd said.

There were about twenty children up to the age of fifteen who attended school in the Minster. There were more men than women, although she wasn't sure of the ratio. Relationships had been formed, but Foster had separated men from women as another way of controlling them. She thought Foster had about thirty followers – mostly men, although there were perhaps four or five women among them. Most were people who were willing to obey orders without question.

'I asked if they would be prepared to kill,' Sandra told Reaper. 'She said some of them would, although not all. Some, she thought, had been carried along by the excitement. But they will all obey orders.'

'That's the first step,' said Reaper. 'Obeying orders.'

'Are we going in?'

'We have to. And it's not just about liberating Abraham and his people. I don't want to fight a battle against Steel here in Haven. I don't want to take him on in the field, either. I want to entice him onto neutral ground where he thinks the odds are in his favour. Where he will bring his best troops, his killers. The men the others follow. The neutral ground is York.'

'So first we have to capture York?'

'That's right.'

'And then you entice him?'

'Yes.'

'How?'

'I'm still working that out. But this remains secret between us. Nobody else is to know. The only leaks I want are the ones that we plan. I want to go into York tonight and remove Foster and his cronies. I think we need to accelerate the action. Take the initiative away from Steel. He won't be able to move his army at a moment's notice, but if he hears of a way of taking the pair of us out and leaving Haven helpless, I'm betting he'd take it.'

'Remove the head of the snake?' Sandra said, with a grin.

'Exactly.'

They buried Rebecca in the communal plot while the three newcomers were being given a tour of nearby villages. The Rev Nick conducted a brief service that was attended by Mary, Reaper, Sandra and Greta. Afterwards, Greta took Mary, who was still overcome by grief and guilt, to be cared for in another village that wasn't on the tourist itinerary.

Tanya and Jenny had returned with nothing to report. Ronnie said a car containing two people had come across the bridge, circled the roundabout, and gone back. Nothing had moved in either direction since.

Reaper called all Special Forces together and gave them instructions. He conferred with Ashley, Smiffy and the Rev Nick and they exchanged and developed ideas. Ash smiled. 'You are a devious bugger,' he said.

'I do my best,' said Reaper.

Arnie, Shirley and Myra returned to the village square in front of the manor house with their guardians Pete Mack, Cassandra and Judith. Sandra, Greta and the Rev Nick went outside to join them. Reaper stood on the steps and shouted authoritatively to Pete, Cassandra and Judith to join him inside. They exchanged looks at his brusque voice; looks that could not have failed to be noticed by the three newcomers.

'Sorry about that,' he said, when they were in the study. 'I was setting the tone. Sandra will be doing a bit of strutting as well, whilst she's out there.' He outlined his plan. 'It's all a bit hit and miss, but it's worth a chance.'

Arnie, Shirley and Myra had lunch in the sunshine outside the Farmer's Boy with Pete Mack and Cassandra, as Ashley mustered the militia. The men and women called to duty all wore military body armour and carried sidearms and L85 rifles. They looked formidable.

'What's going on?' asked Shirley.

'We've heard of a threat from south of the Humber,' said Pete. 'It's just a precaution. As you can see, we're well prepared for all eventualities.'

The militia loaded machineguns and mortars into the back of a wagon, which was then driven over the hill. Half the militia followed the lorry and the rest began building sandbag emplacements at the front of the manor house.

Shirley and Myra did not look particularly reassured.

Two Special Forces Range Rovers stopped in the square and Reaper conferred with the occupants and issued orders that the watchers couldn't hear. Judith came out of the pub with packs of food, thermos flasks and bottles of water, rations for perhaps several days, which were put into the cars. The two teams drove away and Reaper and Sandra walked up the hill towards the front gate.

Across the square, Smiffy directed two militiamen in how to set up mortars in two of the sandbagged positions, and placed machineguns in the other two.

Pete Mack glanced up the hill and said, 'Now Reaper's gone, why don't we go inside and have a drink?'

The three newcomers were directed into the back room of the pub. Arnie and Pete had cans of beer and Cassandra opened a bottle of wine for Shirley, Myra and herself. Before she could pour it, the Rev Nick put his head round the archway that led into the room.

'Sorry to interrupt. Could I have a word?'

He indicated Pete and Cassandra and the two joined him in the other room.

Nick spoke in a conspiratorial voice that was just loud enough to be overheard by inquisitive eavesdroppers.

'Do we have to do this?' he said.

'If Reaper says we do it, we do it,' said Cassandra.

'But surely we can negotiate? This Steel chap, he doesn't seem so bad. If we do as he asks, no one need get killed.'

Pete Mack said, 'This is pointless talk. We have to fight.'

'Why? Because Reaper says so? All Steel wants is food, somewhere to stay. I heard he only wants to spend the winter here. Well, there's plenty of space. His people could stay in Scarborough and leave us alone. All we would have to do is feed them and we can do that. We have a surplus.'

'I don't know,' said Pete Mack. 'Reaper says ...'

Judith joined them from the kitchen.

'Reaper says a lot of things,' said Nick. 'Reaper likes killing. That's the bottom line. He enjoys conflict. But there must surely be another way.'

'You're talking about Reaper's death wish,' Judith said.

'He can have a death wish,' said Nick. 'I just don't want to be part of it. I don't want the people here to be part of it.'

'Easier said than done,' said Pete. 'Reaper's word is law. You know that. Like Cassandra says. If he says we fight, we fight. The Special Forces girls will tell us when they're coming. And we have the militia. We'll give a good account of ourselves.'

'At what cost?' said Nick. 'Besides, without Reaper the militia would run.'

Cassandra said, 'Look, we can't talk now. It's not safe. God knows what he'd do if he heard us. Tomorrow morning he's going to York to see Brother Abraham. We'll talk again then. Although why he has to see Abraham when we're facing a war, I don't know.'

Nick sighed. 'You won't believe this but he's going to do the 55 steps. Reaper has become righteous and what he needs before battle is a noon penance and absolution from Brother Abraham.'

'Cry *God for Reaper, England and St George*?' Cassandra said.

'The man's going mad,' said Judith.

'But who's going to tell him?' said Pete.

Chapter 16

KEV WAS VIEWED WITH CURIOSITY WHEN HE DROVE into Cleethorpes. He had chosen a second hand Suzuki tourer with a 1255cc engine. His black leathers were filthy, because he had rolled in puddles, a muddy field and a gravel patch to take the newness from them, and he hadn't bothered with a helmet. Life was dangerous enough; why should he worry about a traffic accident?

He had taken the M62, turned onto the M18 to cross the Humber, turned onto the M180 to head back towards the coast and ridden straight to the seaside resort. He reckoned any other would-be spy would have approached from the south. Perhaps being so direct might make them think he was genuine, or stupid. Well, he'd been mistaken for stupid before. He could live with that and it might give him an inch of advantage.

Two men in a Transit that had been parked across the road flagged him down on the outskirts of town. One had a shotgun, the other a pistol in a holster at his waist. He was searched for weapons – his knife taken from him – and put in the passenger seat of a Ford Focus. A teenager, who needed a wash and didn't look old enough to drive, was at the wheel. The guard with the holstered gun rode behind on Kev's Suzuki.

'Where've you come from?' said the teenager.

'All over,' said Kev. 'Last place was Lincoln. That's where I heard about you lot. What's this bloke Steel like? Is he okay?'

'You'll find out.'

Road signs warned of the town centre and the youth negotiated a roundabout and took a right. At the next roundabout he went straight ahead. Kev saw that a left turn would have taken them down towards the beach, a pier and a promenade that was lined with what had been described as the circus that followed Steel. He was shocked at the number of people. Cars, camper vans, caravans, trucks, were lined up, with awnings raised, plastic tables and chairs set out. Tents were pitched on the gardens that were between the sea-level promenade and the main coastal road above, along which the youth was driving. Steel's soldiers and camp followers sat in or wandered though the encampment.

Some played football on the beach, others a game of boules; men, and some very shapely women, sunbathed on loungers; others drank, played cards, laughed, argued. Two or three groups were on a crazy golf course. It was as if the plague had never happened and it was a holiday weekend.

The youth turned off and stopped in a side street that was a lot different from the bars, shops and restaurants of the main road. Here were the rear aspects of private hotels, businesses and boardinghouses, backyards that had been converted into car parks, boarded up premises waiting for redevelopment that would never happen. The motorbike stopped behind.

'Out!' said the teenager.

Kev got out. The man on the Suzuki had his hand on the butt of his gun but Kev was not going to argue. The youth led the way across a yard at the back of a green painted building. He opened a door in the side of a garage and motioned that Kev should go inside. He did as instructed and the door closed behind him. The garage was filled with clutter. Rolls of wallpaper, old tins of paint, stiff brushes. Pieces of wood stacked against a wall, shelves that held jars of screws and nails and innocuous tools; a couple of handsaws and a fret saw hung from hooks, a lightweight decorating table was open and filled one side, and a portable workbench was in the middle of the clear space. A deck chair was alongside it. Light came in from a high narrow window.

Kev had a good look around but saw that all screwdrivers, chisels and hammers had been removed. A few power tools littered the shelves but, of course, they needed power. A sander was hardly a weapon unless he threw it. Still it was worth looking.

Eventually, he sat in the deckchair and waited.

A middle-aged man came for him two hours later, about six o'clock in the afternoon. The man had steel grey hair and wore glasses, but was well built. He wore jeans and a polo shirt. Below the sleeve of the polo shirt on his right arm, part of a tattoo was visible. Around his right wrist was strapped a cosh and he looked as if he knew how to use it.

'Hey-ho, me hearty!' Kev said. 'Any chance of a drink?'

'Maybe later.'

The man pointed and Kev followed his directions through a side door into the main house. Before entering, he noticed his motorbike was parked in the yard at the back. He went up half a dozen stairs, along a carpeted corridor and into a room that had at one time been the bar and lounge of a private hotel. The décor was mainly puce which made him wonder if any of its former clientèle had visited more than once.

It was a long room with a bay window at one end looking out onto a street that was more prepossessing than the view out back. The room was empty and seemed spacious until Steel entered through another door beyond the bar. Suddenly, it felt crowded. The man had a presence about him. His wild red hair and beard made him larger than life and he was big to start with. Behind him came a man with a face as sharp as an axe, black hair combed straight back and eyes that were dead. He wore a full-length black leather coat. Kev's apprehension began to grow.

Steel nodded and the man behind him kicked the backs of his legs and he fell to his knees. As he tried to regain his balance, Steel took one step forward and kicked him between the legs. The pain was immense and he rolled forward clutching his groin and gasping for breath.

'Do *not* be sick,' said Steel. 'If you're sick on this carpet, I'll keep kicking your bollocks until they drop off. Then I'll kill you.'

At that precise moment, death didn't seem a bad alternative.

'Now. Who are you?' Kev rolled and gasped and tried to find his voice. 'Don't piss me about or I'll kick you again. Who are you?'

'Kevin Andrews.'

'Where are you from?'

'Leeds, originally.'

'Where've you been since then?'

'I lay low for a while. Then I went to York but I didn't like it. It's run by a religious nutter. So I left and I heard about you. I've come from Lincoln. I heard you were recruiting.' He groaned and tried to sit up on his haunches. 'If I'd known you wanted eunuchs, I wouldn't have bothered.'

The man with the dead eyes said to Steel, 'It's too convenient. What would you do? You'd send somebody.'

Kev concentrated on trying to breath normally and not

be sick. He stared at the man's boots. They were black cowboy boots with heels and pointed toes.

'Do you know the place called Haven?' said Steel.

'Of course. They're next door to York. Run by another nutter called the Reaper.'

'When you left York, why didn't you go there?'

'Well, I'd had a bit of trouble in York. Over a girl. And I'd heard the Reaper was a bit of a stickler so I thought best take my chances somewhere else.'

'I don't like rapists,' said Steel.

'Neither do I. I'm no rapist. It was more like an assault with a friendly weapon.' He winced. 'She didn't object, but her bloke did.'

'Kill him and be done with it,' said Dead Eyes.

'Chef, you have no patience.'

Chef?

'I thought you were recruiting. Look, if you're not, I can just bugger off. If I can find both my balls.'

Steel smiled. It didn't reach his eyes.

'I like a sense of humour. Tell me about Haven.'

Kev shrugged.

'It's a small place. A farm, a few houses. But it's part of a federation that's bigger. Lots of villages, seaside towns.'

'How many people?'

'God knows.' He tensed as Steel seemed to be preparing for another kick. 'Two, three thousand maybe. I honestly don't know. We weren't allowed to fraternise. York was a closed shop. Once you were in, you were in. Went to church and worked. It was no bloody life at all.'

'So why did you stay?'

'It was winter. Harry icers.'

'What?'

'Freezing cold. I stayed for winter. I turned up in November and they took me in. I didn't mind the prayers but they had me humping coal. It was hard work. And they're bloody nutters. All of them. Live in the past. No guns, no petrol, no cars, no generators. Just me humping coal. When the weather changed, I left.'

'After your assault with a friendly weapon.'

'Well, yes. After that.'

'Tell me about the Reaper and his Angel.'

'You mean his daughter?'

'Father and daughter?'

'That's what they say. It's not a sex thing.'

'Tell me about them.'

'I don't know them. Never met them. Only heard about them.'

'What did you hear?'

'That they're good at killing people.'

'Does Haven or the Federation have guns?'

'I suppose so. I never went there. I know we didn't in York. In York they have bows and arrows.'

'Bows and arrows?'

'Crossbows, longbows. Robin Hood. Mind you, you

can do some damage with a crossbow.'

'I'm sure.'

Steel stared down at him for a moment and Kev said, 'Can I stay?'

'It's a mistake,' said Chef.

'Or shall I go?' He shook his head. 'I sound like a fucking song.'

'I think you should stay, Kevin. At least for the time being. Take him away.'

The man behind him prodded him with his toe and Kev got to his feet, still bent over with nausea and pain, and shuffled back the way he had come. When they were back in the garage, he said, 'Look, me hearty, I'm gasping for a drink and I haven't eaten in hours. Any chance of some grub?'

'You were in the navy?'

'Boy and man. Twenty-two years.'

'Where did you serve?'

'*Ark Royal*, *Achilles*, Deeks, among others.' Deeks meant the Royal Naval Detention Centre. Kev sank back into the deckchair, still nursing the pain in his groin.

'You were banged up?'

'Nothing much. I just got caught.'

'Were you in the Falklands?'

'I missed the Falklands.'

'You didn't miss much.'

'Were you there?'

'I was on the *Ardent*.'

'Bloody hell! You had it rough.'

'Rough doesn't describe it.'

HMS Ardent had been sunk in the Falklands War after being attacked by Argentine aircraft.

'Not a lot I can say,' said Kev. 'You lose oppos?'

'I lost two. The best. You never forget.'

'I'm sorry, mate. And then the bloody plague comes along.'

The man hesitated at the door of the garage, as if making up his mind.

'I'm Alec,' he said. 'I'll sort you some scran.'

He locked him in but came back ten minutes later with a flask of coffee, a bottle of water and a cheese sandwich.

'You're a star,' said Kev, but Alec didn't linger.

Kev sat in the deckchair and ate. Thank God for small mercies and a fellow matelot. No ex-sailor could resist acknowledging a fellow member of the service. In other circumstances, they would be swapping stories over several drinks. Maybe they would still be able to swap stories. Alec was his best bet for information.

Dusk was settling when Alec returned. The cosh still dangled from his wrist on its strap and he leaned with his back against the door. When Kev began to get out of the deckchair, he said, 'I'd prefer it if you stayed put.'

Kev raised his hands to show acquiescence and slumped back.

'Where do I pee?' he said.

'There's a bucket in the corner.'

'Thanks for the food.'

The man shrugged. 'What did you do in the navy?' he said.

'Electrician. You?'

'Chippy.'

'Plenty of work for you now, then,' said Kev. 'I'm bleeding redundant.' Alec shrugged again. 'What's the gen about Steel, then? Is it worth joining?'

'Depends what you want. I don't get to do much joinery.'

'The tour's got to stop sometime. There's the population of a town out there. I saw them when I arrived. Sooner or later, they're going to have to settle down. Then you'll be back in demand as a chippy.'

'I'm not sure I want to be.'

'You prefer life on the move?'

'I'm still making up my mind whether I like life at all.'

Kev nodded. 'You lose family?'

'My wife, three kids. The eldest had just started university. The first in both our families to go to university.' He shook his head imperceptibly. 'We were proud.'

Kev remained silent. This was a loss that deserved respect.

'How about you?'

'Wife and daughter,' Kev said. He started to smile as the memories returned, then dipped his head when tears threatened. Dampness in his eyes. He'd controlled it for so long that it was a shock that this casual reminder of his personal devastation could have such a powerful effect. The question had been unexpected and all his carefully constructed emotional defences were down. He sniffed and pinched the top of his nose between finger and thumb so he could also brush away any tear surreptitiously. 'Sorry,' he said. 'I'm fucked if I know where that came from.'

They allowed the silence to stretch. Neither was in a hurry. Kev took deep breaths and put his memories away for a later date. He looked up and grinned at his captor.

'Sorry,' he said again. 'I don't usually cry.'

'Have you never cried? Over them?'

'No.' The grin went. 'I always felt that if I started, I'd never stop.'

'You can't bottle it up forever. It'll have to come out eventually.'

Another silence. Eventually, Alec started to speak in a low even voice without inflection.

'It was the same with the Ardent. Guilt, anger, loss. Why them, not me? I bottled it up after the Falklands for years. Then one night, we were down in Plymouth, the wife and me, getting ready for the annual reunion. It was a black tie job and I always wore a proper dickie. Halfway through the night I liked to loosen it, so it hung there like James Bond. You know?'

Kev nodded.

'I'm in front of the mirror, tying the bloody thing when I started crying. Couldn't stop. I sort of crumpled onto the floor. The wife sat on the floor with me. She just held me. It all came back. The noise, the fire. I'd been aft and was ordered for'ard. A minute after I left, we were hit exactly where I'd been. Mates gone. We lost twenty-two men. I didn't have a scratch. We didn't go to the dinner that night. I never went to another reunion. You'd think that would have prepared me for what happened when the plague came but it didn't. I still haven't cried for Rose and the kids. Still haven't made my mind up whether to join them or not. And that's another guilt trip. Why am I still here making my mind up? Why not just do it?'

'So in the meantime, you joined Steel's army.'

He shrugged. 'If you can call it an army. Maybe one day I'll cry and make a proper decision.'

Kev sniffed again and blinked his eyes. 'I hadn't thought about them for a while,' he said, meaning his own family. 'I conditioned myself not to.'

'What were they called?'

'Our lass was Alison. Our girl was Bethany. Bloody silly name, but Ali chose it.' The dampness returned. 'Bethany was sixteen. I didn't get married until after I left the navy. She was a corker. A heartbreaker. Used to send me mad. The number of lads I gave warnings to. They called me Mad Jack. They all knew I'd been in the navy, see?' He took a deep breath and was in control again. 'All I want now is a peaceful life. And I end up here, getting my bollocks kicked and threatened by a bloke who looks like a serial killer who is called Chef.'

Alec laughed.

'He's called Chef because he likes to carve. People. His weapon of choice is a cutthroat razor. He has a lot of razors. He carries them in a canvas bag, all neat and tidy. They're sharp enough to cut the nose right off your face. That's what he does.'

'Shit. And he doesn't like me.'

'As long as Steel says you live, you'll be okay.'

'I didn't think Steel went in for torture?'

'He doesn't. But Chef believes in making an example. He likes cutting off noses and ears.'

'Are there many like him in Steel's army?'

'It's not really an army. Just a big gathering. Lost people who got together. Steel happens to be leading it. Those at the top give orders and the rest of us have got into the habit of obeying.'

'And if you don't, you lose your nose.'

'That's always a possibility.'

'I think I've changed my mind. Maybe I should have taken my chances at Haven. At least they believe in peace and quiet and minding their own business. After meeting the Chef, village life suddenly appeals.'

'It wouldn't have made any difference if you'd gone to Haven. We're going there next.'

They exchanged a long look.

'And you're not going as farmers?' said Kev.

'Steel takes. He has a lot of people to feed.'

'As I said, sooner or later, his army or gathering or whatever you call it, is going to have to settle down.'

Alec shrugged to indicate it didn't matter to him one way or the other.

'Are there many like the Chef?' Kev asked. 'Blokes who enjoy the violence, I mean?'

'Steel used to own nightclubs. He used to hand pick his bouncers. Always had a good eye for thuggery. He has a hard core of thugs, his storm troopers. Chef is his number two. The rest of us just follow along. Once you're in, you're in. Or you can walk away without some of your body parts.'

'Then it looks like I'm fucked.'

Alec came back when it was fully dark outside. He brought the thermos flask back with more coffee and a bowl of lukewarm stew. He lit a candle stub and remained by the door as before. They swapped stories about their time in the service. About old comrades and outrageous shore leave.

'Why does everybody have to get a tattoo?' Alec said.

'You've got one,' Kev pointed out.

'An anchor on my arm like fucking Popeye and the tail of a fox disappearing down my back passage.'

'Tasteful.'

'How about you?' Alec said.

Kev pulled up the sleeve of his shirt to display a faded banner on which were written two words.

'What's it say?'

'Mum and Dad,' said Kev with a shrug. 'I was seventeen and all these other daft bastards were getting daggers and mottoes like *Death Before Dishonour*. Death Before Dishonour? I had Mum and Dad.' He laughed. 'You're right though. Everybody had one. I had a cousin who came down to Plymouth for a weekend on the lash and decided he wanted one and he wasn't even in the Navy. He wanted an eagle. You know, a big rampant bird of prey. We got him pissed on scrumps and took him to Doc Price. He hadn't a clue. When he woke up he went mental when he saw the tattoo – a budgie on a perch.'

They both laughed, good unfettered laughter.

'What did he say?'

'He never spoke to me again. No loss. He was a prat.'

The chuckles continued until Kev said, 'Actually, I do have another tattoo. Two in fact.'

'What is it?'

'I was very young, very drunk and very stupid.'

'Weren't we all.'

'No, I mean *very* stupid.'

'Not Ludo on your dick?'

'My dick's not big enough for Ludo. I had a tattoo on my arse.'

'Of what?'

Kev grimaced and said, 'A pair of eyes. One on each buttock.'

Alec laughed and said, 'Go on, then. Show us.'

'Bugger off. I don't mind showing them in the pub but not in a half lit garage with one bloke for company.'

'I take your point,' said Alec, still laughing. 'Two eyes?'

'Not just ordinary eyes. Big fluttery come-to-bed eyes. Barbie eyes. I had it done in Amsterdam. I should have gone back and killed the tattooist. You can stick a cigar up me bum and call me Groucho. In fact, I often did. It was my party trick in the mess.'

Alec laughed louder and shook his head. 'One day, I'll get you in a pub and remind you.'

'When that happens, I'll show you.'

Chapter 17

SHIRLEY AND MYRA DECIDED TO LEAVE HAVEN THAT EVENING. They hadn't come to be involved in war, they said. They were looking for somewhere peaceful to settle. Perhaps they would head north. They were given supplies for the road and waved off. Arnie stood in the square with the others and watched them go.

'You staying, Arnie?' the Rev Nick said.

'I'll sleep on it,' he said. 'Maybe I'll head north like the ladies. Maybe I'll stay.' He glanced round in the late evening of summer. Lamps were lit in some of the windows of the cottages. 'This is a lovely place. I can see why you want to keep it, but I'm not sure if it's my fight.'

'Sleep on it, then,' said Nick. 'It's your decision.'

'Where's Reaper?'

'Out patrolling. He never sleeps.'

'Do you approve of him, padre?'

'Reaper guided us here. I was one of the originals. We have a lot to thank him for.' He fell silent for a moment.

'But sometimes, I just wish he wouldn't be so quick to fight.'

'Sounds like he needs religion.'

'Oh, he has that. With Brother Abraham in York. He'll be there again tomorrow at noon. I think the number of deaths for which he is responsible is beginning to prey on his mind. All those people he has killed. He is in need of greater absolution than I can give, which is why he visits Abraham. He takes his guilt straight to God. Just him and Brother Abraham at high noon, doing penance on his knees at Clifford's Tower.'

'What's Clifford's Tower?'

'It's the site of an ancient massacre. Brother Abraham has declared it a holy site and instigated the fifty-five steps.'

'And what are they?'

'There are fifty-five steps up to the Tower and Reaper will climb them on his knees. He's done it before. A prayer on each step. It's a steep climb.'

'Sounds barmy.'

'It's medieval. But that's Abraham's influence. Reaper's done it before and I suppose this time he's doing it in the hope of plenary indulgences before he goes to war again. I sometimes wonder ...'

'What, padre? What do you wonder?'

'Nothing, Arnie. I'm a pacifist and Reaper isn't. We've been in conflict before but we agree to disagree.'

'With respect, that's an impossible thing to do. You still

disagree. You want peace and he wants war. Someone has to give in.'

'True.'

'And Reaper never gives in?'

'It would take an act of God to make Reaper change his mind.'

'Maybe God will talk to him in York tomorrow?'

'We can but pray, Arnie.'

John Steel sprawled on a sofa in the puce lounge bar of the private hotel. An attractive woman in her early twenties lay on the sofa, her legs up, cuddled beneath his arm. Battery lamps were lit and had been placed on the bar and the tables. Chef, without his leather overcoat, sat on a high stool drinking coffee. Sheila and Myra sat side by side on a long settee and Arnie had an armchair. Alec was away from the light, a listener on the periphery, in an easy chair. The lamps gave the gathering the texture of a painting by Edward Hopper.

'I don't like it,' said Chef. 'It's too easy.'

'You don't like anything,' said Steel.

'I can smell a con.'

'I don't think so. They wouldn't risk taking their militia to York for an ambush and leaving Haven wide open. And they can't stage an ambush with half a dozen girls.' He looked at Arnie. 'They *were* girls?'

'That's right. All dressed up like Angel was, vests and

guns. They look the part. But they might not even be there. Reaper sent them out loaded with rations. I reckon they're keeping watch on the other side of the bridge.'

'So,' said Steel. 'He could be on his own. And if he's not, all he's got are a bunch of girls. Maybe he has a thing about women in uniform.'

'You're taking him too lightly,' said Chef.

'He has a reputation, but against what? My nan could have put the frighteners on the locals in this town. Anyway, I don't smell a con. He hasn't had time to set one up. All he's doing is fortifying Haven. The other places will stay out of it. When push comes to shove, the other towns won't send any men. They'll stay put and wait to see what happens. It's human nature. They don't want to provoke anything so that, when it's over, they can be our friends.' He grinned. 'And give us everything we want.'

'We could do with some more women,' Arnie said.

'I'm sure some of their ladies can be persuaded,' said Steel. 'And there will be a lot of widows if it comes to a fight.'

'It's a nice place,' said Shirley. 'They've made it work.'

'I'm very pleased for them,' Steel said. 'We'll try not to damage it too much, so they can keep on making it work for us. But, if we do this right, we won't have to damage it at all.' He looked at Arnie again.' There are those who don't like the way Reaper operates?'

'The vicar's pissed off. Maybe that's partly because this

Brother Abraham has most of the glory at York Minster. But some of the others on the council seem pissed off, too. From what they say, Reaper has gone overkill. Maybe he's losing it. The vicar suggested as much. That's why Reaper goes to York. Bigger church, a bigger God on his side.'

Steel laughed. 'That's a very poetic way of looking at it. Maybe he's gone mad, like that wandering stray told us. Him and Abraham both. Two mad people trying to find salvation.'

'You're talking shit,' said Chef. 'He's setting you up.'

'What? You think I'm going to York to face him down, man to man? Now you're saying I'm mad. If I go to York, I'll be taking plenty with me. Enough to remove him from the game, even if it is a con.'

'It's not a game and it is a con,' said Chef.

'You worry too much. Take here and now as a bonus. We should all have been dead a year ago. But we didn't die. We're the lucky ones. Enjoy the journey. Enjoy the adventure. Enjoy the carvery.'

The last remark gained Chef's attention. 'You've decided about our visitor?'

'Not really. He may have been sent by Reaper or he may be a lost soul. Either way, he's disposable and we can't let him go. In the morning, you can have Kevin whatsisname. Happy now?'

Chef didn't look happy. 'What are you going to do tomorrow?'

'I'm going to York. It's a chance to end it before it begins.

I don't want to go fighting a well-armed militia. You say they're well dug in, Arnie?'

'Around the manor house, up on the hill and by the front gate. Back gate too, I suppose, although I didn't get to look there. Mortars and machineguns.'

'Mortars and machineguns,' Steel said to Chef. 'They could do a lot of damage. It's best if we take them into our protective custody before they are fired at us in anger. Don't you agree?'

'You think you can do this by killing Reaper?'

'Oh yes. Remove him and the rest will be happy to have peace. Especially if we garland it with lies. And once we're in charge, they won't be able to complain. Anyway, they won't have time. They'll be working too hard for us.'

'How will you do it?'

'I'll do it quick. I'll take the Thunderers. Drive straight to this Clifford's Tower just after noon, when Reaper is on his knees. And kill him.'

'And if he's expecting you?'

'If he's expecting me with his little girl soldiers, then they'll get a surprise, because I'll be taking the Donny Boys as well. I'll give them an incentive. I'll tell them they can have the girls.' He glanced at Arnie. 'Didn't you say they were fit, Arnie?'

'As butchers' dogs.'

Steel grinned at Chef. 'Don't you just love it when a plan comes together?'

'But whose plan?' said Chef.

Kev was awakened in the middle of the night by someone unlocking the door. When it opened, Alec stepped inside carrying a lamp. The shadows were deep but Kev could see he still carried the cosh on a cord around his wrist. He stepped to one side and revealed Chef.

The lamplight didn't improve the man's appearance. It accentuated the sharpness of his face so that he looked like a Gothic vampire. He pulled open the leather coat he wore and rested his hands on his hips. It was a pose reminiscent of a Gestapo officer. *Yes, we have ways of making you talk.* He took a razor from his waistcoat pocket and opened the blade with a practised flick of the wrist.

Kev remained in the deckchair. Chef took two steps towards him and kicked him on the knee. He screamed and fell out of the chair and rolled into a corner, tins and pieces of wood falling over. The kick had come from a steel capped boot and Kev wasn't sure whether his knee cap was smashed or not.

'Tomorrow, you'll be my responsibility,' said Chef, casually. The man crouched near him and Kev wondered whether he could reach him in time to throttle the bastard. He turned his head but such a move was not possible. Chef held the razor in his right hand. Its curved blade had a wicked sheen in the lamplight. 'We'll talk then. After breakfast,' he said. 'I'll carve.'

He made moves with the razor in front of Kev's face

before laughing, getting up and walking out. Kev rolled onto his back and looked towards Alec but he had gone. He heard the key turn in the lock.

What another brilliant cock-up he'd ridden into, he thought. Just like his life.

And, as he lay on the concrete, he let the memories in, not the ones from his navy days, but the precious ones from his marriage and his family. He remembered all the good times with Ali and Bethany and the tears came and he didn't try to stop them.

Alec returned to the garage before dawn. He carried a lamp, turned low, and a flask of coffee. He waited until Kev had opened the flask, poured the coffee and begun to sip it before he spoke. 'You're from Haven,' he said.

Kev looked up at him from the deckchair, trying to read his expression in the shadows.

'Have they sent you to question me, matey? Make friends, then question me?'

'You're from Haven,' he repeated. 'We sent people to spy on you and they sent you to spy on us.'

'If I was from Haven, what would happen?'

'Chef would kill you.'

'Chef's going to do that anyway.'

'No, just your nose and ears.'

'That's nice. A comforting thought.'

He sniffed the coffee. He should make the most of his nose while he still had it.

'They said Haven is a good place,' said Alec. 'People work hard but the returns are good.'

'Do they?'

'They say the Reaper has gone mad with all the killing and surrounds himself with girls in uniform.'

'Lucky man. That's the way to go mad. Surround yourself with girls.' Kev sipped his coffee.

Alec watched him. 'You're from Haven,' Alec said, 'and it doesn't matter whether you admit it or not, because Chef will carve you up so badly you'll want to be dead.'

'All right. I'm from Haven. And you're right. It is a good place. A place worth fighting for. Dying for.'

Another silence.

'Have you cried any more?' Alec said.

Kev looked him in the eyes. 'Yes. Thought I better had while I had the chance.' He smiled. 'I feel better. You know why? Because now I can let the memories back in. I can think of them and smile. There'll still be tears, but I have the memories back.'

Alec nodded in understanding.

'How about you?' Kev said. 'Have you decided about life, yet?'

'Not yet. But I'm thinking about it.'

Kev drank coffee and dawn crept nearer. 'Steel will have a fight on his hands, you know,' he said. 'It won't be a walkover. My people are trained, prepared and well armed.'

'Our reports say all the Reaper has are the girls. And they're just girls.'

Kev smiled.' I wouldn't want the girls to hear you say that.'

'Reputations get blown out of all proportion. That's what they say.'

Kev shrugged.

'They also say the Reaper isn't liked any more. That the rest of them at Haven would make a deal without a fight if they could only get rid of him.'

'They say that, do they?'

'They say that.'

'What do you want me to do? Confirm it? Deny it?'

'I'd like to know if he does have support.'

'So you can tell Steel?'

'Steel has already made up his mind. You have a priest at Haven? A vicar?'

Kev nodded.

'The vicar said the Reaper is now best pals with Brother Abraham at York. That he goes there for confession and absolution. That he'll be there today at noon. All alone, except maybe for Angel. There for the taking. That's what the priest said and Steel believes it.'

Nice one, Kev thought to himself.

'Chef thinks it's a con,' Alec added.

The Chef would.

'Steel is not stupid. He's taking his top crew with him.

299

Thirty blokes, all street fighters, all well armed. They're battle hardened. The Thunderers. They all wear the same boots with steel toecaps. When they are on the march, you can hear them coming but there's fuck all you can do to stop them.'

Kev nodded. If Reaper just had Sandra and the team with him, the odds would be dangerous with seven of them facing down thirty.

Alec said, 'He's also taking extra insurance. The Donny Boys. Surprise, surprise, they're from Doncaster. They're a hard gang, been together a year. They don't have a lot of discipline but they're brutal. Steel says they can have the girls. A sort of incentive.'

If Reaper was setting up an ambush, it was in danger of going drastically wrong. And he was sitting in a deckchair in a garage in Cleethorpes drinking coffee.

'Why are you telling me?' he said.

'I thought you'd want to know.'

Kev judged the distance between them, how quickly he could get out of the deckchair and whether he could beat the swing of the cosh that hung from his captor's wrist.

'You wouldn't make it,' said Alec.

'What time is Steel leaving?'

'Nine o'clock.'

'What time is Chef coming to carve me?'

Alec shrugged. 'Sometime after they've gone.'

'You could help me?'

'That would get me killed and I'm still thinking about life.'
'What about my bike?'
'It's still there. The keys are in it.'
'So all I have to do is reach the bike?'
'Then ride it through an army.'

Chapter 18

THE SPECIAL FORCES MET ON THE OUTSKIRTS OF YORK at midnight and left their vehicles down a side street so they would be out of sight of any patrol that Foster might send out. They walked to the apartment in Monkgate that they had used before, ensured a blackout before lighting a dim lamp in the living room, and settled down to wait. Seven of them crowded the small room, but they were off the street and in reasonable comfort. They used the sofa and the armchair and the twin beds and tried to rest.

An hour before dawn, Sandra kicked them alert, although only James was asleep. She had taken the last watch. They checked their equipment and moved out through the darkness, heading north of Monkbar along a road called Lord Mayor's Walk that paralleled the wall towards St John University buildings. They moved into the cover of trees on the grass embankment that fronted the castle wall. Reaper had scouted the area earlier. One of the trees was close to the wall itself, and with the help of a rope he soon climbed the tree until he was level with the crenellated rampart.

He went over it silently and with great care, although he was convinced that Foster would only have a few guards on duty and that those would be at the obvious entry places. Like everything else about the world the man was creating, the security of the city was built on pretence.

The others followed and he watched with approval: Sandra, Jenny, Tanya, Keira, Yank and James, all dark with face paint, all heavily armed, all at a peak of readiness. Reaper was feeling the excitement, so he knew they would be, too. They had studied maps they had found in the manor house library: of the city; the Minster and the Treasurer's House. Both buildings had been tourist attractions and there were several guide books. Mary had added to their knowledge with hand drawn diagrams giving greater detail.

Now they were inside the walls, dawn was approaching and a persistent drizzle fell. The bulk of the Minster was ahead of them and, before that, the back garden of the Treasurer's House. They went over the safety railing onto the sloping roof of a garage in a yard, and lowered themselves to the cobbles below. They went right, away from the Monkbar, and down a short private driveway towards the Minster, keeping to the grass verge to avoid noise. The grand house where Foster was supposed to be sleeping was to their right.

They emerged on another cobbled lane behind the towering church. Tanya and Jenny headed for the front entrance to the Minster, Keira and Yank to the Chapter House at the rear. The Minster was where the people were being kept, so it would be necessary to remove their guards and free them.

Sandra went to the Treasurer's House that was located in its own grounds at the rear of the Minster. The gate into the gardens at the front was unlocked and she slipped inside and went left, round the edges of the shrubbery to reach the building and avoid the open expanse of lawn out front. James remained near the gate, hidden in the bushes, his carbine levelled and ready.

Reaper took a different route onto Goodramgate. His priority was to rescue Brother Abraham before anything else happened. He encountered no patrols. The street was silent, the pavements glistening in the wet, no lights showed. He stopped at the entrance to the enclosed garden churchyard but heard nothing. If Abraham was still in residence, his guards would undoubtedly be sleeping inside rather than outside in this weather.

He stayed on the grass rather than the path and reached the porch at the entrance of the church. The dim flickering glow of what had to be an oil lamp showed within the church. With great care, he turned the door handle. The door was unlocked. He slipped inside, closing the door behind him and waited for his eyes to become accustomed to the gloom.

ANGEL

The lamp rested on a table at the back of the church. Reaper took two steps to the side and laid the L85 that he carried on the floor and out of sight. He removed a Glock from its holster with his right hand. He had no intention of killing anyone if at all possible. Snores came from a box pew a few feet down the south aisle. He leaned over the side and saw the shape of a big man on the bench, a cricket bat propped up against the pew in front. The door to the pew was half open and he took the bat with his left hand and was lifting it high to clear the sides when he heard a noise behind him. A voice, still heavy with sleep, said, 'What the fuck?' and Reaper swung the bat round in an arc as he turned and clobbered a shadowy figure who had sat up in another pew.

The big man from whom he had taken the cricket bat still slept, and Reaper looked into the pew across the aisle to discover the large woman whom he had previously seen on guard duty sprawled unconscious in a heap on the stone flags.

Surely there would be no more guards?

'Who's there?'

Abraham called from the front of the North Aisle where he and Reaper had last met. A match scratched and a candle was lit. The religious leader was illuminated in a halo of light to produce a portrait that would not have looked out of place in one of the church's stained glass windows.

'It's Reaper. How many guards are there?'

'Reaper?' Abraham was surprised. 'Two. There are two guards.'

The man in the pew stirred.

'What is it?' He began to sit up. 'Deirdre?'

Reaper pointed the gun in his face. 'Don't do anything stupid.'

'Where's Deirdre?'

'Taking a nap.' He raised his voice to call to Abraham. 'Are you ready to leave?'

'Absolutely.'

The monk left his sleeping pew and walked briskly down the aisle to the rear of the church, bringing the candle with him.

'Is there anywhere we can put them?' Reaper asked.

Abraham glanced over the side of the pew at the collapsed form of the women.

'Is she …?'

'Sleeping.' He raised the cricket bat. 'And I haven't played in years.'

'The vestry,' Abraham said, and pointed back the way he had come.

'You!' Reaper told the conscious guard. 'Pick up Deirdre and carry her to the vestry!'

He stepped back to give the man room to comply with the command and he crouched and struggled to lift the woman.

'She's a big girl,' he grumbled.

'I either lock you up or I hit you for six,' he said, raising the bat.

The man heaved and dragged the woman into a sitting position; heaved again and put her over his shoulder in a fireman's lift. It wasn't very elegant but then, as the man said, she was a big girl.

Abraham led the way to the small room at the front of the church. Once the man and woman were inside, there was not a lot of room.

Reaper told the man, 'Foster is finished. Special Forces have taken the city. If you have any sense at all, you will stay here until you are let out. Try to escape and you could get seriously hurt.' He levelled the Glock at him. 'Do you understand?'

'Yes.' He nodded several times. 'We'll stay put. Never did like Foster, anyway.'

'Sensible chap.'

He closed the door and Brother Abraham locked it.

'They're not the worst of his followers,' the monk said, in mitigation. 'They just lost direction for a while. Where now?'

Reaper led the way out of the church, the monk following.

'Your people are being held in the Minster. We free them and capture Foster.'

'You're not going to use guns in the Minster, are you?'

'Not if we can help it.' They were outside and the

sky was brightening, despite the rain. Reaper stopped abruptly in the churchyard and turned to Abraham, who had an eagerness in his face, now that he had been freed. 'Abraham, you have to know. They killed Rebecca as the girls escaped.'

The life drained from the monk's face, which went slack with shock.

'Rebecca?' He whispered the name. 'Dead?'

'A bolt from a crossbow in her back. She died instantly.'

'Cedric.' He whispered this name with venom. 'It was Cedric.'

'We took her to Haven and buried her. The Reverend said the words. Mary was with her.'

Tears welled in Abraham's eyes and he turned away and held onto a gravestone. He took a deep breath and his shoulders straightened and when he turned back to Reaper, his face was composed but grim.

'Cedric deserves damnation,' he said, softly.

'He'll get it,' said Reaper.

They left the churchyard, taking a rear path, and headed for the Minster.

The Treasurer's House was a handsome 17th century building. Two wings jutted out at the front while the main entrance was recessed between them and reached up half a dozen stone steps. Sandra crouched with her back against the ivy-covered wall of one of the wings. She had discovered in the last year that there were no such things as neatly worked plans. You started with broad outlines and hoped to get an end result. In between, you adapted. You made instant decisions, that were often a matter of life and death, and about which you could not stop to think until everything was over. Even then, some things were best not thought about.

She looked across the lawn towards the undergrowth and gates where she knew James was hidden. The boy they had found in a public school had matured into a dispassionate sniper. At least, he seemed to have matured and he seemed to be dispassionate, but she knew assumptions could be wrong. Who knew anybody totally? Everybody had thoughts and secrets; fears and hopes and shames, that they kept to themselves.

Who really knew her? She smiled as memories of Jamie surfaced. Even Jamie hadn't known her. Would he have come to know her, had they lived a longer life together?

Once again, she reflected that the plague had given her opportunities beyond her wildest dreams. Anybody's wildest dreams. This was now a different world heading in a different direction. Before, she had worked in Top Shop and dreamed of going to Technical College and then maybe, just *maybe*, on to university. Before, she would have never met Jamie, and if she had, they would never have socialised much less married.

Before, she wouldn't have dreamed of coming to York:

a tourist city full of history and teashops and a superior university that was way above her ambitions. She had actually considered which university might have been suitable. To be honest, whichever university that would have allowed her to sneak in the back door and come out again with a degree. 'The only thing I passed was the school gates,' her mother used to say. 'I want to see you pass everything. I want to be there with the other parents when you get your degree and you throw that mortar board in the air.'

And she hadn't even started the foundation course at Tech.

But she would have done. She had had a plan and the motivation and she would have got the necessary qualifications and sneaked into her local redbrick university and completed a degree and her mum would have been proud. She wondered if she would still have been proud to see her now and she looked up into the persistent drizzle for confirmation. Of course she would. Proud that she had survived and proud she had helped others survive.

Different rules, now mum, different tests. But I think I graduated.

She rotated her head as her neck started to stiffen and wondered when Brother Barry Foster, former medium and hypnotist and now High Sheriff of York, would get up to begin ruling his subjects. The plan – the vague, broadly outlined plan – was that Reaper would bring Abraham to the Minster and that the monk would release those inside by strength of personality, plus the weapons held by Tanya, Keira, Jenny and Yank, and without bloodshed. Once that was accomplished, they could call Foster out and invite him to surrender peacefully. What came next depended largely on Brother Abraham and his followers. They might forgive some of those who had been tempted briefly towards the dark side, and banish others who had displayed signs of dangerous aggression.

The rules here were different to the ones by which she and Reaper operated; this was someone else's community. But someone should pay for killing Rebecca, even though the delineations between right, wrong and insane were not clear. Who was really evil? Who was mad? Could they impose a trial and execution? The possibility had been in the back of her mind for a while, before York had become an issue. As the federation grew, crimes were bound to happen. They would have need of courts and a form of justice that aspired to something slightly more formal than a bullet in the back of the head. The days of being judge, jury and executioner, through which she and Reaper had strode, were coming to an end. Even the Wild West had eventually succumbed to the rule of law. Of course, they had also had Clint Eastwood and his kind of justice had stayed in fashion for an awful long time.

Dawn had slunk in with the rain. The sky was a grey backdrop, with heavy darker clouds, moving across it on a brisk breeze, as if looking for trouble. Had Reaper freed Brother Abraham yet?

Abraham and Reaper approached the Minster obliquely from the rear of Goodramgate, staying under the cover of trees that fringed a grassy area by the Minster Yard. It was a compressed space between the end of the shopping street of Stonegate and the front of the Gothic cathedral. Reaper had considered it as an ideal place to stage his planned ambush of John Steel, but even he had baulked at spilling blood on the Minster steps or even inside the great church itself, and he knew Abraham would have opposed such a plan vehemently.

There was still a chance that blood would be spilt but Reaper hoped they could avoid such an eventuality. He could see Tanya and Jenny either side of the Minster entrance and surmised the guards would be inside, imposing control, rather than outside in the rain, watching for possible danger. He signalled to them, and then he and Abraham ran across the Minster Yard and up the steps to join them, the monk holding up his white robes so that he could run more easily.

'There's movement inside,' said Tanya. 'Although most still seem to be asleep.'

'Where are the people sleeping?' Reaper asked Abraham.

'In the nave. To the left, as you go in.'

'Right,' said Reaper. Tanya and Jenny waited for instructions; Brother Abraham didn't: he pushed open the doors and went inside. 'Shit,' said Reaper.

Tanya and Jenny followed in the wake of the monk, guns at the ready.

'Put down your weapons, brothers and sisters,' Abraham called, in a clear and commanding voice. 'This schism is over. Brother Barry is exposed and deposed. We can return to our peaceful ways.'

Which was when gunshots sounded from behind the Minster in the direction of the Treasurer's House.

Sandra heard sounds within the house and straightened up, her back tight against the ivy-covered wall, her carbine held upright and at the ready. She glanced across the lawn again but still could see no sign of James. She hoped he was still there and hadn't disappeared to answer a call of nature. What had Yank said? Do as I do. Pee.

She grinned to herself and could well imagine Yank doing just that without any feeling of embarrassment. Why should there be embarrassment if lives depended on staying in position? Her thoughts were rambling and she felt the tension; her heartbeat increased. It was always the same. Start the frigging action and she would be fine, but nerves still kicked in beforehand when she had time to consider how many things could go wrong. Plans? Forget plans. *React*.

The doors opened. She waited three seconds and stepped round the corner, the carbine levelled.

'Drop the guns. You're under arrest,' she said, wondering where the words had come from as she spoke them.

Barry Foster, High Sheriff of York, was wearing black velvet trousers tucked into black knee-high boots, a black velvet shirt and a gold cross that hung around his neck on a thick gold chain. Over his shoulders was a black cape. Around his waist was an old fashioned brown leather military belt and a holster that held a handgun. It was an impressive outfit on a very mediocre-looking, middle-aged man with a paunch and a facial wart. With him were two tougher looking men, both carrying shotguns, who did not drop their weapons.

The nearest one raised his towards her, but before he could fire he was flung backwards against the wall and a single shot rang out. The second gunman made the mistake of pointing and firing his gun up the garden and James Marshall's second shot took him in the head and dropped him where he stood.

Foster turned and ran back into the house. Sandra had the opportunity to shoot but she didn't want to put a bullet in his back. Besides, she was still harbouring thoughts of arrest and trial. She ran after him.

Sandra followed him into a great hall with a tiled floor, huge fireplace and large paintings high on its walls. Foster was at the bottom of a staircase that looked as if it led to an enclosed minstrel's gallery. She fired a warning shot that chipped the banister and he stopped.

'You can't escape, Foster,' she said. 'Raise your arms and

I'll take you to Abraham. It's over and you're finished.'

Foster had his back towards her and he looked over his shoulder. He was assessing her. She had seen it before. He was making assumptions. She was a girl and he was a mature man who still had delusions of grandeur. When he did begin to turn, he did it in a way that the holster would remain hidden from her view for as long as possible.

'It's never over,' he said. 'It's just beginning.'

'Don't do it.'

Sandra's gun never wavered and she gave him all the time in the world to change his mind as she saw his right arm move and he took the gun from the holster.

'My dear,' he said. 'I think there has been a misunderstanding. But it is nothing that can't …'

He began to turn more quickly, his left arm raised but his right hand at waist level, holding the gun. She shot him without compunction. Chest shot. He bounced back on the stairs and ended up on the first landing. She took three steps closer, aimed and fired the second shot. Head and chest. Always make sure.

For a few long seconds, she listened to the silence of the house. She sensed it was empty, except maybe for ghosts. Wasn't there supposed to be a Roman legion in the cellar? Well, now they had a new recruit.

Sandra walked out of the house and stopped on the steps. James was in the middle of the lawn, his gun levelled. He lowered it when he saw that it was her and nodded an acknowledgement. She nodded back. Their part of the plan was over.

Reaper ran down the cobbled lane round the back of the Minster and in through the front gate of the Treasurer's House. He stopped because James had turned at the sound of his approach and had him covered. James lowered the weapon. Sandra was on the steps leading into the house, in between two bodies.

'Foster's dead,' she said. 'He's inside.'

He nodded, relief flooding him. He should have known better by now, but every time he and Sandra went their separate ways on a mission, he couldn't help but worry. Once again she had completed her part of the action with minimum fuss and full deadly affect. She came down the steps and onto the lawn.

'You okay, James?' he said.

The youth nodded. His face showed no emotion. Reaper hoped to God he was feeling some inside. He would hate to think he had created a fifteen-year-old cold killer. The time, the situation, the plague, the whole damn world had a lot to answer for.

As Sandra passed James, they exchanged a casual high five. Job done. Mission accomplished. Jesus Christ. The boy was fifteen and she was a nineteen-year-old veteran. What had he created? What had the world created? For a moment he was engulfed by an unexpected wave of doubt.

Was it all worth it?

'How's Abraham?' she said.

'He's okay. I haven't heard any shots. It sounds like he's persuaded the rest of them to give up.'

'The old charisma trick,' she said. 'Maybe we should try it sometime?'

He smiled.

'You think so?'

'Nah. I'll stick to the tried and trusted.' She slapped the carbine in her arms.

By the time they had walked round to the front of the Minster, Brother Abraham was once more in charge and, from the smiling faces, most of the people milling about outside were happy at the change of regime and the return of love and peace and total amateurism.

The monk's presence had worked in persuading Foster's followers to surrender, especially as he had been flanked by Tanya and Jenny. If any had had any doubt, Keira and Yank's appearance through the Chapter House at the rear had convinced them that a peaceful solution would be best all round.

The dozen or so insurrectionists who had surrendered, were being kept separate and under guard in the Minster Yard. They looked anxious and had already split into two groupings of what Reaper assumed were the hardliners and those who had been easily led and persuaded to go along for a ride that had ended unexpectedly.

Abraham joined Reaper, Brother Mark was at his side. The young monk had a bruised face as if he had taken a beating. It didn't seem to have bothered him. He remained slightly aloof, as usual, but he gave Reaper a nod of thanks.

'There is no sign of Cedric,' Abraham said.

Mark said, 'He may be at Monkbar. We are sending people to the guard posts to bring them in.' Reaper raised an eyebrow and Mark added, 'Guards were maintained at four points. Two at each.'

As Reaper had suspected, the security had been nominal.

'Thank you, Brother Reaper,' Abraham said, and held out his hand, and they shook. 'I think it's time that my people joined the federation and found villages in which to live and fields in which to work.'

'What about the Minster? Holy Trinity?'

'Perhaps it's time to put grandeur to one side. God doesn't only live in great palaces. He lives in men's hearts. Perhaps I had forgotten that.'

Reaper still couldn't work the man out. He had shown love, compassion, emotion. He had been as brave, or foolhardy, as a biblical martyr, marching into the Minster and assuming his presence alone would bring people to their senses, if not their knees. And yet he still spouted platitudes as if he was a genuine messenger of God.

'We need to talk,' Reaper said. 'I'm expecting a visitor.'

Reaper, Sandra, Abraham and Brother Mark conferred

on the steps of the Minster. Reaper explained about the confrontation at the Humber Bridge and the ambitions of John Steel. Abraham took the news that Reaper was planning an ambush in York with equanimity.

'So your coming here was not solely to release us from the bondage of the High Sheriff?' he said.

'Not entirely. Although we had motive enough after Rebecca's death.'

Abraham shook his head in sorrow.

'Why kill someone in such a brutal fashion just because she wanted to leave?' he said.

'We knew we would have to sort out this mess before long,' said Reaper. 'More people could have died. We had to come. But the threat of this man called Steel meant we came sooner rather than later.'

'You hope to entice him to York?'

'That's the idea.'

'Why York?'

'Because it's not Haven.'

'That's hardly a charitable reason.'

'York is unsustainable, you know that. Your people have to leave to survive. Society is being rebuilt in the villages of England, not the towns and cities. But York is somewhere that Steel could be contained. We have, hopefully, given him a target, a place and a time. If he bites, he will be here at noon to remove me and we'll be able to remove him and stop a war before it begins.'

Sandra said, 'That is always accepting that at least one of the people who visited Haven yesterday really was his spy and believed the information they were fed.' She shrugged. 'If they were just travellers, Steel won't come because he won't know.'

'There is that possibility,' said Reaper, concerned at Sandra's downbeat attitude. It was unlike her. 'But three people arrived at Haven yesterday, not long after the stand-off at the Humber. We assumed that at least one was a spy, sent by Steel.'

'Why make such an assumption?'

'Newcomers who turn up at Haven are rare, these days. Usually they get passed on from one of the other villages or outlying settlements. But these came directly to us. Two women travelling together and a man travelling alone. The man was the stronger suspect.'

Sandra said, 'Steel always intended to move across the Humber. He had heard the federation was doing well. We think the stand-off has pushed him into speeding up his plans. It's logical that he would send in a spy. We did. We sent someone to join Steel's army.'

Abraham said, 'So let's assume this man Steel does come. You said you were the target, Reaper. How?'

'The spies – if that's what they were – were told that I'm the one who wants war,' he said. 'Everyone else at Haven wants a negotiated peace. We told them that today at noon, I will be here in York, alone, doing the fifty-five steps.'

Abraham's eyes widened.

'Clifford's Tower?'

'They were told you are my confessor. My penance is to climb the fifty-five steps on my knees.' Reaper gave a twisted smile. 'They think I have become a convert. That I've become your disciple.'

'How very flattering,' said Abraham. 'So, what will you have us do?'

If Steel came, Reaper said, it would be along the approach to York that led to Clifford's Tower.

'I want the vehicles moved from the entrance to the city at that point so Steel has a clear run. Ideally, I want him to drive up Tower Street and turn into the square at the top, outside the museum.'

'What if he doesn't do what you want?' asked Sandra. 'What if he sends someone on foot to shoot you from a distance.'

'I don't think that's his style. I think he enjoys confrontation. Besides, he won't risk a long shot if he can make sure by getting up close and making it personal.'

'It's you that's taking the risk,' she said.

He shrugged. Everything was a risk. To Abraham, he said, 'I want the vehicles moving from Monkbar, too, to give us an escape route, if it's necessary. There will be other things, but I need to check the tower itself and the killing ground.' Abraham winced. 'And I want all your people out of York or in hiding by eleven at the latest. This is not their fight.'

Abraham looked at Mark, who nodded. They would do what was necessary.

Chapter 19

AS SOON AS DAYLIGHT ILLUMINATED THE INTERIOR of the garage, Kev once more took stock of what might be either used as a tool to effect an escape or a weapon with which to protect himself against Chef. The motorbike was outside in the yard and, if he got that far, he would be happy to take his chances. The garage was solid and if he attempted any serious hammering or kicking, he had no doubt guards would be sent in immediately to stop him. At about nine, he heard engines start up in the distance. A door opened, voices shouted and the door banged. The engines were revved up and a convoy departed.

Reaper was on borrowed time.

All he wanted now was for Chef to come to enjoy his fun and Alec to stand to one side and give him a chance. Come on, me hearty. What's keeping you?

It was after ten before Kev heard footsteps. He got out

of the deckchair and stepped back into what was left of the shadows. The garage door opened but it wasn't Alec who stepped inside. This was a man he hadn't seen before. Medium height but big with muscle. He wore jeans, boots and a beer belly. He wore a torn tee shirt but he looked nothing like Bruce Willis. He carried no weapon; his arms looked lethal on their own.

'This him?' he said.

Chef stepped round him. 'It is indeed,' he said. He had dispensed with his full-length black leather coat and looked skinny in his cowboy boots, black jeans and a black vest. Skinny but deadly dangerous. His arms were ropes of muscle.

Kev said, 'Look, all I wanted to do was join your lot. If you don't want me, I can soon be on my way.'

'You soon will be on your way,' said Chef, with a smile. He placed the canvas bag he carried on the workbench and unrolled it. It contained eight or nine cutthroat razors. He chose one, took it out with care and opened the blade. 'This is hand-made in France. Sheffield steel and an olive wood handle. A Thiers Issard.' He pronounced the words with a French accent and inspected the razor with affection, then folded it and put it away. 'Too good for you,' he said. 'We need something a little more prosaic.' He chose another. 'This is a German one. Utilitarian, carbon steel and celluloid handle.'

He moved it in the air in front of him as if making

practice moves.

'A little carvery with this to loosen up the wrist and then, if you're good, I may use the Thiers Issard to finish.'

'You're a maniac.'

Chef smiled at him. 'That's been said before and I take it as a compliment. Now, you won't feel a thing. At first. The pain comes later. About ten seconds later.'

'Do you want me to get him?' asked Torn Vest.

'I don't think he'll give us any trouble, Vincent. I'll make you a deal,' he said to Kev. 'Cooperate and I'll be quick. Fight me and I'll cut your face to ribbons. You'll need a sewing machine to put it back together.'

He moved forward and Kev stiffened as if in panic, his arms stretched wide along the shelves at his back. He closed his eyes and held his head up, as if doing as Chef had instructed, and heard the man's footfall in front of him.

Kev opened his eyes and swung his right hand with as much force as possible. It held a cordless nail gun he had found among the abandoned tools. He had set it to rapid fire and hoped, as he pulled the trigger, that the batteries still had something left. If not, the weight of the gun itself should knock his attacker back. The power surged. Chef's nose spurted blood from the force of being hit in the face, and his forehead shuddered as 90mm nails were thumped into his skull.

He fell backwards, the razor dropping from his fingers, and Vincent in the torn vest gaped in shock before the cosh swung and he fell in a heap across the body of his boss. Kev dropped the nail gun and found he was having difficulty breathing. Deep breaths, he told himself, and stared across the garage at Alec who was staring back.

'We'd better go,' said Alec.

'How did you know that I'd put him down?' said Kev, still breathless.

'I didn't. But I reckoned an old Jack wouldn't go down without a fight.'

Kev nodded.

'We'd better go,' Alec repeated.

In the yard, a second bike was alongside Kev's.

'We take it nice and easy,' said Alec. 'My face is known. If anyone stops us, we're taking messages to Steel. Okay?'

'Okay.'

Kev could feel himself begin to shake at how close he had been to mutilation. Concentrating on riding the bike would help and, once clear of the town, they would have to ride fast. Time was running out.

Tower Street and Monkbar had both been cleared. The team brought their Range Rovers within the walls and left them in the half empty car park behind Clifford's Tower.

Abraham's people had responded willingly to Reaper's requests. Sandbags had been found and filled. York's propensity to flood after heavy rainfall meant there was always a ready supply. They had been stacked to provide further cover alongside the Second World War field gun that stood in the corner of the square on the raised frontage of the old museum entrance. There, they had created a nest for a light machinegun that was manned by Tanya and Jenny. An advertising board from inside the museum was propped against its front to disguise its existence until it was needed. It said proudly: *Welcome to the Castle Museum – the best day out in history.*

The modern glass-fronted entrance to the museum was behind them. The nearest panel had been smashed in and the jagged edges knocked clear, to allow the girls a line of retreat if things went wrong. They had plotted a route through the back of the museum to the banks of the river and the castle walls.

The high walls of Clifford's Tower would not provide the necessary fields of fire into the square. They might have been fine for sitting out a siege and pouring boiling oil from their broken battlements, but they were not suited as a place to site automatic weapons. At the top of the fifty-five steps, there was a concrete platform in front of the small doorway into the Tower. More sandbags had been placed here on both sides and had been disguised with more signs, this time from the gift shop inside. The sandbags did not have to be high because the elevation alone provided protection.

This was where Yank and Keira were located with automatic L85 rifles. They had no escape route but they could retreat inside the tower and barricade the door if necessary and wait until the militia arrived from Haven. At least, that was the plan but, as Sandra knew only too well, plans seldom went to plan.

James had a position on the museum roof which had a solid stone wall around it, intermingled with stretches of balustrade. He had declined to use a sniper's rifle because he would be so close to his target. He had both a carbine and an automatic L85.

Reaper moved the vehicles in the car park, placing two near the base of the mound to give him cover if he had to come down from the steps quickly. He also familiarised himself with an escape route through the car park and into the Coppergate shopping centre.

The rain had stopped. The clouds were no longer uniform and were breaking up. Glimpses of blue sky promised a pleasant afternoon, if they lived to enjoy it. Everything they had planned was on the assumption that Steel would come to York with a small force, maybe a dozen men. Why would he need more? That was why they had brought no mortars or grenades. And surely, it would be too difficult to organise a bigger flying column at short notice. A lot was riding on assumptions.

The steps and the grass mound upon which the Tower

stood were wet and treacherous. Reaper wore a long navy blue waxed coat with a storm cape over the shoulders. He had a Glock strapped to each thigh and carried an Uzi sub-machinegun on a strap hidden beneath the open coat, which was draped over his shoulders like a cloak so that it could be shed quickly.

Brother Abraham had insisted on being part of the subterfuge and waited with Reaper and Sandra at the bottom of the steps in clean and distinctive white robes. A wooden cross hung around his neck and he carried a bishop's crook. A volunteer from among his flock was across the road in Tower Street, hiding in the trees. Another lookout was further away, on the other side of the Tower Street – Bishopgate roundabout, keeping watch for the approach of Steel's men, whether they came on foot or in vehicles. They were both equipped with personal radios and Reaper also held one to receive their warning.

An alarm was raised from a different quarter when Brother Mark arrived in a hurry on a bicycle. The skirts of his robe were flying and his sturdy legs peddling as fast as he could across the car park.

'We've found Cedric,' he shouted.

'Shit,' said Sandra. 'Perfect timing.'

It was 11.30.

'He's at Monkbar and he has hostages. Children. He demands the freedom to leave. He knows what's happening.

He knows Steel is expected at noon and he has given us the same deadline or he kills the children.'

Reaper and Sandra exchanged a look.

'I'll go,' she said.

'He's not alone,' said Mark. 'There are three others. Two have guns.'

But Sandra was already moving, Mark running in her wake. She climbed into one of the Range Rovers and the monk got in beside her. His body odour was immediately apparent and, as she switched on the engine, she also lowered the windows. Now was not the time to hand out a lecture on personal hygiene. But later?

'Where are they?'

'In a shop, just inside the gates. We have men on the walls. Two have shotguns, although they've never fired them before, and others have longbows.'

'Who are the hostages?'

'Two girls, aged ten and eleven.'

The situation was going from bad to worse.

'Guide me,' she said, and the monk pointed which road to take. 'What does he want?'

'A car and to be allowed to leave.'

'Will he kill the girls?'

'He is an evil man and I think he will. As a last act of evil pleasure.'

Her mind was racing and a course of action was

presenting itself in a logical sequence. She stopped the Rover in a long, open square where, she suspected, a market had been held in ages past.

'Direct me to the Treasurer's House. I don't want Cedric to know I'm here.'

He pointed and she drove, slightly less in haste, as she outlined what he was to do.

Sandra left the Rover in the wide private drive that led alongside the Treasurer's House to the section of castle wall from which they had dropped early that morning. She led Mark up onto the castle wall and they climbed over it, dropping onto the gently sloping grass embankment on the other side.

'That one,' she said, pointing to a silver Mercedes saloon that was parked at the side of the road.

Brother Mark hoisted his robes and ran to the gate. She crossed the main road that ran parallel to the wall and took up a position in the bushes and trees that filled the open space between traffic lights and the start of a row of houses. On the end wall was an ancient advertisement, painted on the red brickwork: *Nightly Bile Beans Keep You Healthy, Bright Eyed and Slim.*

So did hunting down scum like Brother Cedric.

At 11.45 a radio message from an excited lookout alerted Reaper that someone was coming.

'They're early,' said Reaper.

Abraham began to move to the top of the steps but the sound of a motorcycle made him pause. Pete Mack braked his Harley Davidson fiercely in Tower Street and turned up the approach road to meet them.

'They're on their way,' he said. 'But there's more than expected. Maybe eighty. Maybe a hundred.'

Pete had been watching on the route from the south, near the junction of the M18 and the M62. It was the first time he'd been able to use the Harley, which was his pride and joy, with a real sense of urgency. His exhilaration at the ride was tempered with the news he brought.

Reaper said, 'Sandra's gone to Monkbar. A hostage situation with the bad bastard who killed Rebecca. Tell her. The odds are too steep. Tell her to stay back and watch the outcome. She will need to get back to Haven to organise resistance. Make sure she goes, Pete.'

'How do I find Monkbar?' said Pete.

Abraham pointed.

'Go towards the Minster, he said. 'It's just to the right.'

Pete engaged the gears and set off again, across the car park.

Reaper shouted up to Yank and Keira.

'Change of plan!' With so many to fight, the Tower could become a death trap, just as it had 800 years before. 'Join Jenny and Tanya.' They picked up their weapons and ammunition and came down the steps.

'What's wrong?' asked Yank.

'There's more than we thought. Maybe too many. Set up behind the field gun. We'll see how they play it. Wait for them or me to start it. Then take out anyone in the square. If it gets heavy, get back to Haven. They'll need you.'

'What about you?' said Yank.

'There's still a chance to take out Steel. After that, I'll get moving, too.'

'Luck Reaper.'

'You, too.'

He nodded to the two girls, who turned and ran along the road towards the field gun.

'James!' Reaper called. The young man showed himself on the roof. 'The odds have changed. Steel's bringing a small army. If you get a chance, put him down. But don't get trapped up there. There'll be too many of them. Get back to Haven. We'll re-group there.'

James raised an arm in acknowledgement and sank back behind the balustrade.

'And now,' Brother Abraham said. 'I think it's showtime.'

Reaper stopped him from climbing the steps with a hand on his arm.

'These odds are suicide, Brother. You should get to safety.'

Abraham smiled. 'This is my city and this is a holy site.

I believe this is a holy cause, good against evil. We stand against evil in different ways, Brother Reaper, but we stand against it together. I shall add authenticity to your charade as well as a little godliness. And I can always seek refuge in the Tower.'

'In that case, I'm glad to have you along, Brother.'

Abraham walked up the steps. After a moment, Reaper followed, but stopped a short way from the top and knelt. Abraham reached the concrete platform, faced outwards and spread his arms like an Old Testament prophet.

'How's this?' he said. 'Impressive enough?'

Reaper grinned.

'While you're at it, you might actually say a prayer,' he said. 'I think we're going to need one.'

Abraham nodded and joined his hands in front of him and bowed his head. After a moment, he said, 'Will you hear my confession, Reaper?'

'What?'

'My confession. I can't think of anyone else who would understand.'

Reaper was confused. 'Is this really the time?'

'Considering that there may not be another, I think it is. Will you hear me?'

Reaper glanced at his watch. 'Go ahead,' he said.

'Abraham is not my real name. I chose it when I gave myself to God. My real name is Colin Hazlehurst.' He took a deep breath, as if preparing for a great revelation. 'Before the plague, I was a journalist.'

'Jesus Christ,' said Reaper, in shock.

Abraham made the sign of the cross between them to dispel Reaper's blasphemy.

'I was a member of that very profession that fed the lie, that fed the madness of modern society. I was a member of the tabloid Press. What changed me was a road to Damascus moment that happened on the Docklands Light Railway.'

Reaper glanced up at Abraham to see if this was a wind-up but the monk's eyes were closed and his expression was serious.

'It started with a newspaper story I was writing. A feeble attempt to mock God and His plague. The deaths had started, although this was in the early days of the pandemic. I was writing a "what if" story about the end of the world, without for one moment thinking such a thing would happen. As part of the story, I went online and was ordained by an internet church. A free and painless rite of passage that took two minutes and cost nothing. I ticked the appropriate boxes and became Brother Abraham. My holy orders were granted by an ethereal message – hypertext through hyperspace. You can't get closer to God than that. It made a very amusing part of the story I wrote.'

'You were ordained over the internet?'

'I became Brother Abraham of the Church of the Eternal Light. It's based in California – if anyone has survived. It was a gimmick for a story. And no, I didn't take it seriously, either.

'Then the situation became worse and the possibility of apocalypse was not such a far-fetched idea but others refused to accept the inevitable. Life and lifestyle blinkered them. But my eyes had been opened. My Docklands Light Railway moment. I was on my way home when I knew the world was over. It came to me, a blinding flash of divine revelation.' He paused, reflecting on the moment. 'I never returned to the office. I threw my phone away, my first rejection of the trappings of society.

'This was two weeks before the end. Life was staggering on towards an inevitable conclusion. Then I realised the importance of my ordination. I went back online and read the philosophy of the Church of Eternal Light. It was simple enough, a combination of humanism, benevolence and Christian principles. I immersed myself in a search for truth. I looked for it in Buddhism, Islam, Judaism, Christianity, Hinduism. And I found Him back in the Church of Eternal Light and its philosophy of basic humanity. I opened my heart and God entered. A simple God who delivered a message of good and evil. A God people could understand.

'Before the plague there were too many gods, too many beliefs, hatreds, wars. My God is the One God who is neither Muslim nor Christian nor of any particular persuasion. He embraces all, for God is a concept that belongs to everyone. As all around me died, God allowed me to live. He told me to pray to Him and to help others who wished to follow a truer path than before.'

Abraham had been speaking quietly and without fervour. He had been confessing the accident of his position. He sighed and said, 'That is why I came to York and that is my confession.'

They exchanged a long look; Abraham's was expectant and hopeful.

Reaper said, 'Do your followers know where you were ordained?'

'No one asked.'

'Probably best not to tell them.'

'Probably,' agreed the monk. 'Do I have your absolution, Brother Reaper?'

'You do, Brother Abraham.'

'Then I shall offer another prayer for our salvation.'

Hell, thought Reaper, kneeling on the wet steps. It can't do any harm.

He armed the Uzi.

Sandra favoured the carbine she had learned to shoot with and leaned against a tree for stability. Across the road was a toyshop with a window full of antique dolls, then a bicycle store and then the parked Mercedes that, even now, Brother Mark was telling Cedric was waiting for him. She hoped Cedric would not suspect a double cross. He was in a bad situation and human nature would make him want to believe what Mark was promising: an escape without a shootout. His followers would likewise want to accept terms rather than fight; they were amateurs, after all.

She knew what she had to do: kill again without hesitation. Amateurs they may be, but they had chosen Cedric and violence and had crossed the line without hope of redemption by holding children as hostages. There could be no doubts, no second chances. Once again, she was judge, jury and executioner.

A woman climbed over the wall in the same place where she and Brother Mark had jumped down. She stared anxiously across the road into the trees but did not see Sandra. She took up a position at the side of the bicycle store, leaning her back against the wall and resisting the urge to look around the corner. She continued to stare across into the trees and, when her body stiffened, Sandra knew she had been seen. The plan was taking shape.

Two men appeared at the corner of Monkgate. One was young, one middle-aged. Both wore track suits. One carried a rifle, the other a handgun. They hesitated on the corner by the second hand shop, stared up the road and one pointed.

'It's there!' he shouted.

The men were joined by Brother Cedric, still favouring his crossbow, and a young woman who held the pony tail of a little girl in one hand and a knife in the other. The young woman had a sharp face that might have been attractive but for the harsh lines of anger and desperation. Her hostage was too terrified to cry, her eyes and mouth wide in fear. Cedric was grinning and the group began to move at a fast pace towards the promised car.

Already the plan was working because Mark had negotiated the freedom of one child in return for the car. But, of course, they would not let the second one go.

Sandra focussed through the sights on the woman with the knife and blanked her mind to any thoughts of compassion. She squeezed the trigger: a chest shot that sent the woman spinning backwards to crack her head on the pavement. The knife fell from her hand but she maintained the grip on the girl's hair, pulling her to the ground with her. The other three stopped in shock. The man with the rifle pointed it across the road towards the trees but couldn't see Sandra. Another chest shot put him down. The younger man dropped the handgun and raised his arms. Too late. She shot him, too.

Cedric crouched, the crossbow at the ready but without the benefit of a target. He backed up until he was against the glass of the toyshop, dozens of eyes from dead dolls staring at him.

'Bastard!' he shouted, and fired the crossbow bolt in final, desperate anger, and Sandra remembered how he had killed Rebecca.

The chest shot raised him from his crouch. The head shot that followed smashed him back through the glass of the window and he lay, half in and half out of the display, two more dead eyes staring into eternity.

Sandra walked steadily across the road. She let the carbine hang from its strap and took the Glock from its holster. The woman peeped round the wall from the side of the bicycle store. The little girl now started crying and the noise seemed to break the tension. The woman ran to the child, scooped her up into her arms and continued running towards Monkbar. Sandra inspected the bodies and delivered three head shots.

Brother Mark and Pete Mack came round the corner from Monkbar. They stopped and stared at the bodies. Then shooting from the other side of the city caught all their attention.

Chapter 20

THE SHOTS FIRED BY SANDRA COINCIDED WITH THE RADIO message that Steel was coming.

Reaper dropped the PR on the floor and told Abraham, 'They're here.'

The brother stood straighter.

A dark green Hummer turned off Tower Road and came towards them slowly. It had a sheet of steel welded to the front. Behind it, Reaper saw two 4x4s. They had four-door cabins with truck beds in the back. Two men were standing in each truck bed. The first pair had a machine gun resting on the cabin roof. The second pair had rifles. These cars also had steel sheets attached to the front. Reaper turned away his head and maintained the posture of praying. The vehicles had entered the square behind him. Others parked on the approach road and an assortment of 4x4s went past on the Tower Road and he heard them turn right towards the Hilton Hotel. They were making sure. They were surrounding him.

The cars behind him had stopped but the engines continued to tick over with a gentle rumble.

Doors opened; boots crunched on the road.

Brother Abraham spread his arms wide, the shepherd's crook in his right hand, every inch the prophet and not at all like a journalist, and shouted, 'Who dares disrupt a holy penance?'

'So you're Brother Abraham!' someone laughed. 'We've no beef with you, Brother. We want the Reaper.' The voice was loud and confident. 'I assume this is him?'

Reaper knew he was living on the edge and, perhaps, by the grace of Abraham's God. His body was tense in the expectation of being hit by a bullet at any moment. He was unhurried as he got to his feet. He wondered how long he would have when he turned around and whether he had chosen the correct weapon. The Uzi was notoriously difficult to aim. He wondered if he would have time to run for cover afterwards. But first, he had to kill Steel.

He turned slowly. Three vehicles were in the square. The Hummer and the one with a machinegun were facing the Tower. The third was parked broadside behind them. The men they had carried had taken up positions behind the vehicles to cover all directions. All the doors of the two vehicles facing him were open to provide added protection

– except for the passenger door in the Hummer.

Four other vehicles were stationery on the approach that led up from Tower Road.

'Are you the Reaper?' the man said, in his loud voice.

He was big, wore army fatigues and a floppy camouflage bush hat that hid his hair. He was not Steel.

Reaper saw that the machinegun was trained on him, as were the rifles of at least four others. This was suicide time, without a diversion of some kind. But he had told the girls and James not to fire until he did.

'God is the judge of all men …' shouted Abraham, in a voice that made even Reaper jump, and diverted the attention of the men below. Thank God for religion, he thought. He shed the coat and opened fire.

He held the gun down as firmly as possible but the spray was erratic. He hit at least two men, including the chap with the big voice, and made others wince and duck rendering their return fire wild and unsteady. He aimed most of it at the front passenger window of the Hummer where he guessed John Steel was sitting.

As he flung himself left off the steps, he was hit in the chest. The Kevlar vest saved him from death but the pain was numbing. The hit added to his momentum and he went sideways quicker than he had intended, rolled on the grass, found a grip with his toes and propelled himself down the embankment to find cover behind the cars he had parked below to escape the bullets.

Even as he ran and scrambled and dived, he was aware that a battle had started in the square behind him.

The solitary wait James had had on the rooftop had seemed longer than it had actually been. It was time during which the view over the city and the river had made him remember his family and, of all things, a day at York races in the autumn before the virus – a wonderfully happy day. His father had treated him as an equal, even though he was only thirteen, his mother had been elegant and beautiful and his younger sister had left her tantrums at home. Thirteen. When was that? A lifetime ago.

But once the wait was over and the action started, everything went into fast-forward mode. He watched Brother Abraham attract the men's attention, saw Reaper fire the Uzi and chaos reigned. James first took out the two men manning the machinegun. Two clean head-shots. He ducked and ran as return fire from rifles chipped the masonry near his head. He lay flat, a foot back from the balustrade, and looked for the red-haired figure of Steel.

The girls behind the field gun had opened up, causing further consternation among the men behind the vehicles. Men from the cars parked on the approach road spilled out and ran to join the fight, taking cover by the vehicles or at the corner of the Crown Court building. A fresh crew now manned the machinegun and James made them his next priority. He put one down and stopped its chatter before return fire sent stone chippings into his face like shrapnel. For a moment he was blinded by blood and, in his confusion, the carbine slipped from his grasp and went over the side of the building.

He was desperately angry with himself, and desperately worried about the safety of the girls. He rubbed his eyes clear and grabbed the L85. The machinegun was again firing at the sandbag and field gun emplacement. He stood up and leant on the wall and fired bursts from the automatic rifle into the back of the truck, silencing it once again. His determination was such that he was unaware of the bullets that hit the concrete and stone around him as the enemy responded.

James had crouched to change magazines, then, rising again to fire more bursts at the gun itself to render it ineffective, he saw the red curly hair of Steel among the vehicles. At last, he had his primary target. He aimed the gun, standing upright for perfect balance, and was flung backwards by a burst of fire that took him across the chest. His fall continued into blackness and his last regret was that he had missed.

'Bugger,' he thought.

Yank and Keira fired short bursts from behind the cover of the field gun's armour plating. Jenny maintained an almost constant fire from the light machinegun as Tanya fed the ammunition.

The noise was deafening, the acrid smoke and smells engulfed them, and their weapons grew hot, but the enemy was not attempting to attack. They were simply returning fire. The girls could keep this up as long as the ammo lasted.

They worked together through sign language because they couldn't hear themselves speak. They had seen Reaper go sideways off the grass mound, but had he been shot or was he throwing himself in that direction? Gunfire had also splatted the wall of the Tower around Brother Abraham as the monk had ducked inside and slammed the door.

Yank saw the carbine fall from the roof and her heart contracted in anguish, only to leap again when James resumed firing. It made her more reckless in attracting the return fire in their direction rather than upwards at their youthful comrade. Then the gunfire above them stopped and the enemy concentrated solely on them. James was down. They all knew it, they all felt the pain, they all knew they could be next.

Doors closed on one of the 4x4s and it began to move towards them, straight across the central area of tall grass. Two men were in the back, firing rifles over the roof, but they ducked when Jenny turned the machinegun on them. When she lowered the sights, the bullets hit the steel sheet welded to its front.

Yank abandoned her position and ran into the Museum. She dodged behind the cafeteria and went as far to the left as she could to get an angle on the approaching vehicle. She fired through the glass frontage and raked the side of the vehicle, hitting the driver. It didn't stop, but the driver's foot pressed the pedal hard and the vehicle veered violently to the right, headed straight for her and crashed into the side of the building. She changed magazines but had only a steel sheet to aim at. One of the men in the back leant over the cab roof to fire at her.

Shit, she thought. Is this it?

Then she was aware of Keira, stepping clear of the cover of the field gun to get a better line of fire, and putting burst after burst into the other side of the 4x4, until she went down, flung backwards into the museum.

Yank was consumed with anger. She left cover, used a concrete planter as a stepping-stone, and leapt over the steel sheet onto the bonnet of the car, to see that the men in the front of the vehicle were either dead or badly wounded, then onto the roof of the cab. The two men crouching in the back looked up in shock. She blasted both as bullets came through the roof around her feet. Someone inside was still alive.

She jumped backwards into the truck bed, firing into the cab as she did so and kept firing until the magazine was empty, only to be hit in the back as she reached for a fresh magazine. The blow put her down and her back hurt, as if it had been thumped by a sledgehammer. But she knew she was okay, that the vest had done its job. She reloaded, her head in the lap of one of the men she had killed. Then she rolled over and fired a short burst over the back of the truck bed – which, she realised instantly, was a mistake. The side of the truck was no real protection against bullets and she had alerted them to the fact that she was still alive.

But was Keira?

Yank leapt back the way she had come and ran into the shadows of the museum frontage and round the cafeteria. Her partner lay on her back, arms spread, ankles crossed like a grounded angel. Her eyes were closed and, for some reason, Yank took that as a good sign. You die with you eyes open, don't you?

'Make it, you Irish bastard,' she said, her words lost in the deafness and noise of firing, touched her fingers to her lips and transferred the kiss to Keira's forehead, then ran back to the cover of the field gun to continue the battle.

Jenny was shouting something to her but she couldn't hear and shook her head. Yank was crying with anger and she fired burst after burst over the gun, changing magazines, and firing again, until she realised that only two guns were firing back. This was holding fire. Containment. Most of the enemy had gone in the other direction. Were they chasing Reaper?

The shooting from James and the girls was enough of a distraction to aid Reaper's initial escape as he took cover among the vehicles in the car park. Ahead, towards the Hilton Hotel and the city itself, he could see a line of armed men spread across his path. A couple fired in his general direction but most hadn't seen where he had gone. He crabbed sideways, further to the right and the river.

He could hear a limited pursuit behind him but most of those in the square seemed to be engaged in returning fire towards the girls. More shots were fired, but came nowhere near him. With luck, some stray bullets might cross the car park in either direction and hit his foes.

As he ran, dived, rolled and scrambled, he wondered whether he had managed to hit Steel, whom he was sure had stayed inside the Hummer while his subordinates got out. The man was not as macho as he had thought. It had been a clever move to stay out of sight until he knew exactly what risks he was facing. Reaper hadn't had that luxury, but at least he was in one piece and running. But where? Back to Haven, as he had instructed everyone else? Or could he hole up for one more try at Steel?

There were three entrances into the Coppergate shopping mall: to the left, next to the Hilton Hotel, was the route he had ridden with Brother Abraham on his first visit to the city; to the far right, on the other side of an underground car park entrance, a walkway went alongside the river before going beneath the shops; the third was directly ahead and went down the side of Fenwick's store and then became a short underpass into the piazza. This was the one he chose. ·

Two men were directly in his way, others were nearby but looking outwards. He let the Uzi dangle from the strap around his neck, took the two Glocks from their holsters and ran straight ahead without hesitation. He took one shot with each and both men went down as he continued running towards the underpass. The shouts behind meant pursuit was close and, as he entered the piazza, he knew he would be an easy target if he kept running. Perhaps he could find a refuge from where he could tempt Steel into showing himself.

Bullets went past him and hit the paved stones at his feet. Other men were in the lane by the side of the church. They fired and smashed the windows of Topshop. He went through them, past mannequins that lay like bodies amid the debris. He took refuge behind a pillar and fired back at his attackers. Not surprisingly, they took cover before returning fire.

The men facing him were not trained soldiers and were probably not prepared to die for the cause of John Steel. They would prefer to keep Reaper pinned down and wait for his ammunition to run out before contemplating anything as drastic as storming the store. For the moment, it was a stand off; Reaper kept his head down, changed the magazine on the Uzi and wondered if Steel would appear.

Sandra and Pete ran to the Range Rover. She opened the boot and threw back a blanket to reveal an arsenal of weapons with which she started arming herself.

'Reaper said if it went wrong, you should go back to Haven,' Pete said. 'He said you would be needed to organise resistance.'

'Right,' she said, continuing to strap guns from her shoulders and grab extra magazines of ammunition. 'You drive.'

Pete didn't ask where she expected him to drive. He knew where they were going. As he was about to close the boot, Brother Mark appeared and reached inside and took a combat shotgun.

Sandra looked at him questioningly.

'How does it work?' he said.

'Get in and I'll show you on the way,' she said.

As Pete got behind the wheel, the noise of battle changed. It was no longer frenetic with automatic and machinegun fire. It now sounded more like a siege.

'This way,' said Brother Mark, pointing.

Tanya and Jenny were now using L85 automatic rifles. They knelt amidst a flooring of shell casings. Yank touched

Jenny's shoulder, pointed at the enemy and raised two fingers to indicate the number of guns they faced. Jenny, face taut with strain and dirty with residue, nodded. Yank pointed at herself and at the tree in the middle of the square. She mouthed, 'Cover me' and ran back into the museum, past the body of her friend and around the cafeteria to her former position behind the crashed car. She looked across at the girls and nodded and they both began firing in sustained bursts.

Yank left cover and, crouching low, ran through the tall grass which gave her partial concealment. She made the tree just as she was spotted and ducked behind its trunk as bullets chewed through the bark and scythed the grass. They were still pinned down and neutralised from the action unless a miracle happened or Yank tried a suicidal charge. Why not? she thought, as grief and battle anger took hold of her.

Then the miracle happened.

Brother Abraham appeared from the entrance of Clifford's Tower. He began to come down the fifty-five steps at a cautious pace. In his hands he held a sword. Yank began to fire again, to cover the monk's approach from their enemy's rear. She attracted return fire but Tanya and Jenny joined in as an added distraction and Abraham speeded up his descent.

He reached the first gunman and swung his weapon as

the man realised he was under threat and began to turn. He hit him across the neck. The second gunman turned as Brother Abraham lifted the sword and approached him for another strike. Yank stood up from cover, aimed and fired, and took the man in the back, causing him to discharge his rifle over the head of the monk and smashing the blade of the sword.

The three girls ran to the bunker of cars. Yank realised with a shock that there were a lot of bodies. Brother Abraham was breathing heavily and looked with surprise at his broken blade.

'It's a Viking broadsword,' he said. 'It's only a replica. It doesn't even cut.' The girls glanced past him at the man he had struck. 'I think I broke his neck.'

To make sure, Tanya put a bullet in him.

The girls were all dishevelled, dirty and out of breath. Abraham's robes were unsullied and he looked remarkably clean in the circumstances, but a fire burned in his eyes.

'They're still shooting,' he said. 'Reaper's still alive.'

They ran across the car park towards the sounds of fighting. Three girls carrying L85 automatics and a fiery monk with a broken sword.

Reaper used the Glocks. Single shots, always at a target, nothing random or wasted. He had reloaded the Uzi with the spare magazine and would save that until the end.

In the meantime, he kept moving from one side of the window to the other, using the cover of clothes racks and broken furniture and his bullets to keep the enemy at bay. If nothing else, he might give the girls and James a chance to escape; it was Reaper after all that Steel wanted.

He saw a man with red hair in the lane by the side of the church and fired two quick shots but without effect. His desire to kill Steel put his own survival at the back of his mind. He felt dispassionate and distanced from the situation he was in, and the fact that he didn't rate his chances of getting out alive didn't bother him unduly. He might find a way out of the back of the shop and go on the run through the city, but he had to give the others as much time as possible and he still had a chance, slim though it might be, of nailing Steel.

A bullet scored his arm but he hardly felt it. He had been hit several times, mostly in the vest. If he lived, his bruises would give him hell. The wounds he had taken on his arms, legs and one that had scoured his neck, were minor irritations. If he lived, he would survive them. If he didn't, then what did they matter?

If he died, he was dying for good people, and besides, he'd had a year of life that actually meant something, whereas those immediately before had meant nothing but pain, anguish and guilt. He thought of Greta and what might have been, and he thought of Sandra and his heart swelled with pride. He knew that, in his situation, she would do the same; that the young girl was a true warrior with both courage and compassion. God, but he was proud of her. Tears dampened his eyes and he laughed at his sentimentality and the thought that, by a quirk of serendipity, his last stand was being enacted in Topshop, the chain store where she had worked. For a few seconds he stood tall and fired both guns recklessly before it dawned on him that he was behaving like some Wild West cowboy.

He moved back into cover when bullets came too close. The clouds had broken, he could see blue sky and the sun was about to burst forth in all its glory. He grinned as he changed the magazine on one of the Glocks. The last magazine. At least, he had a nice day for it.

Sandra instructed Pete to stop the Range Rover at the top of the lane that led down into the mall from where all the shooting was coming. They were all equipped and Brother Mark knew the simple rudiments of the seven-shell, pump-action shotgun and how to reload.

As she slipped partway down the lane, she surmised from the way the firing was being directed that Reaper was holed up in premises at the far end and on the left; everyone else was facing him in the arc of shops and churchyard to the right. She went back to the Rover and gave her instructions.

Reaper had six bullets in each Glock plus the one magazine in the Uzi that hung round his neck. Not long before the final curtain. What was the song? *My Way* by Sinatra, the anthem of pub singers everywhere. Not for him. He spaced his shots from the handguns. What music would he choose for *his* final curtain? Something loud to wake the bastards up. No tears, no regrets. A Stones record would be good. *Jumpin Jack Flash* or *Brown Sugar*. Maybe *Sympathy For The Devil?* He took more shots and the Glocks clicked on empty but he thought he had seen Steel's distinctive red hair behind the church wall on the far side of the square. Maybe he could still take him.

He put the handguns in their holsters and pulled back the slide on top of the Uzi to arm it. He had a clip of forty bullets that would burst out at ten per-second. Four seconds of continual fire and he would be empty. He was determined to make them count.

The Range Rover rolled gently down the slope, attracting shots from Steel's men before coming to rest against the wreckage of the burnt-out fast food outlet. The clouds above parted at speed, as if they had been waiting for stage directions from God. The sun finally broke clear into an unblemished sky. Its brightness shone down in a beam of light that, by some miracle of refraction, hit the windscreen of the Range Rover to be deflected with laser intensity onto the broken shards and slices of still upright glass in the shattered shop windows. The result was a starbust of brightness that blinded everyone in the piazza. They blinked and squinted and wondered at the dazzling light that was brilliant enough to be a portent of divine intervention. And from its corona stepped an Angel of Death.

Sandra walked forward, an Uzi in each hand, firing indiscriminately as the guns bounced erratically in her grip, but providing a terrifying barrage of 9mm bullets. On her right side was Pete Mack, holding a light machinegun with pit bull determination, its deadly stutter chewing brick, concrete, wood, glass and flesh. On her left marched a bearded monk with wild hair, blasting anything in sight with 12 gauge buckshot. When his gun clicked empty, he dropped it and reached for the second shotgun that was hanging around his neck. Sandra dropped the Uzis and swung the L85 forward from its strap and continued firing in short bursts. She wore one Glock on her right thigh and a second slung cross-belt style in a holster across her chest.

The three stood side by side and produced a terrifying storm of firepower. Reaper stepped from the shop window and joined them and restricted his Uzi to short bursts to extend his effectiveness.

It was too much for Steel's men, and those still able to get to their feet, broke and ran, turning the pedestrian access points into rat runs as they sought a way out. Steel tried to rally them but they brushed past him. At this point, he would have run, too, except that Sandra shot him in the leg. He went down and no one stopped to help him.

Post-percussion deafness made the piazza a silent place and the four allies walked to the prone figure of John Steel. He rolled onto his back and stared up at them. Sandra stood over him and her outline was blurred by the halo of sun above her. He shook his head as if puzzled that the battle he'd thought he had won had been turned to utter defeat by a girl.

'Angel,' he said.

And the Angel shot him. One bullet in the head.

More shooting came from the direction in which the enemy had fled and, without a word, the four ran off in pursuit. When they came out opposite the car park, they saw the remnants of Steel's army, leaping into parked 4x4s outside the Hilton, some returning fire at a small band approaching from Clifford's Tower. Tanya, Jenny and Yank were blasting away while Brother Abraham, a broken sword in his right hand, held his arms outstretched above him as if in a rapturous prayer or entreaty.

They joined them, Brother Mark pushing cartridges into the shotgun he still carried. Sandra handed spare magazines to Reaper for his Glocks, and they fired as the vehicles reversed backwards down the slope into Tower Street, colliding in their desperation to get away. They began to drive forward, going back the way they had entered York, only for the drivers to brake in disbelief.

Coming towards them, and filling both sides of the dual carriageway, was a fleet of cars, Land Rovers and trucks that spread out to block their escape. The newly arrived convoy stopped and its occupants climbed out and levelled weapons: Smiffy had the right flank behind a machinegun mounted on a military truck; Ashley commanded the centre with another machinegun on an army Land Rover; Gavin Price and Kev held the left flank by the river with a group of militia with automatic rifles.

Between them were not just Haven militia but friends and neighbours from the federation: The Prof and Alan White from the 'Brains Trust', Bob Stainthorpe and Nagus Shipley and a contingent from Bridlington; Preacher Charlie Miller and a group from Filey, and many more from the hamlets and villages that had come together in the hope of building a better future. They pointed their weapons like a firing squad at the vehicles attempting to flee.

The thugs in the 4x4s braked and tried to reverse again but vehicles crashed into each other and panic set in.

Sandra stepped forward and, above the chaos, she shouted, 'No prisoners!' She opened fire and all followed her lead. The barrage was devastating, added to by grenades launched by Kev from an L85. The guns eventually fell silent, as if from shock at the carnage they had wreaked, even before Sandra raised her arm.

Greta Malone, the Rev Nick, Cassandra, Judith and Kev ran from the newly arrived force's lines.

'Is anyone hurt?' shouted Nick.

They must have noticed that Keira and James were missing.

Yank started running towards the museum.

'This way,' she called, and the medical team followed. Kev stayed.

'You made it.' said Sandra.

'I made it.'

Reaper looked past him at the people from the federation.

'What happened?' he said.

'I knew Steel was bringing his top people but I was too late to warn you. All these had gathered at Haven by the time I got there. I supposed they answered the call.'

'We didn't make one,' said Reaper.

'They answered it anyway. When I told them what Steel had planned, we came at top speed.' He glanced back. 'Looks like we were just in time to make a difference.'

Sandra changed the magazine on one of her Glocks and looked down at the mess of smashed and shot vehicles below the grassy knoll in Tower Street and at the bodies that lay among it, some still; some moving. She pulled back the slide to put a bullet in the chamber and clicked the trigger to remove the safety.

'Someone's got to do it,' she said, with a glance at Reaper.

'Christ,' said Tanya, in a low voice. 'Hasn't there been enough?'

No sooner had she uttered the sentiment than a small hole appeared in Tanya's forehead as a shot rang out. Tanya fell backwards on the turf without another sound.

Jenny dropped her weapon, sank to her knees and tried to cradle Tanya's head but the back of her skull was missing and Jenny stared in horror at the gore on her hands.

'No,' she said.

Sandra walked down the slope and Reaper followed. He was out of ammunition again and took a gun from one of the fallen and the two of them went between the cars and the chaos and did what had to be done. From beyond the lines of the vehicles that had arrived just in time to stop the escape, the people of the federation watched in horror.

Chapter 21

A WEEK LATER THEY WERE BACK ON THE ROAD. Reaper and Sandra were in the lead Range Rover on the M1, Tanya and Yank in the vehicle behind. Returning to routine and making their calls.

A lot had happened since they had broken Steel at York. Brother Abraham had encouraged his followers to join the federation and, in truth, most hadn't needed much persuasion. The city had largely been abandoned and more farms and villages had been occupied.

Steel's army had been a different proposition. Its people had been used to an itinerant lifestyle where the threat of violence was always present. A few of the foot soldiers who had fought at York had escaped and made their way back to the main body still encamped at the coast. The Rev Nick and a conciliation team travelled from Haven the day after the action. Kev and Alec had been among them and Reaper and Sandra had gone at the head of a small military presence. Nick had insisted they attend. Even he acknowledged the power of legend and the growing fame of Reaper and the Angel.

Talks lasted two days, after which more than four hundred had decided to follow the federation example and settle into the villages and countryside nearby. They would remain south of the river and attempt to integrate with survivors already there and work the land and the sea. That was the future, after all, and the federation promised to help.

Others had drifted away in groups and headed south and west. A contingent left for Windsor, to investigate the rumour, passed on by travellers, that Prince Harry was head of a 'Government of Redemption'. Seventy or eighty people had gone north, looking for new beginnings, although half of them still lingered within existing federation lands and seemed destined to remain.

Reaper drove. Clapton played on the car stereo. They said nothing, each alone with their thoughts and the loss they still felt.

They reckoned they had faced eighty of John Steel's hardcore army and they had survived and been victorious because they were better trained, had better armaments and were more committed to their cause. James had been shot in both arms and received a head wound and facial scarring, but he had made it. His recovery would be slow.

Keira had died, along with Tanya. They had been taken home to Haven.

On the evening of the battle, the close-knit fraternity of the 'Special Forces' had sat together on the grassy slope outside the guardpost near the front gate. The others, even Dr Greta Malone, had left them alone. They had drunk beer and wine and too much vodka, and had remembered the two they had lost.

Yank had said, 'Keira had a VIP pass into heaven. She did the First Fridays. She told me. It's a Catholic thing. It's a guarantee that you get straight in through the Pearly Gates with no waiting.' The laugh caught in her throat. 'Keira will have flashed that and taken Tanya in with her. And if St Peter has objected, she'll have shot the bastard.'

Kev had cried: tears for the girls and for his wife and daughter. When they wouldn't stop, he had left the group and walked back over the hill to the manor house to sit by James's bed, keeping a nightlong vigil, despite Dr Greta telling him to get some sleep.

'But I wasn't there,' he told her. 'I wasn't there.'

To try and purge the guilt he felt, he had sat by the bed and prayed for the comrades who had become his family. He would have willingly given his life to save Tanya and Keira. If he had been there, he might have been able to do exactly that.

Jenny and Yank had eventually retired, taking the

double bedroom in the mobile home, sleeping together for comfort. Reaper had drunk his share but felt stone cold sober. Sandra was showing the effects of too much alcohol. She had tried for temporary oblivion with a vengeance.

'How did we do it?' she said.

'They were overconfident. They weren't trained. They were just armed yobs.'

'There were eight of us. We shouldn't have won.'

'We fought for each other, as well as for this place. We fought for a future. If you like, we fought for our dead, too. The ones buried down there last year. Who wanted what we still want and who gave their lives for it. We already have a heritage, Sandra. A history. In one short year.'

'I keep asking the same question. Can we do it again?'

'If we have to.'

Reaper pulled out the folding bed in the mobile home and they curled up together, as they had on the first night they had met, Sandra safe in his arms.

The next morning, they had buried Keira and Tanya. The Rev Nick had said the words at a subdued service. Yank and Jenny held hands, both girls crying. Reaper and Sandra stood side by side with faces set in stone. Greta was next to Reaper and took his hand. Her touch was a reminder of humanity and he had taken hold of Sandra's hand as well. Kev, who the previous day, had nail-gunned an enemy to death, blubbed without shame.

Life was not fair. But they already knew that.

Everyone who had gathered in defence of the federation and all the residents of Haven had attended the funeral. Brother Abraham had also come to say farewell to Rebecca. He did not presume to intrude on the service. He stood off a distance with Mary, the surviving member of his 'trinity'.

Reaper remembered the day he had led the small group of survivors into Haven. Their arrival had coincided with a funeral. Jamie had been burying the people who had previously lived there. Nick had said the words then too, and Kate had sung *Amazing Grace* over the graves. A few short months later, he and Sandra had been here again when Kate herself had been buried, along with Jamie and others who had died in the cause of freedom. This time it was only two that they were committing to the earth and God's mercy.

Only two.

They pulled off the M1 at Trowell Services. Percy Radcliffe was subdued when he greeted them and Martha had an anxious look as she dispensed coffee. Travellers had told them of the Battle of York. They exchanged gossip and rumour and skirted the question that was on their minds until Martha eventually broached it.

'Keira?' she said. 'Tanya?'

And they told them they had died and the couple cried and the visit was over.

They got back on the road, silence in both cars: no music, no Clapton, just dark thoughts and despair that had been revived. They took the A52 and Reaper tried to tell himself the trip had been worthwhile. They had to get back into a routine and they couldn't avoid being the bearers of bad news. But he did not look forward to telling Maisie Day and Brian.

As it happened, he didn't have to.

He stopped the car alongside the tables and chairs on the grass verge. Maisie was sitting in one of the chairs as if she was a rag doll, arms hanging over the sides, legs splayed inelegantly. Her eyes stared and flies had gathered in a cloud around her face. They got out, guns at the ready. The second car had stopped a hundred yards behind.

Sandra went to Maisie and waved her hand to clear the flies from the bullet hole in the woman's forehead. She exchanged a look with Reaper and he went to the caravan while she went to the approach road from the village. The caravan was empty. So was the approach road. Reaper waved for the second car to join them. The anger showed on the faces of Jenny and Yank when they saw the body.

'Why?' said Jenny. 'What's the bloody point?'

Reaper said, 'This is recent. They could still be here.'

'I sure as hell hope so,' said Yank.

'We'll check Maisie's house,' Reaper said. 'Then go on to Arnold's.'

Normally, they would stop on the A1 to visit with Maisie and Brian and if the couple hadn't been at the caravan, they would drive into the village to find them, so they knew its layout. Cromwell was a blip by the side of the A1. A slip road led off the south-north highway and became Main Street, that ran for about half a mile before rejoining the A1, where Maisie had located her cafe. Most of the houses in the village were built along each side of Main Street, along with the white stoned parish church of St Giles. More houses straddled the road that went west from the middle of the village towards the neighbouring hamlet of Norwell. It was a handsome village with handsome houses. A respectable village with history. Arnold, the red-faced farmer, had told them about it, when they had met.

He had lived in the district all his life. Generations of his family had worked the land.

'Cromwell is one of the Thankful Villages of Nottinghamshire,' he had told them. 'There are four of 'em. *Thankful* because we had no losses during the Great War.'

But they had losses now.

Arnold and Shirley had seemed an odd couple. He was deliberate in speech and she was a small, slim, attractive woman of fifty-two who had been a solicitor in Newark. They had been content together.

Maisie and Brian lived at this nearer end of the village

while Arnold had moved into Shirley's home near the parish church.

Reaper and Sandra ran up the right side of the road past the caravan park; Jenny and Yank up the left until they reached the first of the small houses shared by Maisie and Brian and where Brian had built hen huts and a sty for a pair of pigs in the back garden.

All was quiet and Sandra went to the front door and she was not surprised to find it unlocked. In she went, followed by Reaper. Jenny and Yank edged round the side of the house into the garden at the rear. The house had not been ransacked but items had been broken as if someone had caused the destruction almost casually. Reaper ran upstairs, but the bedrooms were empty.

'Reaper!' called Sandra.

As he came back down the stairs, Sandra pointed through the French windows: Yank was in the middle of the lawn indicating she and Jenny had found something.

They joined her and went past shrubbery to the bottom of the garden. One of the hencoops had been knocked down and the chicken wire broken. Two hens were dead, while the others pecked around. The sty was partly brick wall and partly timber fence. The fence had been knocked down. Inside were two dead pigs and Brian. The young man was naked, covered in dirt and mud as if he had been forced to wallow. Brian and his pigs had been shot. Flies had gathered.

A grim-faced Jenny was standing guard.

'Jesus Christ,' whispered Sandra.

They looked at each other and needed no further instruction. They set off at a trot for the house occupied by Arnold and Shirley. •

Jenny and Yank went ahead, off the road and through the back gardens. Reaper and Sandra followed Main Street, although using the cover of gateways, trees and the occasional abandoned car. The village was quiet but, as they approached the large detached house that Arnold and Shirley shared, they heard the sound of music. It was muted and appeared to be coming from the rear of the house, which was set back from the road. A Land Rover and a Nissan 4x4 were parked on the drive. At the side of the house was a Land Rover truck with military markings.

They took quick glances through the windows to see that the rooms at the front were empty. Reaper tried the front door; it was unlocked. He pushed it open and Sandra stepped past him and went inside, moving sideways to put the wall at her back. He followed, closed the door behind him and stepped the other way. The house had wooden floors and panelling. They were in a large hallway, a wide staircase ahead of them and a corridor heading towards the back of the house. Room doors were closed. The music was coming from the rear and reverberated through the wood panelling: Abba's *Dancing Queen*.

Sandra was first down the corridor. Two doors were open at the end. The one facing led into a kitchen. The one to the right was where the music was being played. She exchanged a look with Reaper and went round the door jam. Once inside, she took one step left, to give Reaper space to join her. Both had their rifles levelled.

Shirley was wearing only a slip. She sat in an armchair, her feet tucked beneath her, arms held protectively across her chest, her hair dishevelled, tears running down her face. As she looked up, Sandra saw a pain that she recognised: no relief that they had come; only resignation for what had happened.

Two men were in the room. Both wore camouflage trousers and khaki vests. One sprawled on a sofa, a can of lager in one hand and a cigar in the other. The second soldier held a bottle of whisky and had been dancing by himself to the music. The remains of food were on a low table – the carcasses of a pair of roast chickens, baked potatoes, the remnants of a salad, chunks of bread. More cans and bottles littered the room.

'Who the fuck are you?' said the dancing soldier.

He was big, muscular and had a shaven head. His tone was belligerent and unafraid, despite the guns they held.

The room had open French windows that led into a large conservatory, whose doors were also open. On the lawn outside, a third soldier was in the act of zipping up his trousers after relieving himself on the grass.

Reaper said quietly, 'We need one alive.'

Sandra shot the standing soldier through the head, sending him crashing backwards against a sideboard, knocking a tin of scones and the battery-operated CD player onto the floor. The music stopped. She knew the man was dead but still put a second bullet into his chest.

'Hey!' shouted the soldier outside.

He wore his uniform tunic, as well as his camouflage trousers. He had the stripes of a corporal on his arm and he was reaching for the Browning at his waist as he came running through the conservatory.

'Don't,' said Reaper.

The man stopped and glanced behind him, perhaps looking for an escape route, and saw Yank and Jenny emerge from the undergrowth with weapons raised.

'Corp?' shouted the man on the sofa, who had dropped the can and was getting to his feet. He was medium height and had an athletic build but his face was vacuous and puzzled. He still didn't realise he was dead.

'Stay put, Davy,' said the Corporal.

Sandra looked at Shirley who was crying fresh tears.

'Where's Arnold?' she said.

'They shot him.'

'Did they ...?'

'Yes.'

Sandra lowered her carbine and placed it on the ground

behind her. She took the Bowie knife from the sheath on her right leg, held the blade down by her side and stepped towards the soldier called Davy. He was about four inches taller than her.

'That's Reaper,' she said, in a conversational tone. 'And I'm the Angel. Heard of us?' She saw the recognition and the fear in his eyes. 'The thing is, Davy, we only need one of you alive. And you are not the one.'

Sandra brought the knife up in a vicious thrust between his legs, cutting genitalia as the blade went deep behind the protection of the pelvic bone and into the soft flesh around his anus. He screamed, and when she pulled the knife free he fell to the floor, his hands holding himself, trying to stop the blood and pain, his feet scrabbling on the wooden boards.

'Outside,' said Reaper, and the corporal retreated through the conservatory and went back into the garden. His hand still hovered over the butt of the Browning. 'Remove the gun and drop it on the ground.'

The man hesitated.

'Or shall I give you to the Angel?'

The corporal lifted the gun from its holster with two fingers and dropped it on the grass. He backed away, under Reaper's direction. Further down the garden was a bench beneath the shade of a tree. In other circumstances, this would be an idyllic spot in a lovely garden. Even the grass had been trimmed to a reasonable length. Arnold, Reaper remembered, had used a scythe.

'Why don't you put your hands in your pockets,' said Reaper. After a moment's hesitation, the man obliged. 'Now sit on the bench.'

The corporal backed away and sat down.

Yank took up a position to the left and several feet away from Reaper, holding her gun cradled in her arms. Jenny went inside the house.

'How many of you?' Reaper said.

'Three.'

Reaper spoke to Yank. 'Check with Shirley.' And then to the corporal, 'Where's Arnold?'

'He's in the field.'

The man moved his head sideways to indicate a nearby field.

'Dead?'

'Yes.'

'Why?'

'Why?'

'Why kill him? Why kill Maisie? Why kill Brian?'

'It … got out of hand.'

'You're a corporal. You were in charge. You let it get out of hand.'

'I didn't know about the couple down the other end of the village. Not until later.'

'Brian was naked and dead in a pigsty.'

'That was Brannie.' The man shrugged. 'He has weird ideas.'

The yells and pleas for help from the man Sandra had knifed had been echoing into the garden. Abruptly, they changed to high pitched screams intermingled with the sound of a rhythmic thumping. Then they stopped.

'What about Shirley?' Reaper said.

'We ...' He was at a loss. He knew there was no mitigation. He looked back towards the house and shrugged. 'Once Brannie started, no one could have stopped him.'

'Angel did.'

Worry showed in the man's eyes at the use of the word *Angel*.

'I'm Reaper. Have you heard of us?'

'Yes. That's why we were sent. Recon.'

Yank came from the house. 'Just the three of them,' she said.

Reaper nodded. The corporal began to shake with fear.

'You came north because of us?'

'We'd heard stories.' He shrugged. 'Daft stories. One man and a girl. The Reaper and the Angel.'

'Well now you know they're true. Except that it's one man, one girl and a pair of banshees. Who sent you? Where are you from?'

'General Purcell of the New Army, sent us. We're from

Redemption. It's the seat of the new British Government.'

'With Prince Harry?'

The corporal twitched. 'That's right. Prince Harry.'

'A new British Government? A new army? How big is the army?'

'I don't know. It's big.'

'Be more specific.'

'Four companies. Battalion strength.'

'Army, RAF, Navy?'

'Mainly Army and RAF blokes.'

'All service personnel?'

'Yes.'

'Do you have aircraft?'

'No.'

A commotion at the house made Reaper turn around. Jenny was trying to hold onto Shirley and calm her but the small woman did not want to be placated. She broke away and ran through a gate in the hedge that led to the field where the corporal had indicated that Arnold was lying dead. Jenny went back into the house as Sandra came out and walked down the garden to them.

'When did you get here?' Reaper said.

'Yesterday.'

'You've done a lot of damage in twenty-four hours.'

'It was Brannie. He was always a wild man.'

'Are there are a lot like him in the New Army?'

'Like Brannie? No. They're just ordinary squaddies. Do as they're told.'

'Like Davy?'

'He's easily led.'

'Like you?'

'It got out of hand, I told you.'

'Why were you sent?'

'The General wanted to know about you.'

Shirley came back into the garden, the gate banging behind her.

'No, Shirley,' said Sandra, and Reaper turned.

She strode down the garden quickly, like a wraith in the stained nylon slip, Arnold's double-barrelled shotgun in her hands. It was pointed at the corporal.

'Shirley,' Reaper said, but stood to one side, in case the tremble in her arms and hands transmitted itself to the triggers. 'Don't do this. We need information.'

'Bastard,' she said, ignoring everyone but the corporal.

Reaper reached to grab the gun but she pulled the triggers and discharged both barrels into the soldier's chest, blowing him backwards off the bench.

Nobody moved. The scene became still life. Reaper could appreciate why Shirley had done what she had done but wished he had had more time to question the corporal before the inevitable sentence had been carried out.

Jenny stepped from the house with an armful of clothes

for the distraught woman who dropped the shotgun and sank to the grass in tears. Sandra knelt to comfort her.

Reaper walked to the gate and looked into the field next door. Dead animals lay around. Shot for fun. For target practice. Arnold lay among his animals.

Yank was at his shoulder.

'Shirley beat the other bastard to death with a saucepan. We didn't like to stop her.'

Reaper nodded.

'We'll take her home.'

Sandra came through the gate and joined them.

'Jenny's finally calming her down. She'll get her dressed.' She noted Arnold's body. 'It never ends, does it.' Then, to Reaper, 'What did he say?'

'They were from the new British Government. They were part of the New Army. They'd been sent to find out about us. They came from a place called Redemption.'

The three of them let the stillness of the afternoon settle over them for a moment, even though the view was of a field littered with the dead bodies of animals and the corpse of an elderly farmer. Maybe they would never find a stillness like it again.

'So,' said Sandra. 'Now we go looking for Redemption.'

Jon Grahame

Coming soon …

The final instalment of
the Reaper trilogy…

JON GRAHAME'S
REDEMPTION

MYRMIDON